When It All Falls Down

An erotic novel by

Jennifer Robinson

ISBN: 978-0-578-44982-1

When It All Falls Down

This is a work of fiction. Names, characters, places, and incidents either are the products of the author's imagination or are used fictitiously. Any resemblance to actual persons, living or dead, businesses, companies, events, or locales is entirely coincidental.

For permission requests, please contact the author via the "Contact" page on the following website:

www.authorjenniferrobinson.com

Proudly self-published through Divine Legacy Publishing,
www.divinelegacypublishing.com

Dedication

My grandma Mamie Jackson

My grandparents Green and Dorothy Hamilton

My great nephew Cameron J. McGhee

The city of Americus and Sumter County

Chapter One

I pulled up to the cemetery and immediately knew this was a terrible idea.

It'll get easier, they said. *It won't always hurt this bad*, they promised.

Meanwhile, a whole year later, visiting my brother's grave wasn't any easier. I hadn't even gotten out of the car yet and I felt the heaviness of his loss keeping me stuck in the car. I wanted to pull off, go back home, and get ready for work but I couldn't. Not today. I needed to talk to him today.

I got out of my Audi and grabbed my grey pea coat from the passenger side. As I made my trek to his gravesite, I wrapped my green scarf around my neck. The joy of a southwest Georgia winter: it was January and it was just now cold enough for a coat. When I was home for Christmas last month, it was just cool enough for a light sweater or jacket. Winter in this part of Georgia would last about three months. Then it would be hell hot for the next nine. When I was younger I wanted to move up north where there were true seasons because it was ridiculously hot down here for most of the year.

Wanting to look anywhere but at where I was going, I glanced to my left. I still wasn't used to the empty space. The building where I attended Head Start had long since been torn down. Head Start and Barnum Funeral Home made Ashby Street and now one part of that duo was gone. Just another reminder that my hometown of Americus, Georgia was changing. It wasn't necessarily a bad change, just different. I made my way through Eastview Cemetery toward Jayshawn's grave. I wanted my parents to put a bench out here, but I hadn't been here often enough for it to get any good use out of it. I was still trying to process it.

"Hey baby brother. I said I wasn't going to come out here today, but I think you were pulling me here. Maybe you knew I needed to come today."

My voice came out stronger than I anticipated. I was trying to be strong, but the weight of the feat was draining me. I sat down on the ground, my legs too heavy to stand anymore. I was glad I had on black pants. At this point, it wouldn't have mattered if I had on white; I'd just be dirty talking to my brother. Being in close proximity to him made it harder to breathe.

"One year," I eked out. "It's been a year and I still can't believe that you are gone. I just don't understand."

It had been 365 days since he died, and I still felt the same emptiness that held me hostage that day. Actually, it wasn't emptiness; it was a hurt that I didn't think would ever go away. My brother's death ripped my heart out of my chest and stripped me of my sanity. We were only two years apart. He often joked that I tried to be his mama even though I wasn't old enough to be. I was the oldest, so I took it upon myself to try to be his protector. But a year ago today, on January 21st, I failed him.

"Daddy still can't talk about you. Mama will, only in small doses. When I see Renee, I still see the hurt from losing the love of her life, but Jadira is doing great. You'd be so proud of your baby girl. Midori is the only one that seems to be doing okay, but you never know when it comes to our sister."

The words felt like they were strangling me; it was hard to even speak to him like this. Speaking of my brother in the past tense was one of the hardest things I did daily.

"I'm trying to get Blaze on the map but not in a celebrity, stuffy kind of way. I remember when you came that time and brought some of your friends, one of the biggest compliments I received was how laid back the place was. Folks stop by after work just to hang out and for one of Peaches' famous concoctions. I changed some of the decor, made it more comfortable. You'd love the place now, baby bruh. I want to try some new things though, get more people in and turn more of a profit."

Telling my brother about my bar and lounge made me feel proud. He was one of my biggest supporters and even put in some sweat equity to help me get the place up to par. I sort of inherited Blaze a few years ago. I worked there as a bartender just about every weekend. When Kevin, the owner, got sick, his stupid ass son took over and in the span of a few months almost bankrupted the place. He gave himself a ridiculous salary but neglected everything else. When Kevin was able, he fired his son and put me in charge. Not to brag, but I was a natural born leader but not in a mean, condescending kind of way. I was organized, smart, and majored in marketing at Georgia Southern. I knew I could run Blaze, and I was so glad when Kevin realized it as well.

It took me a while, but I got Blaze back on track and to show his appreciation, Kevin left Blaze to me in his will. His son didn't seem to mind because he really didn't want the responsibility of a business. I was very fortunate to not have to start a business from the ground up, and in a few months we'd be celebrating Blaze's ten-year anniversary in Midtown Atlanta.

"Even with Blaze doing well, it's still hard for me to be happy. I miss you so much, Jay."

For years, it was just Jayshawn and I. You'd be hard pressed to find siblings closer than us. Our sister Midori was ten years younger than me and we weren't as close as Jay and I were. Even though he was gone, Midori and I hadn't gotten any closer. Since I was in Atlanta, Jay and Midori had a great relationship, which I hated to admit made me a little jealous. It was hard for me to go to college at Georgia Southern in Statesboro because all of my life, my whole world was right there in Americus. Jay wouldn't let me stay home and go to Georgia Southwestern.

"Come on, sis," he told me. "Sure, GSW is a great school but get out. You've been here forever. It's time to see what's outside of this little town."

Because he gave me his blessing, I was able to go. And I was so glad I did. I left Americus in 2006 and I hadn't lived there in over ten years. And nothing, and I mean nothing, could ever get me to live there again. Don't get me wrong, I loved my little small town. It's not that I'm too good for Americus. It's just that I'd gotten a taste of the city and Atlanta was home now. I tried to go see my parents at least once a month but since Jay died, it had been harder and harder for me to come.

"I thought I'd find you here."

I looked up from my place next to Jay's grave and saw my sister, Midori. *So much for alone time.*

I stood up and wiped off the back of my pants. "Were you looking for me?"

"Not really. I've called you a few times, but you didn't answer," Midori responded.

"Why aren't you in class?"

"I didn't feel like going today," she reasoned.

I studied my little sister's face. She was the clone of our mother while Jay and I resembled our father. Staring at my sister was like looking at my mama and I saw the same sadness mama got when we talked about her baby boy. Midori had an obvious beauty that she took to heart. Because she was a 90s baby, she felt like she had to be on all the time. 20 inch sew ins. Face beat more often than not. Michael Kors bags and watches. Pink and Polo made up most of her wardrobe. Midori didn't seem to realize she didn't need any of that. She put you in the mind of Lauryn London. Same complexion, same smile. She was very popular in high school and I'm sure she was turning heads at GSW while majoring in sociology.

I hated that my parents bought her a reliable car, a 2015 Honda Accord, because it gave her the ability to run up and down 75 North. She came to Atlanta damn near every weekend because her boyfriend Rashard went to Clark Atlanta. She was planning on transferring next semester and I was trying to talk her out of it. Midori is a smart girl, beautiful on top of that, but she would become too easily distracted in Atlanta. And I didn't have time to babysit her.

"Midori, you can't just not go to class because you don't feel like it. You don't want to get into that habit," I lectured.

"Monica, calm down. I don't need you to tell me what to do. It's just one day and I can miss three. I read it in my syllabus."

I rolled my eyes at her. One thing she hated was for me to try to tell her what to do. Mama always thought we'd be much closer than we were because we were born on the same day, ten years apart. Imagine my disappointment when my mama had my sister on my tenth birthday. That was not the present I wanted. Growing up, I tried to help her, but Midori was definitely a Gemini; her moods changed like the seconds on the clock. Mama said I was the same way and maybe I was, but I also wasn't a spoiled brat. "Okay. Well, I'm getting out of here. I gotta open Blaze in a little bit."

"You're leaving? You're not going to see mama and daddy?" she questioned.

"Yeah, I'm going to stop by." I was frustrated that she interrupted my time with Jay. I planned on going by the house to see my parents and the school to see my niece. We FaceTimed weekly, and I followed her mama on social media so I could keep up with everything she was doing. My mama and daddy tried to go to all of her events, but Renee kept Jadira in some of everything. I guess keeping her busy didn't give her time to think about her daddy being gone.

"I still can't believe he's gone," Midori said staring at our brother's headstone. We stood there in silence for a few moments. My sister shut down when Jay died. She rarely talked about him to anyone. "Why didn't you stop him from leaving?"

I whipped my head in her direction wondering where this was coming from. "What do you mean?"

"If you didn't let him leave Blaze that night, he'd still be here."

I grabbed a hold of my sister's words. They didn't have anywhere to rest inside my brain because I wished I would have tried harder to get him to stay in the city. I asked him twice and he refused both times. Midori knew this. I'd told this story a million times. "Midori, shut up. You know I asked him to stay with me."

"All you had to do is make him spend the night instead of letting him drive all the way home. That's all you had to do."

"It's my fault some drunk nigga got behind the wheel? Jay didn't want to stay with me. I asked him, but he said no. Don't you dare try to blame this on me."

Midori wiped her eyes and bent over to move a leaf from Jay's grave. "Whatever you have to tell yourself to be okay. But even mama and daddy wondered why you didn't make him stay."

She left me standing out there, guilt rising up in me and coming out as the sausage biscuit I grabbed on the way down here. I wiped my mouth and almost ran back to my car. The anxiety and pain I felt earlier was nothing compared to what I felt now. *Was I really the reason he died? Could I have saved him?*

I replayed that day over and over in my head and no matter how much I tried to convince myself it wasn't my fault, there was a little voice telling me that maybe it was.

***

"Peaches, I thought we got a shipment of that liquor in the other day? How are we already out?" I called to my bartender.

"It's in the back, Mo. I only put a few bottles out."

"But why are you letting them get so low? You know I hate when you have to leave the bar to go to the back when the crowd is thick. You need to make sure you have everything ready to go for the night."

"Why do ya think I'm here now? I didn't just start working here yesterday, ya know," Peaches replied, her voice laced with irritation. "You're really trying me like I'm a buster right now and it's pissing me off."

I paused for a second to try to get myself together. This was so unlike me. One thing I prided myself on was not being a micromanager. I made sure I hired people that could handle their jobs without me having to stand over them and make sure they did it. In the two years she'd been here, Peaches has proven to be one of the best bartenders and bar managers I'd ever known. Not only did she handle the bar, but she made sure the wait staff did what they needed to be doing. It took a lot of pressure off me. So, for me to be there now trying to tell her what to do was counterproductive; I had other stuff I needed to be doing.

"I'm sorry, Peaches. Today is just not the best day." I came from around the back of the bar and sat down on the other side. I rarely sat from the customer's view point, but it was a good distraction to take in the bar's sporty elegance. I wanted everyone to enjoy my signature Mo Mack Experience. Atlanta sports team paraphernalia decorated the space, but not just jerseys and pictures. Because I'm extra, I commissioned unique and custom depictions of Atlanta sports. It didn't hurt that my boyfriend Nick was the artist. He helped do most of the pieces but also requested some of his colleagues to contribute as well. I prided myself on showing love to the home teams in a unique way.

"What's wrong?" Peaches asked, pausing her inventory to talk to me.

One of the first lessons Kevin taught me about this business was to draw the line between employees and employer. He preached that your employees should never be your friends. For the most part, I followed this advice but not with Peaches. She was different. She didn't know everything about my personal life, but she was someone I could talk to from time to time.

"I went to my brother's grave this morning," I began. "Can you fix me a vodka and cranberry?"

Peaches expertly fixed my drink and waited for me to continue.

"One year ago today, my brother walked out of here and died." I picked up my glass and took it to the head. I tasted just enough of the vodka to scrunch up my face after the familiar burn hit my throat. "You know my sister said it was my fault? She said I should have made him spend the night."

Without me even asking, Peaches gave me a refill. "How could it be your fault? Jay was a grown ass man. What were ya goin' to do? Wrestle that giant to the ground and make him stay? It was the drunk bastard from around the corner that's to blame."

I downed my drink quickly and she started to fix another one, but I put my hand over the glass. I didn't want to be tipsy before the sun went down. "I know that. Or at least I thought I knew that. Midori said daddy and mama blamed me, too."

I heard Peaches exhale deeply. "Look. You can play the blame game all ya want but it won't change anything. It won't do anything but have ya miserable. It's bad enough that he's gone. Don't add to it, Mo."

In the back of my mind, I knew Peaches was right. But it was the thoughts in the front of my brain that were giving me grief. "You're right. Midori's just...I don't know. I guess she's grieving like the rest of us."

"Fuck Midori and whoever else feels like they can heap this on ya," Peaches said with her arms folded across her chest. "And I say that as respectfully as I know how."

I laughed at Peaches because if this was her attempt at being respectful, I'd hate to see her speak her mind. It's always the little ones that have the biggest attitudes. She might be about 5'1" tall and couldn't weigh more than 110 pounds-and that was soaking wet. Her beautiful caramel skin was covered in tats and piercings that gave her a certain sex appeal. I knew she had about 30 tattoos and I was trying to catch up with her. She looked sweet as pie but when she spoke and that hood fell from her mouth, you knew she wasn't to be played with. I had to teach her a little business etiquette, but most of our customers became accustomed to her. She was known to 'go ham on that ass', which was one of her favorite things to say. About everyone and everything. One of the things that made Peaches,Peaches had an IDGAF attitude. She truly didn't care who rocked with her or not. I envied that about her.

Before Jay died, I was all about my business and I didn't leave room for much else. I was definitely no nonsense. After losing my brother, I lost a little bit of my edge and I became more sensitive. There was no way that shit my sister said to me today would have had me feeling like this before. I would have given her my two cents and went on about my life.

My boyfriend Nick liked that I wasn't so bossy all the time, as he described me. He wanted me softer, less blunt, but that really wasn't my personality. He would also prefer that I didn't hold back with him, but I would probably never fall in love with anyone else again; a casualty of giving your heart to the wrong person.

With my man on my mind, I decided to go see him. It was almost four and our happy hour crowd would be showing up in a little while. I had time to go home, change, go see Nick, and then get back here. "Thanks for listening Peaches. I'm gonna run home and change. I'll be back."

"Okay, Mo." Peaches got up and headed back to her side of the bar. "Oh, and if Cierra is late again today, I'm going ham on that ass. I'm not dealing with her bullshit excuses anymore. I can't work both ends of the bar and the servers if she ain't here."

"Let me talk to her first and then we'll go from there," I replied, thankful for the reprieve of work to get my mind off of Jay.

I headed to my office to get my bag when I heard my phone ringing with my mama's ringtone. I had to dig way down in the bottom of my bag to try to find it, but I was having no luck. *I need to clean this purse out. Then maybe I can find something in here*, I told myself.

I finally found my phone, but it stopped ringing before I could answer it. I didn't want to call her back, but I knew better. I took a deep breath to prepare myself for mama to fuss at me. I knew Midori told her I was in town. I opened the door to my office and ran smack dab into Nick.

"In a rush I see," Nick said grabbing my shoulders and making sure I didn't trip.

I was relieved to see him but the look on his face told me he wasn't too thrilled about having to track me down. I smiled up at Nick trying to transfer some of my fake happiness onto him, but it wasn't working.

As he stared down at me, his 5'10" muscular frame seemed daunting compared to my 5'5" height. If only I could get him to smile that beautiful smile, that smile that seemed to illuminate his dark chocolate skin, I'd know he wasn't mad at me anymore. Even with the scowl on his face, he was sexy. His freshly maintained dreadlocs that he usually kept pulled back into a ponytail were hanging to his shoulders. I loved when his hair framed his face. He was mad at me, but I was still happy to see him.

"Hey, King. I was on my way to see you," I gushed. Nick loved when I called him King. I did it more now than I did before; this was part of the new me he liked.

"Is that right?" His facial expression didn't change at all. "After two days, you finally decided I was worth seeing?"

I knew it was coming, but I was hoping he wouldn't be that upset about it. I'd been avoiding Nick. "It's not like that. Don't you know what today is?"

Nick stood his ground and crossed his arms. He wasn't having any parts of me getting out of this. "I know full well what today is and had you been around, I would have asked what you needed me to do. But just know I'm still waiting for an answer."

I leaned against the door of my office fumbling with my hands. Getting nervous like this was something I never did before, and I started to get mad at myself. I hated feeling emotional because it made me feel weak.

"Today isn't the day for this, Nick." I tried to be nice. *He's not going to do this to me today,* I assured myself.

"I wasn't trying to do this today. I told you that you need to move in with me two days ago and you've been missing ever since," he countered.

Part of the reason that I was apprehensive was that he didn't ask me to move in; he told me that's what I needed to do. I wasn't the submissive type, which usually pissed him off to no end. A lot of our arguments transpired because Nick demanded things of me and I refused to fall into his traditional relationship role where I did everything my man wanted because he was a man. I wasn't a feminist by any stretch, but I wasn't the type to forgo my happiness for his sake either.

I really didn't want to argue with him and add him to the list of people that had pissed me off today. "Look, that's not something I can just agree to without giving it some thought. It's a big step."

"But it's the next logical step. We've been together long enough. I don't understand why we are still living in separate places. I gave you a key to my place, but I don't have one to yours but that's another argument for another day. Doesn't it make sense to stop paying bills in two places and start building for our future?"

"Nick, I just don't know if I'm ready for that yet." I was very honest and open with him about my past, but he didn't seem to give a shit about that.

The reason I couldn't be submissive with Nick was because I did that with Devin and it got me nothing but the most gut-wrenching pain I ever experienced-until my brother died. A few months before I met Nick, I was nursing my very devastated heart because I fell in love with Devin Eaton. He was my first serious boyfriend and I gave it my all. We moved in together and I was more than happy to be wifey and step-mama to his daughter. Everything was going good until I started asking when we were getting married. I had the same reasoning as Nick; it was the next logical step.

Devin finally proposed but he told me a wedding was out of the question. He was 100% against dropping $10K for a one-day affair. Devin grew up with his mama barely living paycheck to paycheck. Even though he made decent money with his landscaping business, he couldn't see the point of shelling out big bucks for a wedding. I tried to cut corners everywhere I could, but it wasn't enough for him. I finally relented, convincing myself that I wanted to be married more than I wanted a wedding. We made an appointment to go to the courthouse, much to my disappointment, but it's what Devin wanted. I showed up for our 10:00am appointment but Devin never did.

I called and texted him a million times, but he was nowhere to be found. I scoured the news and social media trying to make sure he was okay and not lying dead somewhere in a ditch. The next day, he texted me to tell me he was going to work things out with his daughter's mother. Last I knew they moved to Tennessee, opting to get as far away from me as possible. I don't blame them with the way I harassed Devin and his baby mama. I just couldn't concede defeat. I replayed our relationship over and over in my head and I determined giving your all was for the birds. I let him control me, control us, and I ended up with nothing but a restraining order.

Losing Devin like that broke me down something awful. I loved him more than I ever loved anyone else. He was my everything. When he left me, I shut down emotionally. Nick somehow found his way in, but I vowed to never give my heart completely to anyone else. I would never experience that hurt again.

Hearing Nick repeat his same speech from the other night still freaked me out. I'm not even sure why I was surprised he wanted this. Nick told me on our second date he wanted to get married and have kids. I smiled politely and changed the subject. When I told my best friend Keyalani that Nick wanted me to move in but I was undecided, she questioned my sanity.

"Monica, girl are you crazy? Do you know how many women would jump at the chance for their man to talk about building for their future?"

On some levels, I knew she was right. Nick was every sane woman's dream. He was smart and an insanely talented artist. Instead of showcasing his art in huge venues, Nick decided to teach art to high school students. He was worth much more than he was being paid, but he really believed in the power of art and the doors it could open. His passion for working with kids was heartwarming. A few times a year he and some of his friends taught classes for kids in different mediums and then they host an art show to showcase their talent. He had a friend that had an art gallery and he cleared the space for the kids to display their work. It was a beautiful event, one that I looked forward to attending.

"Nick, I'm...I just need time to think, that's all. You're asking me to give up my condo. I'd have to put it on the market and what if it doesn't sell? And why do I have to move out of my place?"

He dropped his head and clinched his fists. "Now you're just making up excuses, Monica. My space is bigger, and I need the room for my art. You know that. And do you really think I'm dumb enough to believe you'd have a hard time selling a corner condo in Midtown? What's the real problem?"

"I don't think you're dumb at all. I'm just asking you to be patient with me. I did this once before and it ended terribly for me. I'm not trying to go through that again. And I cannot make this decision today. Not today. It's too much today."

"Whatever, Monica. Between your brother and your ex, you have the most excuses for why we can't move forward. I'll be glad when you stop using them as excuses for everything you don't want to do."

"Nick, that's not fair! You know I'm-"

"You're having a hard time," he interrupted me, proof that I said that a lot. "But how long am I supposed to pay for mistakes I didn't make?"

I sat silently because Keyalani had scolded me about this a number of times. My mind knew it wasn't fair to keep punishing Nick for what Devin did; it was my heart that refused to believe they were two different people. I just couldn't make myself trust that Nick wasn't going to play me like Devin did. And as far as my brother went, it was too new and too fresh for me to even try to deal with.

"And I'm not insinuating that you should be over losing your brother. What I am saying is that you're never going to heal if you keep yourself chained to his death. You haven't even cried yet. I'll talk to you later."

Nick walked away leaving me confused by what he said. The fake happiness I had a second ago was now replaced by real anger. I waited a few minutes for him to leave before I followed suit. I was grateful to live in close proximity to Blaze so traffic wasn't a total nightmare. I walked into my condo and fell across my bed.

Nick was wrong. I wasn't trying to hold on to Jay's death; his death held on to me. Martin Jayshawn Mack was my best friend. I talked to him every day. If I had a problem, he was my go-to for advice. Losing him suddenly wasn't easy for me, not when he was such a big part of my life. Nick was an only child, so he didn't understand how I felt, how bad this hurt. I'd give anything to feel some sort of normalcy again.

But he was right about one thing: I hadn't cried for my brother yet. At all. Not one tear had fallen from my eyes. Since he died, I had lived in a state of shock. He encouraged me to let it out and a year later, and I still haven't been able to shed a tear for my brother.

I kicked off my shoes and hugged my body pillow. The day ended up being very exhausting and I was worn out. I was going to allow myself five minutes to rest my eyes then I was going to get ready to go to work.

I woke up to Nick's ringtone on my phone. He told me to open the door. Groggily I went to my front door and let him in. "I have to go to work," I said.

"You're exhausted. Just rest, baby."

I didn't even try to fight him on it, another casualty of the new me. I went to my bedroom and sank back into my 600 count sheets, knowing I needed to rest but also wanting to go to Blaze. My body refused to let me get up though.

Nick tucked me in, kissed me on my forehead, and started to walk out, probably to go the living room to watch Netflix.

"Baby, come hold me. Please."

He didn't even hesitate before he took off his clothes and got into bed with me. Being in his arms made this bad day seem more bearable.

"I can't be here for you if you push me away," he gently scolded me.

"Sometimes it becomes overwhelming and I don't want to keep burdening you with this. I'm trying. I really am."

Nick pulled me in closer to his body, and I could feel the rhythm of his heart. "I know you are Queen and you're not a burden to me. You never have been, and you never will be. I am here for you, no matter what. But if you need time alone, tell me that. I can respect that. I can't respect you disappearing for two days."

My heart thudded in my chest because Nick continued to prove how much I meant to him. After Devin, love sucked. I stopped caring about love. I stopped wanting a relationship. I was fine having a cut buddy to call when I needed an orgasm. Nick showed up when I wasn't trying to be involved with anyone and his persistence won me over. I fought him for months, but he was determined to be with me.

Nick scared me at first because we seemed to be opposites. I didn't even think I was his physical type. I'd seen pictures of women he dated before and my milk chocolate skin was shades darker than his ex. A man as fine as Nick was used to an obviously gorgeous woman on his arm. Not saying I'm not pretty, but I just wasn't into make-up, weave, and name brand clothes. I had the body to dress more provocatively, but I chose not to unless it was a special occasion.

We both had locs but while his were maintained, mine were purple and I rarely made the time to do maintenance on them. We were both educated; we both had master's degrees, but that was where our similarities ended. Nick was a neat freak and I was not. He liked to stay home and paint and I liked to be out in the crowd. He preferred home cooked meals, and I rarely used my kitchen. Nick wants to get married, have 2.5 kids, a dog, and a house with a white picket fence. I want to live in my corner condo with a gym in the building and I've never wanted kids.

With all of our differences, Nick was in love with me. And at that moment, nothing else but him loving me mattered. Even if I didn't quite feel the same.

Chapter Two

"Okay everyone, that's about all I have. I need everyone to share the events on their personal pages. Invite as many people out as you can. Let's make sure we are well prepared for the crowds with as little delays as possible. Peaches will let everyone know how our specials will run."

I finished addressing my staff and headed back to my office. I didn't have to stay and listen to Peaches give directions; we already established how to make sure our customers didn't run into long wait times. I've spoken to my cooks, Quan and Tank, about making sure we had wings and fries flowing constantly. Focusing on what I could control, I needed to finalize this DJ for Friday night and we'd been playing phone tag for most of the day.

Next week we would be celebrating Blaze's tenth anniversary. I wasn't stressed because we had been planning this event for months. Now that it was around the corner, there was nothing left to do but execute. I left yet another voicemail with my potential DJ before straightening up the papers on my desk. At home I didn't mind clutter, but at work organization was one of my strong suits. I needed everything in order.

I was so very excited about Blaze's ten years in the game. With the way businesses closed down all the time, I was fortunate to have a steady flow of customers day after day. But...there was still room for improvement. I had plans to renovate parts of Blaze, the ladies' room in particular. I also wanted to be able to do things like karaoke and open mic nights, and I wanted to re-vamp the menu and hire a chef. Right now, we served simple appetizers; wings, fries, fried green tomatoes, spinach dip. It wasn't anything to write home about, but it served its purpose. But I wanted something else, high end, more of a dinner menu. I had the mindset to plan these things and how to execute them. It wasn't that I didn't have money, Blaze was turning a profit every month, but making such a huge investment was a risk.

I stopped thinking down the road and prepared my-self for the upcoming anniversary party. Instead of having one big party on the weekend, I planned several events throughout the week. From ten cent wings to an old school party, I was preparing to have an epic week at Blaze.

I was so engrossed in the paperwork on my desk that I jumped when my cell phone rang. I was hoping it was my potential DJ but instead it was Nick. I was slightly disappointed but only for a brief second.

"Hey baby, what's up?" I sang into the phone. I pushed away from my desk and crossed my legs. I was good at multi-tasking but Nick would start an argument if I wasn't giving him my undivided attention. With the way he'd been kind to me the past couple of days, I was going to give him the pleasure of being the center of my world right now.

"Hey Queen. I was just thinking about you, and I wanted to let you know," he replied causing me to smile. I was a grown woman, damn near 30 years old, and lines like that shouldn't have that kind of effect on me. It was so high school and cheesy. But that was Nick…an old school romantic.

"Aww, thank you King. It's great to be thought about," I gushed. "What you got going on tonight?"

"I'm coming to get you in a little while so we can spend time together."

The silence that ensued was more than awkward. It was damn right disrespectful. Nick knew how I felt about not being in the building for at least part of the night. If I didn't stay to closing every night, I was usually here to close at midnight doing whatever needed to be done around here. I wasn't one of those owners that felt like I was above washing dishes or wiping down a table. I did whatever needed to be done to make this place run smoothly. Nick knew that and here he was telling me to leave my job.

"Nick," I began weighing my words carefully. I didn't want to start an argument although his demand was enough to make me mad. "You know I can't just not be at work. I'm the owner and not the behind the scenes kind either."

"Well, you have the night off tonight. Peaches said so." Nick wasn't moved by the speech he'd heard a million and one times. He understood this was my life, at least I thought he did. I didn't keep traditional hours. We didn't date like other couples; we had to settle for weekend brunches or a quick dinner in my office while I worked. We'd been making it work; I'm not sure why Nick was trying to change things now.

I snorted in the phone. "She can't give me the night off. I'm the-"

"You're the boss. Yes, I know. She knows. Everyone that's ever met you knows. But being the boss shouldn't mean you never get to spend time with the people you love."

Before I could ask him what he meant by 'everyone that's ever met you knows', Peaches came to my office.

"Hey why don't ya get out of here. We can handle it tonight. We have a big week next week so why don't ya get rested up?"

"Are ya'll in cahoots?" I asked laughing.

Peaches looked at me clueless. "Yo, I don't know what that shit means but Nick asked if we needed ya and I told him we didn't. Not tonight anyway."

Nick decided to chime in to plead his case. "There are no major sporting events going on tonight. And Wednesdays are usually pretty chill up there. And before you ask, no I'm not coming up there. I always come up there. It's time you do something for me."

I don't know how he knew that was about to come out of my mouth, but he shut me down before I could even form the words.

"Mo, just go. We'll be good. Enjoy ya man, girl. Get ya some for the ones of us that don't have that always there dick," Peaches inserted.

"Peaches!" Sometimes she was so crass.

"What?" she replied. She wasn't even aware of why I was saying her name. "Girl, I wish I had a man around to take me on a date. And give me that D. I'm about ready to go ham on somebody's ass."

I heard Nick laugh, and I couldn't help but to grin myself. Peaches really didn't give up too much information on herself. Hell, there were times I forgot her real name was Calandria. I knew she had a son that was born extremely premature and he passed hours after he was born. She told me that one time and she never talked about it again. I also knew at one point her man was locked up and apparently Peaches was a ride or die chick. I, on the other hand, didn't grasp the concept of riding and dying for a nigga in jail. But hey, whatever floats her boat.

I knew I wouldn't be able to keep fighting the both of them. "Okay, okay! You guys win! Give me about an hour."

I could practically hear Nick smiling through the phone. "Naw, Queen, I'll be there soon. There's a spot I want to check out near you."

"Okay baby. See you in a little bit." We hung up the phone and I decided to finish the last little bit of paperwork I had left. But I noticed Peaches was still standing in my doorway. "Yeah, you and Nick are working together I see."

Peaches rolled her eyes at me and sucked her teeth. "Whatever, Mo. Ya got this man, he's fine as fuck, and he wants to spend time with ya and you'd rather be here? Why?"

I pondered her question and I didn't have a real answer. Before Nick, I had Blaze. It was what I loved. It was what I worked my ass off for. I was almost at the place I wanted to be in my life. If I asked Nick not to paint or draw, he'd probably die right then and there. So, I didn't get why he couldn't understand that I loved Blaze like he loved his art.

"This is what I love to do, Peaches. I have an obligation. This is my job. I can't just blow off work cause my man wants to cuddle."

Peaches cocked her head to the side and gave me a blank look. She truly didn't understand. "But you the

25

boss. Ya don't *have* to be here. I'm just saying. A man that fine will get snatched up quick cause you're too busy here. Don't say I didn't warn ya."

She left my office, leaving me to ponder over what she said. *Would Nick leave me because I didn't spend enough time with him?* I let the thought linger for a second then let it go. I wasn't everything Nick wanted me to be, but he fell in love with me anyway. So there was some reason he was still with me. But I didn't have time to dwell on that; Nick would be here shortly, and I had time to mingle with a few patrons before he got here.

I grabbed my purse to put behind the bar and locked my door. Peaches was the only person that had a key to my office because she handled the money at the end of the night if I was not around. It was only a handful of people here tonight and that wasn't unusual for a Wednesday. I tried closing on a Wednesday once and I caught hell from my loyal customers. Since Wednesdays were pretty chill, it was more of the business and girls night out crowd. The people that didn't want to be bothered with a lot of people. The people that could have a good time and still get home before 9.

I mingled with a few of my customers, some who were regulars. A group of stay-at-home moms came out once or twice a month to get out of the house and I started a special just for them which guaranteed they would come back. I used to assume that stay-at-home moms didn't do much. But, after having a conversation with some of the ladies, I learned there was a lot that went into it, especially the ones that home schooled their kids. So, the Wednesdays they came to Midtown, I hooked them up with a drink, wings, and fries for $10. They didn't even have to ask for it. When my hostess spotted them, she made sure their server knew why they were here: some time away from the house with some girl talk and good drinks. My servers fought to get this group because they tipped very, very well.

I chatted with my ladies before going to sit at the bar to wait on Nick. I checked my phone hoping that I hadn't missed a call from my DJ. At this point, I was prepared to move on to someone else because he obviously didn't want this money.

"Peaches, can you get the lady a drink? Whatever she wants," a patron sitting at the bar called to Peaches.

Peaches rolled her eyes, obviously annoyed with this customer. This happened from time to time and contrary to what Nick thought, I didn't tell everyone I was the boss. "No thank you sir. I'm good. I'm about to go."

"Oh, word? Where are we going?"

I laughed heartily at the boldness of this stranger. "WE aren't going anywhere. I'M going on a date with my boyfriend."

"Boyfriend, huh? Is you happy?" he asked in his best T.I. impression.

Again, I laughed, entertained by this guy. And then I looked at him. *Damn he was fine.*

Even sitting down, I could tell he was tall as hell and muscular to boot. His skin was like honey, and I was usually not attracted to light skin men. But the most striking thing about him was his eyes. They were noticeably light brown and…intense. He was staring at me, and I felt uncomfortable. Exposed. Naked. I had to immediately averted my gaze and fumbled with my phone in the process. I didn't want to give him access to me like this.

"Hey Queen, are you ready to go?" Nick kissed me on my jaw, startling me. "You okay?"

"Y-y-yes," I stammered. "You just scared me."

I got off the stool and told Peaches I'd see her tomorrow. I looked briefly in the direction of the stranger and once again his intensive stare did something to me. I quickly looked away again and let Nick whisk me out of Blaze.

It didn't take long for me to get the stranger out of my mind because Nick escorted me to Nina's, a restaurant that just opened up the street. The owner, Nina, has frequented Blaze numerous times and I was glad that Nick finally gave me the opportunity to check the place out. As a business owner, I found importance in making allies rather than enemies. Atlanta had enough people for us to all win and I didn't see the need in putting down another business to highlight my own. Besides, Nina's Caribbean cuisine was nothing like the wings and fries we served.

We walked in to Nina's and I was immediately in love with the décor. The red, black, and yellow ode to her homeland reminded me of the trip I took to Jamaica a few years back. Either Nina had an awesome decorator, or she just moved from the islands last week. Impressed was an understatement.

"Mo! So very glad you could come! Here, have a seat and I'll get you a menu," Nina exclaimed when she saw me. She had lived in the states for years, but she still had a slight Jamaican accent that I loved. Nina was in her early 40s, but she didn't look a day over 25.

"Thank you, Nina! The place looks great and I mean that. You did a phenomenal job with the décor," I gushed as Nina beamed with pride. "Oh, and this is my boyfriend, Nick."

Nina and Nick shook hands before we took our seats. "Nice to meet you, Nick. Here are your menus; I'll be back to check on you in a few minutes."

"Thank you, Nina. Again, the place looks great!"

Nina moved along to greet other patrons while Nick and I looked over the menu. "So how was your day?", Nick asked.

I was still skimming the menu and having a hard time deciding between the Jamaican jerk chicken or the curry goat. "Umm...you know. Same ol', same ol'. How was yours?"

"It was good. Preparing for the kids' next showcase in March. There's this one kid, Jarrell, that I thought was a lost cause at first. Rude, disrespectful, mean as hell. Turns out he's in foster care and is just tired of being moved here and there. He's had a rough child-hood...absent father, mother strung out, separated from his siblings. I don't see how this kid hasn't killed himself or anyone else yet. His foster parent noticed some of his drawings and signed him up for the pro-gram. After he saw that Chris and I weren't going to give up on him, he started softening up. Mo, you have to see this kid's work. It's insane."

Hearing Nick talk about his passion was always a breath of fresh air. With social media and reality shows, most kids thought their only way to make it was to be a rapper, drug dealer, model, or side chick. To see kids really passionate about art gave me hope for our future generation.

Nick pulled out his phone and showed me some of Jarrell's art work. And the kid was really good. His best works were done with charcoal even though he was good with painting as well. Nick also told me Jarrell was becoming interested in photography, so he was reaching out to a friend of his to spend some time with Jarrell.

"It's amazing how this kid has turned around. Even his art has changed. Before, his drawings were dark, and the sadness seemed to leap off the page. But now, his content has changed. He drew a picture of his foster parent and she cried. Mo, you should have seen how proud he was. I don't think he's ever had anyone tell him they were proud of him."

"Wow, babe, that's amazing. I can't wait for the showcase to see what he and the others have done," I said. "And you're amazing for donating your time and talents to these kids."

As usual, Nick dismissed my compliment. He was very humble and hated when I doted on him like that. "If I don't use what I have to influence someone else, what good is what I have? I just can't wait to be able to share what I love with my own kid."

I tried to hide my surprise, but I was sure Nick caught it. Fortunately, I was saved by the waitress arriving to take our order. I opted for the curry goat and Nick, the jerk chicken. I also got an appetizer of beef, chicken, and vegetable patty.

"I haven't been able to secure a DJ for next Friday night. People complain that they can't get work and here I am offering this dude a chance and he can't even get back in touch with me," I said choosing not to address Nick's last statement.

"Well, move on to the next babe. There are plenty of DJ's out there that want the work. Reach out on social media, I'm sure you'll have plenty to choose from."

"Great idea, Nick! I'll do that!" I started to make a post immediately but decided against it. If I posted it now, my notifications would blow up and I wouldn't be able to enjoy my dinner or my man.

Nick and I continued to make small talk until our appetizer arrived. Nick wasn't a fan of the patty, but I thought it was good. About ten minutes later, our food came out. I took pictures of our meal to post on Blaze's social media pages to drive some business to Nina. My curry goat was delicious, and I was glad this place was up the street from me and I could get this on the regular. Nick's jerk chicken was good as well. Before we left, I found Nina to compliment her again and to let her know the food was delicious.

Nick was parked near Blaze but he wouldn't even let me look in that direction. We got in his car and I knew we were heading to his place. As much as I didn't want to admit it, it was good to get away from Blaze for a night and relax. Running a business was as rewarding as it was draining.

At Nick's place, I went to his bedroom and changed into the pajamas I kept over here. I was sprawled out across his bed checking Blaze's Instagram posts when I felt Nick climbing on the bed. He straddled me from behind and began massaging my back. I dropped my phone and closed my eyes, loving the strength of his hands.

"Mmmmm baby that feels so good," I exhaled.

Nick didn't speak; he just continued to rub my back. He moved my locs from the right side of my neck to plant soft kisses on my exposed skin. Once again, I exhaled deeply, loving the way he was touching me.

"I love having you here like this. I can't wait for you to move in."

My eyes flew open and my moment of pleasure was now over.

"Nick, why do we have to talk about this now? Why can't we just continue our evening without getting into all that seriousness? And I haven't agreed to move in."

Nick paused and then moved to sit on the side of the bed next to me. I turned on my side and propped my head on my hand to look at him. He was a combination of upset and frustrated. I just wanted him to go back to kissing my neck because he was turning me on.

"Because you've never given me an answer. I think I've been more than patient with you and this situation," he snapped.

I really wanted to go off, but I didn't want to escalate the situation. I needed him to scratch the itch he created. I crawled on the bed to where he was sitting and straddled him, so I could look in his eyes. I kissed his lips and he tried to resist me, but he couldn't. When my tongue slipped in his mouth and I heard him moan softly, I knew I had him where I wanted him. I began to grind slowly against him, getting more and more aroused by his hardness between my legs.

"Mo..." he whispered. I loved to hear him say my name like that. "I shouldn't have to beg you for this. Move in with me. I need this every day."

And just like that, my arousal disappeared again. I stopped my slow grind and got off him to go to the bathroom.

"Where are you going?" he called after me.

I ignored him and stomped to the bathroom. It had been close to two weeks since we'd had sex and I needed this bad. But I wasn't going to get any if he kept pressuring me to move in. Accidently, on purpose, I slammed the bathroom door, closed the toilet lid, and sat down.

"Yo, I've told you I don't like for doors to be slammed," Nick almost yelled as he burst into the bathroom.

I closed my eyes and slowly counted to ten to stop myself from going off on him. "I'm sorry, Nick."

"What the hell is your problem? We were talking about you moving in and you storm off to the bathroom and slam the door? You don't even have the decency to respond?"

"We were not talking about it. You were. I have told you I need to think about it. Stop pressuring me and give me time to think!" I spat. I was done being nice to him.

Nick shook his head slowly, letting me know he didn't understand my logic. "Mo, what's the deal? We've been together for over a year. I want to be in the same place with you. Is that so hard for you to understand? I have plans in my life that include you-that include you as my wife and the mother of my children."

I've always known that's what he wanted. But for some reason, he was pushing it hard. I was nowhere near ready for that.

"Nick, I'm not saying I don't want that, but I am saying I don't want that right now. I'm at the height of my career. Blaze is doing great and I have plans to make it even greater. I can't even think about marriage and kids right now."

"Wow, tell me how you really feel," Nick responded with sarcasm.

I started to play with my locs, a nervous habit I developed after Jay died. "This isn't new to you. I've told you this before. Plenty of times. I'm not sure why you are having a hard time getting it."

It's not that I didn't want to be someone's wife someday, but not now. Not for another few years. Getting married meant a wedding and I didn't have time to plan a whole wedding right now. Not to mention I still wasn't over what Devin did to me. And being a mama? My whole life would have to change. My family was in Americus and Nick wasn't that close to his mama so we wouldn't have any help here. And I wasn't ready to give up my business to be a parent.

"So many women complain there are no good men, but you have one, one that wants to marry you and have a family with you and you don't want that. You blame it on your business and your brother. On top of that, I'm paying the ultimate price for something someone else did to you. Unbelievable."

My ringing phone stopped me from giving him the business. I wasn't other women and he knew that about me. I'm the same person I was when he met me. I wanted to ignore my phone, but it started ringing again with Midori's ringtone. I would have ignored it, but it was the excuse I needed to get out of this conversation.

I walked out the bathroom, making sure not to touch Nick on my way out. I got to my phone just as it stopped ringing, but it started right back.

"Midori, why are you calling me back to back?"

"MO! HELP ME! COME HELP ME!" she screamed.

"Midori, what's wrong? What happened?"

"Just come get me please! From Shard's apartment. Mo please hurry!"

"You're in Atlanta? Why?"

"STOP ASKING ME ALL THESE DAMN QUESTIONS AND COME GET ME!!"

She hung up and I thought for a second about not going. I wasn't in the mood for her tonight. I started getting dressed when Nick asked where I was going.

"I'm assuming Midori got into it with Shard. My mama would kick my ass if I left her to deal with this shit alone. So, I'm going to go get her."

Nick exhaled deeply. "Hold on, I'm coming with you."

* * *

Nick and I pulled up to an apartment complex in Washington Park and located Shard's apartment. I had to call Midori three times to get her to tell me where she was. We hadn't even parked good before she came running out. Her left eye was black and swollen and there was dried blood on her face.

"Let's go. Let's just go!" she cried while hopping in the back of Nick's car.

If she thought I was just going to let this black eye go, she had another thing coming. "Naw, Midori. Where is Rashard? I know damn well this nigga didn't put his hands on you."

I was out of the car and heading towards the apartment she ran out of. My sister was a hot mess and needed to learn a thing or two, but I didn't take Rashard hitting her too lightly. I was livid. I could hear her in the background begging me to forget about it and to just take her home.

I walked into the apartment and it looked like World War III had taken place. Furniture was over turned, and pieces of broken glass were near the front door. I looked around in disbelief and tried to imagine what could have taken place here. It was then that I saw feet in the kitchen.

I ran over and found Rashard on the ground and bleeding from his head, just as I heard Midori come back in behind me. "Oh my God, Midori what the hell did you do? No, don't answer that! I don't want to know! Did you even call 911?"

Her tears let me know that she panicked and hadn't. I pulled out my phone to call an ambulance while I felt for a pulse. Owning a bar and lounge, I thought it would be a good idea to be certified in first aid in case something happened. Rashard had a pulse and he was breathing. His wound looked superficial at best, but he was unconscious.

An hour later, Nick and I were sitting in the waiting room of Grady Memorial, ignoring the need to finish our conversation. I hated that my sister almost killed her boyfriend, but it got me out of talking about why I didn't want to move in, get married, and pop out children.

Midori finally emerged from the back with a prescription for pain meds. We spoke with the police and I couldn't tell them anything because I had no idea what happened. No charges were pressed because neither would press charges against the other. The police weren't bothered because it was Atlanta; there were more pressing things to attend to. I didn't even look at her as we got in the car to leave. I asked Nick to drop us off at my apartment even though I needed him to make love to me; my sister was in no position to be alone. Plus, Nick would want to talk, and I didn't want to talk about that.

Midori headed straight to the guest bathroom to take a shower and I sat on the bed in the guest bedroom waiting for her to get out. I checked in with Peaches to see how the night went and she told me everything was good because it was a slow night. I was relieved because I didn't need any problems with Blaze tonight; Midori and Nick were enough.

She finally emerged from the shower and laid across the bed.

"Midori, what happened? Why are you in Atlanta tonight anyway?" She sighed heavily, and I hoped she knew to expect this. I wasn't going to just let this go.

"I was coming up here this weekend anyway, but I decided to come a day early to surprise him. I have a key to his place and when I walked in, he had another bitch in there. He claimed they were studying but I knew better. I just lost it."

I shook my head, but truthfully I wasn't surprised. I didn't know where she came from, but my sister was certifiably crazy when she had a boyfriend. Boyfriends that she changed like she changed panties. I didn't understand how she got so crazy so fast; she seemed to be in love with someone else every other month.

"Damn, I'm sorry. That was foul of him, but you didn't have to hit him like that. You could have killed him and been in jail."

"I know. I don't need a damn lecture from you. It doesn't matter. It's over and now I have to figure out what I'm going to do."

"What do you mean?"

"I withdrew from GSW, and I was going to transfer to Clark Atlanta to be with Rashard."

"YOU DID WHAT?" I screamed. I knew I didn't hear my sister say she withdrew from college. In January. Hell, the semester had barely begun.

Midori got up and headed to my kitchen with me on her heels. She had another thing coming if she thought I was going to be quiet about this. She rambled through my cabinets until she found some chips and sat down at my island to eat. Her nonchalance was pissing me off.

"Listen. You are too smart for this. Why would you do that? Why couldn't you wait until May? Why are you putting yourself behind like this?"

Midori was staring off into nothing, bouncing her leg as she ate her chips. "Mo, I don't even know if I wanna go to school. It's boring to me. I don't even know what I want to do with my life. Rashard and I talked about me just coming up and finding a job."

Listening to my sister talk was draining the life out of me. I just wanted to grab her and shake her. I crossed my arms in front of me to stop myself from being charged with shaken sister syndrome. "Atlanta isn't the place you can move to and not have a plan. Talking about finding a job and actually applying for jobs are two different things."

"I have an interview on Monday and one on Thursday," my sister said matter of factly.

As I processed what she said, the realization of what was happening hit me. "So you were planning on moving up here this weekend? Have you told mama and daddy? And if you and Rashard are over, where are you planning on living?"

"Yeah they know. Kind of. Okay, no they don't," she began. Her eyes darted everywhere but she refused to look at me. "I was hoping I could live with you."

"MIDORI!" I began but paused before I cursed her out from here to kingdom come. I knew I should have packed up her shit and got on 75 South heading to Americus. But right now, I stared at my sister, my sweet, clueless sister and silently thanked her for this mess. Because so long as she was here, Nick couldn't pressure me into moving in. My sister's stupidity just saved me.

I let the silence linger so as not to give away my secret satisfaction in her situation. "Ugh, Okay, Midori. But only temporarily. And you have to find a job. Quick."

I left Midori sitting at my island while I headed to my bedroom. I'd never tell her so, but for once I was grateful for the drama she created.

Chapter Three

I thought living with my sister when we were kids was bad, but this was as bad as it got. I knew I was not the cleanest person in the world but damn. If I had to pick up her shit out of my living room one more time, I was going to punch her in the throat. If I had to wipe toothpaste off the sink one more time, I was going to drop kick her in the face. I was sick of Midori living with me.

Luckily, I was consumed with work and I always had a safe haven in Nick's place. Blaze's ten-year anniversary week went on without a hitch, but I was so glad it was over. I made new connections including landing a new DJ in Tyrin, a student that goes to Georgia State. Even though he was only 21, Tyrin kept my grown and sexy crowd rocking that night. I was probably going to hire him as my official event DJ because he contributed to the Mo Mack Experience. I'm sure he got a few numbers from women old enough to be his mama.

Anniversary week helped me to realize I really needed to get on the ladies' bathroom renovation. Two stalls were hardly enough and there weren't enough mirrors for the women to make sure they still looked fly. I needed to start looking for a contractor to get this project underway.

Because Midori wouldn't keep a job longer than a week, she was always at my apartment. So, I spent more time at Nick's. I was trying to do better and spend more time with him. He loved the days I got off work while the sun was still out. Most evenings I came to his house, he had dinner waiting for me. We would drink wine and talk, and I had to admit, it was great coming home to him like this. But I checked in with Peaches constantly to make sure everything was running smoothly. I did agree that Wednesdays would be my early day so that we could spend time together.

Tonight was Wednesday but Nick cancelled our date because this weekend was the art showcase for the students he's been working with. Instead of going to his house and being alone, I decided to brave my own place with my sister there.

I walked into my condo to trap music blasting from my sound bar followed by loud laughing and talking. *Was this child having a party in my house?*

I made it to my living room and almost started choking from the thick cloud of smoke that hit me in the face. There were about seven kids in my house. I saw cups and paper on the floor and on my living room table. One girl had her dirty ass feet on my cream-colored sofa.

"Get. The. Hell. Out. Of. My. House," I said through clenched teeth. I tried my best to be calm because I didn't want to embarrass my sister, but her ass was pushing it.

"Yo, Mo! What's good, sis? You wanna hit this?" Midori asked stupidly while trying to hand me a blunt.

I pushed past her and went to turn the music off. I don't know whose iPhone I almost threw across the room, but I really didn't care.

"Mo! What are you doing?"

"Party's over. Get out. All of you. Get out." I acted like I didn't even hear her.

Midori's face was a mixture of confused and high as she looked at me with her head cocked to the side. No one moved; they just looked back and forth between Midori and I. We stared each other down, both testing the will of the other. If Midori wasn't stupid high, she'd probably get pissed. I put my hand on my hip and held my gaze until she rolled her eyes at me.

"Ya'll gotta go. My sister acting like I don't live here too and I can't have a few friends over."

"Bitch," I said before I knew it. "You just live here. You don't clean up and you don't pay a single bill in MY house. So, until you contribute in some way, you don't get to have anyone over here if I don't want them here and you certainly will not smoke in my house."

Midori popped her lips and walked towards her bedroom. She slammed the door leaving her guests out there with me. They figured out I wasn't one to play with and it only took them a hot second to gather their things and leave.

My living room was in disarray, my house smelled like weed, and my sister was a big ass baby. A high one at that. I didn't have the energy to deal with this shit tonight. *I should have just gone to Nick's*, I told myself

I went to my bedroom to take a shower and to wash away the stress Midori was heaping on me. I guess I should have been relieved that she was out of the bed. A few days last week I don't know if Midori left the apartment. She was in the bed when I left for Blaze and she was sitting around when I got home. I chalked it up to her trying to get over Shard. Whatever it was, tomorrow we were going to have a heart to heart and she was either going to find a job or she was going back home.

* * *

"Midori, we need to talk," I began when she finally got up the next day. I planned on making her breakfast, but she didn't get up until almost noon. She looked like she hadn't really slept.

"Damn, Mo, I'm just getting up. Do you have to start already?"

She walked around the island to the fridge, and I noticed she didn't have on any pants.

"Girl, if you don't go put on some pants! I don't want to see you in your damn draws!"

She popped her lips and went to her room. When she didn't come back, I went to find her.

"I told you we need to talk," I announced standing in the doorway.

She sighed heavily and crossed her arms. "Okay so talk, Mo."

"Listen. When are you going to find a job? Because you sitting here doing nothing all day isn't going to work."

"All these jobs want you to work every weekend. And close at that. I have a life, I don't have time for that."

I scrunched up my face. "What do you mean you don't have time for that? You don't have time for what? Working? Making money? What else are you doing with your time? You aren't in school and you aren't cleaning up…what else do you have to do?" I rattled off. This girl was seriously pissing me off.

"Calm down! You're as bad as mama! I just want to have fun and hang out with my friends. I can't do that if I'm not getting off work until 11:30 at night. I miss all the parties, all the fun, everything."

I couldn't believe the words that were coming out of my sister's mouth. Were all 19-year olds this…lazy? "You wanted to be grown and move your ass to Atlanta, so this is what you have to do. You will not stay here for free. You will either find a job or get in someone's school. Life isn't all about fun, Midori. You're almost 20. You need to learn some responsibility."

Dumbfounded, she just looked at me. I don't know what about me gave her the impression that I would be fine with her being a couch potato. I called my sister a few times a week to check on her. I always asked about school and work; she shouldn't be surprised at all.

"Of all those kids that were here, how many are in school? Or work?" I quizzed. She refused to answer me. "Probably all of them. Except you. They are doing what they have to do, and you'll be stuck looking crazy with no money and no education. They come party with you, but I guarantee they aren't blowing off a paycheck to come smoke weed."

"I don't expect you to understand," she spat, and I assumed I hit a nerve. The truth will do that to you. "You do nothing but work. Didn't you use to party when you were my age?" She was trying to get me feel sorry for her, but I felt nothing of the sort. She was too old to free load off me. Not when she was capable.

"Yes, Midori, I did party when I was in college. But I also went to class and work. I'm not going to lie…I did miss class sometimes and I did miss a few days of work." I wanted to lie to her and pretend I was the model student but that wouldn't help her. "I also knew I wasn't going to be a career student and I wasn't, under any circumstances, going back home. So, I got it together. Which is all I'm trying to get you to do."

Midori rolled her eyes at me and headed back to her bedroom. "If Jay was here, he'd understand." She mumbled under her breath, hoping I didn't hear her.

I could have let the comment go but that really wasn't in my nature, so I followed her. "You're right, he would understand. Everyone let you do what you wanted to do, Midori and that's part of the problem. You are spoiled. You are entitled. You think things are supposed to be handed to you and I don't know why. Mama and daddy came from nothing and earned everything they have. They sacrificed so we didn't have to struggle like they did. Jay worked hard to provide for his family and I have worked hard to get Blaze where it is now. Nothing was handed to us. For some reason, you think you just have to sit there with your hand open. If that's what you want, you are going back to mama and daddy. You will not do that here."

Midori laid across her bed but refused to acknowledge me. She didn't have to, though. I meant what I said. "You have a month, Midori. School or work. I will compromise on you having friends over, but I will not come home another day to kids smoking weed in here. And you will clean up behind yourself. I am not your maid."

I left her to wallow in self-pity and I went to go get ready for work. My morning with my sister was just the beginning of a stressful day. Today we started our

March Madness specials for the college basketball games and Peaches had a stomach virus. My other bartender, Nashonna, had to take over. She was decent; just not as good as Peaches. Then on top of that, a food inspector from the health department showed up. I run a tight ship, so everything was good, but I just didn't have time to deal with that today.

I've learned that my customers weren't usually die-hard college basketball fans; they preferred a laid-back atmosphere with drinks and food to watch the first rounds of games. But by the time the Elite Eight and Final Four came around, it became a different atmosphere.

I stayed near the bar to help Nashonna out as much as possible, but I saw that she had it under control, so I mingled with my customers. I was chatting with a few regulars at the bar when I noticed a patron looking at me. I recognized him as the man that tried to buy me a drink a while back. I hadn't seen him in here since then, but with the anniversary my mama could have come in here and I wouldn't have noticed.

I continued greeting people and finally made it down to him. "Hey there! How are you doing tonight? Everything alright?" I made a mistake of looking directly in his eyes and felt…something. I couldn't quite describe it, but it made me instinctively clench my legs.

"Yeah, I'm good. I'd be better if you let me buy you that drink," he winked.

"Hey, Mo, can you watch the bar for a second? I need to go change this customer's order really quick," Nashonna called to me. I was grateful for the interruption because this customer was doing too much without doing anything.

"Yeah, go ahead. I got it," I told her while walking behind the bar.

"Oh, so you work here. That's why you won't let me buy you a drink?" he asked.

"Yeah, I don't typically drink while I'm working. But thank you though."

I fixed a few drinks and talked to some customers, but I felt him looking at me. *At least my ass looks good in this dress,* I reasoned. Because I knew I was being watched, I decided to be a little extra with my movements. I was so enthralled in being extra that I didn't even notice he wasn't there anymore. And for some reason, I was a little disappointed. I knew that Nick loved me and loved my body, but I liked that another man took notice of me. It was nothing wrong with a little harmless flirting. But his eyes were something else. Almost dangerous even.

* * *

I came to Blaze around eleven the next morning for our liquor shipment. Peaches usually took care of this, but she was still out sick. I got everything checked in and then ordered the things we needed in the kitchen.

It was still early and even though I wanted to go get a pedicure, I knew the nail shop would be packed. I called my nail tech and as I suspected, they were busy. I didn't really have anything to do until I came back to Blaze this evening, but I was impatient. Pedicures were my peace, my solace. I didn't want to wait, and I didn't want them to rush. I usually went on a Monday, but I didn't get the chance this week. Since a pedi was out of the question, I decided I would surprise Nick with lunch because he'd been busy getting ready for the art showcase the next day. Before leaving Blaze, I checked our social media and my email.

As usual, there was a lot of spam and party promotions but there was an email with a subject of *Wanna take Blaze to the next level?* That definitely got my attention. I opened the email and read it in disbelief.

Someone named Andre Restin was asking for a meeting to discuss a potential investment opportunity for my business. He said he's been in a few times and liked the vibe and he wanted to help me take Blaze to the next level. He made some observations about my business including the numbers of the businesses around me. I was impressed with his observations of what I was doing and what a number of bars and clubs were doing around me. I checked out my competition, but I always believed that Blaze had its own niche in an older, mature crowd. Mostly young professionals and I was fine with that. I wasn't interested in a younger crowd, but I also knew word of mouth alone wasn't going to cut it to get more customers.

I was skeptical, but my interest was definitely piqued. Andre provided his number for me to contact him. I thought for a second and then dialed his number. It went to voicemail.

"Hi, Mr. Restin. This is Monica Mack at Blaze. I got your email and I'm interested in meeting with you to discuss Blaze. This is my cell so call me back or email me. Thanks."

I left Blaze en route to Nick's school to deliver his lunch. He was grateful for the Chick-fil-a and even more excited to see me. He reminded me that the show would start at 6 tomorrow. I assured him, for the thousandth time, that I would be there. I understood he was just excited, more so for Jarrell than anyone else. He didn't tell any of the kids, but he asked friends from the Art Institute of Atlanta and Full Sail in Florida to be there to speak to the kids about attending college, careers in art, and possible scholarship opportunities. He felt that Jarrell could earn a free ride somewhere; that's how talented he was. Nick was so excited about this showcase, more than any of the other ones he'd hosted.

As soon as I got in my car, Andre Restin was calling me back. "Hello?"

"Monica, this is Andre. I'm sorry I missed your call. How are you today?"

I switched on the Bluetooth function in my car and braved Atlanta traffic to get to my condo. "Hey. I'm good. So tell me more about this business plan. And what makes you so interested in my business?"

"Straight to the point, huh?" he laughed. "I'm always looking for new ways to invest and your business caught my eye. I'm in real estate and while that has been very profitable, I am looking for a more long-term investment."

"Long term in what way? Cause if you're looking to buy Blaze, this conversation is dead." I didn't consider that at first but if this man thought my business was for sale, he was sadly mistaken.

"Not looking to take your club. Or buy it. Or even be involved in the day to day operations. I would just help you draw more people in and make more of a profit. I'd be a silent partner."

I paused, taking in what he was saying. It seemed too good to be true. "Mr. Restin, I have to be honest.

I've been taught that if it sounds too good to be true, it probably is. I've worked my ass off to get to where I am now, and I will not lose my business to any shady business deals."

"I promise I am not trying to take over. All I want is a return on my investment and more. But this isn't a conversation we need to have over the phone. I want to set up a meeting and we can talk about everything in detail. You can also check my credentials so that you will know I am not a scam artist."

My brain was working a mile a minute. This is what I needed, but I was skeptical. "Andre, I don't know…"

"Monica," he interrupted. "Just meet with me and after that if you aren't convinced, then you can walk away."

He definitely had me interested and I figured I owed it to myself to see what he was talking about. "Okay, when do you want to meet?"

Andre and I decided to meet on Monday morning at Blaze to discuss his proposal to add to my business. I locked the meeting in my phone and set out to finish my day.

Lord, don't let this man be trying to get over on me.

* * *

I arrived at the venue for the art showcase at 5:30. Nick would kill me if I was anywhere near late. Since I knew Nick would be occupied, I asked my friend Keyalani to come with me. She was single and on the prowl so any event that would allow her to mingle with men, she was down for it.

Keyalani and I were roommates at Georgia Southern and I hated her guts at first. But I had no reason to. She was just as nice as she could be; she was just plain and boring. The more we talked the more we discovered that we had almost nothing in common. Little did we know that this friendship would bring balance to our lives. Lani was my voice of reason and I was her voice of take a chance. I got her to try and love sushi and she taught me how to pick my battles and not fly off the handle at everyone. She understood me, she didn't always agree but she got my personality without judging me. When Jay died, she was my saving grace. After I played the strong sister when people came to the house, I was drained. Lani sat with me and massaged my scalp until I went to sleep. She really defined friendship for me, and I loved her to death.

Nick insisted the show be treated like it was real and for these kids, it was. So, I donned a strapless black hi-lo dress and gold heels. I knew my man would appreciate my ode to his fraternity colors. It was chilly, so I had a shawl wrapped me that I decided I'd keep on. It was an event for kids and they didn't need to see all my cleavage. I'm sure Nick would appreciate it though.

I told Keyalani the show started at five, so she came rushing in at 5:30pm. "Hey girl. I'm sorry I'm late. I couldn't decide what to wear."

I laughed at her because Lani would be late to her own funeral. I swear she had a mental condition that prevented her from doing anything, and I do mean anything, on time. She looked around and saw there weren't that many people here yet. "Not that great of a turn out this year, huh?"

I laughed again. "It doesn't start for another 30 minutes, Lani."

She shot me an evil look. "Mo! Do you know how I rushed to get here?"

"If it started at 5, you were late but now you're on time. Aren't you proud of you?"

Keyalani rolled her eyes and adjusted her royal blue jumper that hugged her hips and thighs like a glove. In college, Lani and I used to be the same size but over the years she has gotten thick. I was slick jealous of her body.

I found Nick to let him know I was here. He gave me a quick peck and then went back the business of hosting. He was incredibly sexy in his tailored black suit, black shirt, and gold bow tie. His locs were pulled into a ponytail and hung casually against his back. Watching him work, speaking to the kids and other guests was always a sight to behold. His pride was all over his face.

I knew he wouldn't be by my side much tonight, so Keyalani and I made our way to get some food.. The buffet style meal was beautifully arranged, and the food looked almost too good to eat. Meatballs, ham and cheese sliders, and pigs in a blanket for the kids. Cocktail shrimp, caprese salad skewers and brie, apple, and honey crostini for the adult palate. I was impressed with the menu and fixed a skim plate since most of the guests were just starting to arrive. The caterer left cards on the table and I snagged a few for any future events I might need a caterer.

By 6:30, the event was in full swing. I joined the other guests in moving through the gallery, looking through the art, and talking to the artists while Keyalani studied the men that didn't sport wedding bands and seemed like they were alone. I loved that the kids weren't shy to answer questions or explain their pieces. The clear star of this exhibit was Jarrell. His displays included paintings and photography.

One of the best pieces of Jarrell's was a family painting. In his interpretation of family, Jarrell said the people in the painting were kids he met in one of the 6 foster and group homes he lived in. The colors, the faces, and the details of the features...he really made them feel like more than just spots on a canvas.

Another great picture was a black and white photo of his current foster mother. She was standing at the sink washing collard greens, an apron wrapped around her waist, with a boy that looked like he was eight or nine years old. Jarrell said the boy was also in foster care and had only been in the home for about a week when this picture was taken. She had a slight smile, as if the little boy said something funny while his face held seriousness as he tried to mimic the movements of the woman. Her eyes looked happy, content to be sharing a simple moment with a child that has experienced the horror of being removed from his home, his stability and thrust into the care of someone else. Jarrell was able to capture her attempt to make him feel at home. It was beautiful.

I had intentions of going to Blaze but I was having such a good time, I stayed for the entire event. It was refreshing to have an evening of not working and supporting my man and spending time with my best friend. Nick continued to play host until the last of the guests left. Satisfied with one or two prospects, Keyalani left to go play private investigator on social media. We hugged before she left, and I promised that we needed to do lunch one day next week. When everyone was gone, Nick grabbed me and gave me a big hug while lifting me off the ground. I laughed at his enthusiasm.

"You guys did a phenomenal job, babe. Even Lani was impressed, when she wasn't trying to be noticed. I know these kids will remember this night for the rest of their lives."

"I'm so proud of them. Especially Jarrell. He is a shy kid, but he interacted with people well. Even the reps from Full Sail and the Art Institute were impressed with him. All of them. I think Tianna is seriously considering going to Full Sail and majoring in graphic design. Her mom and I are trying to figure out how we can get her down there for a visit."

Just hearing the excitement in his voice made me so proud to not only know him, but to love him, as well. "If it's financial, I will sponsor her. Or Blaze will anyway."

"Are you serious, Monica?" he asked staring at me intensely.

"Of course, baby. I love this event and if this will help get her to college, then I'm in."

Nick grabbed me again and kissed me deeply. "Thank you, Monica. I really appreciate how supportive you are. I love you."

I blushed and leaned in for another kiss. "I love you more, King."

Nick and I left the venue and stopped to get something to eat before heading to his place. I got in the shower while Nick uploaded pics of the event to social media. When I got out of the shower, Nick was sitting against the headboard waiting for me. I didn't even bother to put on clothes. Instead, I crawled on the bed until I straddled him. As I leaned down to kiss him, his hands traveled down my back before grabbing my ass. I moaned in his mouth because I always loved the way he touched me.

Needing to be in control, Nick rolled me over on my back. He was a passionate, gentle lover. The way he kissed me, the way he touched me made me feel like I was the center of his world. Nick made love to me with such an intensity that I hadn't experienced with anyone else.

Nick learned my body and knew how to stroke to make me claw at his back as I traveled to ecstasy. His manhood was thick and filled me up as if he was made just for me. I closed my eyes and held on to his body as mine teetered on the edge of release. I moaned out my pleasure as Nick took me to another world.

My body finally reached the point of no return and I could tell that Nick was getting close as well. Just as mine ended, his was beginning. He slipped out of me long enough to place my legs on his shoulders. I held on to him, his movements getting more frantic as he pushed deeper and deeper into the wetness he created. He pounded me, hard and fast, signaling his climax was so close. I moved my hips in his rhythm. I knew he needed to release but he was pushing me towards another one.

"Yes, baby," I moaned in his ear. "Right there. Oh God, King! Right there!" Nick loved it when I talked to him, encouraged him. And that's all he needed to finally give me what I craved. I loved feeling Nick throbbing inside of me. His release was enough to carry me to bliss once again. As he grunted in pleasure, Nick whispered, "Monica, let's get married."

My eyes flew open and I was caught in a matrix of unyielding pleasure and catastrophic confusion. I tried to hide the terror in my eyes, but I knew I did a terrible job. I looked for Nick's face but only saw Devin staring back at me. Remembering how he up and left me came hurling back into my memory and I thought I was back in the hallway of the courthouse trying to wrap my head around Devin not showing up. So, I did what I did best...I ran.

I went to the bathroom and sat down on the side of the tub for a few moments trying to get my thoughts together. Knowing me all too well, Nick came in the bathroom a minute later. I held my breath waiting for him to talk; I didn't trust myself to speak.

"Don't worry, Mo. I'll get you a ring."

Still unsure of my voice, I looked everywhere except for at Nick. It wasn't that I didn't love him because I did. Although I couldn't admit that I was in love with him. The relationship was going well...but we haven't been together long enough to be talking about this. It was just that...marriage wasn't something I wanted in my life. At least not right now. I had a great example of marriage in my parents and grandparents, but my generation didn't value marriage like baby boomers.

To people my age, marriage was an event. It was about doing the most for social media. Marriage was about hashtags and trying to outdo the last wedding you attended. It was not about love or even financial security, it was to be able to have a Shug Avery moment and declare "I's married now!" A girl I graduated with spent every bit of $15,000 on her wedding and was filing for divorce not even a year later. I'm not about that life.

"Nick, we've talked about this and I am not ready for that. You already know that," I finally admitted.

Nick's face registered anger first but then morphed into hurt. I hated to see that look on his face, but I didn't want to lie to him. Not about something as serious as marriage.

"Monica," he began. I could tell he was thinking about his words before he spoke. I could also tell he was not happy with me right now. "I am almost 32 years old. I don't have any kids because I never wanted to be a baby daddy. I want my children to be with my wife. I have waited to meet the woman I know will be the life partner I need. That woman is you, Monica. I don't understand why you're letting someone else keep you stuck in something that happened years ago."

"We've talked about this before. We've only been together a little over a year. Let's just enjoy getting to know each other. I'm not saying ever. I'm just saying right now isn't the time. Blaze is doing great things and I am looking to do more. I can't think about being a mother and a wife when I'm trying to grow my business."

"So you're saying that you'd rather have a business than a husband and kids?" he almost shouted.

I exhaled loudly and rubbed my temples. "I don't get why you don't understand me. I watched you tonight and the passion of working with these kids and art was all over your face. You were proud. This is what you are meant to do." I reached out to touch his hand, as if my touch could drive my point home. "Well, that's how I feel about Blaze."

He snatched away from me, his gaze piercing and cold. "The only difference is my passion isn't limiting me from doing other things. I can love art, the kids, and still be a husband. Your passion won't let you do the same. So, no, I guess I don't understand. And you can keep blaming it on Blaze, but I know that's not the only thing. Dude hurt you. I can understand that. But it's not fair to blame that on me. Good night, Monica."

He left the bathroom without looking at me. I know I hurt his feelings, but I had to be honest with him. I looked at myself in the mirror. I studied my face, and I prided myself on being truthful and not just agreeing to marriage because it was expected. At the same time, I felt like shit for hurting the man that wanted to do nothing but love me.

If I knew how to forget about how Devin left me, I would. But I just couldn't trust that Nick wouldn't do the same thing. Nick wooed me the same way Devin did and look where that got me. No damn where. I wasn't about to experience that kind of hurt again.

Chapter Four

"YOU SAID WHAT?" Lani practically yelled at me. "Girl, what's wrong with you?!"

"Keyalani, keep your voice down. We're in public!" I scolded.

We were having lunch at Mary Mac's Tea room and of course the place was crowded. I looked around embarrassed, but it seemed most people were engrossed in their own personal conversations and their lunch and not worried about us at all. But still. I didn't need her acting all crazy in public.

"I'm just saying, Mo," she began while finishing off her fried chicken. "I meet loser after loser. Playboys. Married men. Down low men. Trifling men. Stupid ass men. Men that send dick pics though messenger. Men I can't even get to take me on a date and you're turning down marriage? Why?"

I sighed heavily. This is one of the areas we butted heads the most. And you would think that we would be complete opposites when it came to marriage. Lani grew up in a single parent home, her father running off to marry someone else when she was barely a month old. She saw her mama struggle with relationships before finally settling on being the other woman. Yet, Lani believed so much in love and cried at weddings. Even if she didn't know the people. Me, on the other hand couldn't fathom marriage right now even though my parents' relationship was like Marriage 101. I saw firsthand how wonderful marriage could be, but it scared me to death. Devin made sure of that. Everything Lani did and everywhere she went had the ulterior motive of finding Mr. Right while I wasn't even looking for love when I met Nick. All she wanted was to meet a decent guy and here I was, freaking out because my man wanted to make me Mrs. Monica Pierce.

"Lani, marriage has never been my life's dream. You know that. And I'm not saying I will never get married; I'm just saying I owe it to myself and my business to be all in. You'd think Nick would appreciate that I don't want to neglect him. He has enough to say about how I work now."

"Why can't you do both?"

"I probably could, but Nick would have to understand that running a business is not a 9-5," I countered. Nick made no bones about my hours. He hated that I came in as late as 2 am. And now that Andre is trying to make moves, who knew what kind of hours I would have to put in. "I told you about this investor guy. This is major Lani and I don't think I should have to give that up just to be someone's wife."

"Make your moves, Mo. I am proud of you and I know Nick is, too. But," she paused.

I recognized that pause and avoidance of eye contact. "Just say it. But what?" She worried so much about hurting my feelings that she often didn't say things. I told her plenty of times that I had tough skin and she needed to learn to speak her mind.

"Blaze can't hold you at night. Blaze cannot beat that thang up. Blaze cannot listen to you. Comfort you. You need Nick for that."

I inadvertently rolled my eyes. It was such a habit. "You sound like Nick now. I haven't even agreed to move in, why do we have to jump to marriage?"

"Whatever, Mo. You have to do what makes you happy. I know a lot of this has to do with Devin, but Devin and Nick are two different people. Just know if a man like Nick wants a wife and kids, he's going to do just that. With or without you."

I didn't want to admit that she was right. On the surface, Nick and Devin were two different people. But my heart couldn't tell the difference in Nick proposing and Devin leaving me. "Keyalani, you are so dramatic," I chided trying to mask the hurt of her words. "I agreed to get off work early on Wednesdays for him. Doesn't that count for something? I'm making progress!"

"Progress would be letting go of Devin's hurt and letting Nick in completely. Go listen to *Previous Cats* by Musiq Soulchild. That's exactly what Nick is going through and it's not fair. You're not even giving him a chance."

"Lani, that's not fair. How am I just supposed to get over that?"

"No one said it would be easy, but it seems like you aren't really trying. Nick hasn't done anything to warrant this."

"Maybe he hasn't, but Nick is a dominant guy and he can't deal with the fact that I'm not docile and eager to jump to do what he says. What if he expects me to give up Blaze once we are married because he wants his wife to be home when he gets there? He's already making demands and we've only been together for just over a year!"

Lani's ringing phone saved me from the dissertation she was about to unleash on me. Keyalani was an RN for an OB/GYN and she was getting ready to go back to school to become a nurse practitioner. I was sure her phone call was related to that.

Lani placed her phone on mute and told me she needed to go and handle some paperwork for school. She gave me a quick hug and left the restaurant. I was happy to be spending time with my friend, but I was glad she was gone. It was draining to keep talking about why I wasn't getting married any time soon. At least I would have a good distraction today; I was meeting with Andre in about an hour.

I paid our bill and headed over to Blaze to prepare for him. I was engrossed in payroll and other paperwork when Peaches knocked on my door. "Hey Mo, someone's here to see you."

I heard the irritation in her voice. It was probably because I usually made her aware if someone was coming to see me. "Okay, cool. I'll be out there in a minute."

I glanced at the clock on my cell phone and saw that he was 15 minutes early. *That's a good sign*, I silently commented. I opened my camera and checked my face, popped a mint, and got my pad and pen before heading to the front to meet with Andre. The closer I got to him, the slower I walked. I knew this was a scam. Andre was the guy that tried to buy me a drink. Twice.

"I don't know what kind of games you're playing but I am not the one," I explained. I was beyond irritated that I actually took this man seriously. I was also irritated because he looked damn good. Better than he did the nights he came in here.

"Whoa, calm down, Monica. I'm not about games, I'm about money," he assured me. And he was certainly dressed like money. I wasn't the type that could calculate the cost of a suit just by looking at it, but I knew Andre's suit came from a high-end place. The only jewelry he wore was a watch, and it looked to be a very expensive watch. Even his attaché looked like it cost a pretty penny. "I told you that all we had to do was meet and if you weren't convinced, then you could walk away."

I know it wasn't professional to roll my eyes but that's exactly what I did. I rolled my eyes at Andre Restin. Part out of irritation, part to avoid looking into his sexy ass eyes. "So, what were you doing in here? Spying on me?"

"Spying? No," he assured me while adjusting his tie. "I was simply taking in the crowd, the environment. I was seeing how your people worked. Listening to conversations. And seeing how you handled business. I had to make sure this was worth my time and my money."

Peaches was listening to our conversation with disdain on her face. Andre didn't notice her but before he did, I asked him if he wanted a drink.

"Just water, thank you."

Peaches handed him a bottle of water and we moved to one of the tables away from the bar. When we sat down, I made the mistake of looking in his eyes. I forgot not to look at them and now I had to fight this growing arousal.

"Okay, Monica. This is what I know. Blaze has been around for a while. Ten years to be exact. You threw one hell of an anniversary celebration and I know we can get you that kind of crowd weekly. I also know that you could do much more business than you are now. Your patrons are a young professional's crowd, you need to cater more to them. Music, food, drinks, events. They aren't looking to get wasted, they just want to unwind after a long day and get away from the kids on the weekend."

I had to admit that he was good. He had my business down pact. But...I needed to know how all of this research became action. "What does that mean exactly? Anyone can rattle off facts but how do you take this beyond talk?" Maybe my tone was unnecessary, but I had to let him know I was about business.

He seemed undeterred by my callousness. "I'm glad you asked. I put together this proposal for us to go over." He opened his attaché and pulled out an official looking report. If this man was a scam artist, he was damn good at it.

For the next hour, Andre and I talked business and most importantly numbers. I think I was more impressed because of some of the things he was proposing: renovations to the bar and adding a chef with a whole new menu. That alone was the selling point. But the most important proposal was buying the empty space next to Blaze as an addition. My eyes went wide as I tried to picture the space he was suggesting be used for a VIP section. He was selling me on having this space for private parties. I questioned some of his calculations and Andre praised me for my attention to detail. The more we talked, the more lucrative his plan sounded. But I wasn't going to let him know that.

"Andre, this-"

"Dre," he interrupted. "Call me Dre."

"Okay, Dre, all of this sounds good. It's very impressive but it would be irresponsible of me to jump into this without giving it some thought. This is my livelihood. I have people depending on me. This is how my employees pay their bills. I need to be sure." Dre smiled at me, his eyes boring into mine. I looked away first hoping he didn't know the effect he was having on me. *Men are clueless, right?* I silently assured myself.

"Monica, I'd expect nothing less. Take your time and look over everything. Call me if you have any questions."

He stood up and held out his hand to shake. We'd been meeting for over an hour and I had a lot to think about.

"Thank you, Andre. I mean, Dre. I'll give you a call once I've made my decision."

Andre and I walked by the bar. I sat down on one of the stools and he left. I leafed through his report on Blaze and again, I was impressed with the detail he put into this.

"So you're selling the place? Just like that? No notice, no warning, nothing? You know how fucked up that is, Mo? Did you even think about us? I bet you didn't. As long as you-"

"PEACHES!" I was surprised at her. I thought she knew me better than that. "Now you know I'd never sell Blaze!"

"So what was all that about?"

"He's an investor. He wants to help us grow," I said. I rattled off some of the details of the meeting-leaving out the money part. Even saying it out loud, it sounded too good to be true. The look of skepticism on her face told me she didn't believe me. Or him.

"He's a business man," I answered. "He said we are sitting on a gold mine. You know I want to make some changes and do more things here; his money would help us do that."

"So he's just going to give you money and that's it? He's not going to try to come in and take over?"

"He said he's going to be a silent partner. All he wants is a return on his investment and some profit."

Peaches shrugged and went back to stocking the bar. "Well, do what you do."

"Damn, you sure changed you mind mighty fast," I joked.

"I'm all about the money, Mo. And if this cat is gonna get us more money then I'm with it."

"I haven't decided yet. I'm going to look over this stuff again and talk to some folks before I do this."

"Okay, cool," Peaches said nonchalantly. She seemed...unbothered but almost like she trying to prove to me that she didn't care. "What are we going to do for your birthday?"

I was glad that she changed the subject because I didn't think I could think about Andre anymore. I mean...his plans for Blaze.

* * *

The next few weeks were mad hectic. My birthday was coming up and of course, I was going to be party-ing at Blaze that weekend. I booked Tyrin again because he was dope at the anniversary party. Peaches had drink specials and my regulars were spreading my party on social media. I was beyond excited.

Ever since I was a little girl, my birthday, June 2nd, was like a national holiday. It wasn't that my parents threw these elaborate parties for me, but I just loved my birthday. I loved celebrating closing one chapter and starting another. This one was extra special because I was turning dirty thirty.

I wasn't one of those chicks that got all bent out of shape about their age. I didn't mind telling anyone my age, not only because I still looked damn good, but also because I was proud of where I was. I have accomplished a lot in thirty years and I planned on celebrating my birthday to the fullest. Of course, the only person who had an issue with me celebrating my birthday at Blaze was Nick.

"Mo, you do this every year. I want to take you out of town for your birthday. Don't you want to do something different?" he lamented.

We argued about my birthday for days but in the end, he realized I wasn't changing my mind. It was too late. Because I wanted to make him happy, I did cut my celebration at Blaze down to one day instead of the whole weekend that way I could spend part of my birthday with him. He wasn't too thrilled, but I took off Monday too to appease him. It can never be said that I don't compromise. Knowing that I'd never been, Nick booked a quick trip to New Orleans. I was excited about that too and that was why I loved birthdays.

I woke up Friday morning to a barrage of texts, calls, and social media posts telling me happy birthday. I smiled that everyone was showing me love. Nick's voicemail was the sweetest and I texted him back to let him know how much I appreciated him in my life. I hadn't even gotten out of the bed yet and my birthday was already off to a great start. As much as I wanted to lay around in bed all day, I had a busy day ahead which included getting my hair done.

I started my dreadlocks years ago because I wasn't a fan of doing my hair. The get up and go of my hair was one of the many pluses and I rarely did anything other than some moisturizing. I hadn't gotten my hair done in close to six months but because it was my birthday, I needed to do something to it. My loctician, Asia, understood my sporadic hair moments and made time for me. She did Nick's hair, too, just more often because he liked the maintained look of his locs.

I took a shower and threw on a sundress to head to my appointment. Midori was in the kitchen and I was surprised she was even up. She was looking in the fridge. She wasn't going to find much in there because I hadn't gone to the grocery store in a few days. I made a mental note to cash her some money to buy some groceries.

"Hey, I'm going to get my hair done. I'll be back," I called to her before walking out the door. She didn't say anything because she was probably still pissed that I gave her that ultimatum. But she had been holding up her end of the deal. She would start her summer classes at Clark Atlanta sometime that month and she was working part-time at Publix. When she wasn't at work, she was in her room doing what, I don't know. I rarely saw her but so long as she was upholding her end of my deal, I was fine with our limited interaction.

I got to my appointment early because Asia and I had to catch up before she even started on my hair. Every time she washed my hair, I wondered why I didn't get this done more often. I've had my locs for almost 4 years and it was getting harder and harder to wash my hair myself. But Asia's hands were anointed.

Asia hooked me up with some curls and I was sitting under the dryer. It was then I remembered why I hated getting my hair done; dryers were the of spawn of Satan. I hated them. I was checking emails and social media when my phone rang with a call from Andre. We'd kept in touch here and there. Nothing special, just me letting him know I was still interested, just thinking. He always let me know it was no rush. But I always kept it impersonal and texted him. So, it was a little weird for him to be calling me.

"Hello?" I almost shouted over the noise from the dryer.

"Good morning, Monica. Happy birthday!" I heard through my earbuds.

Hmmm...he must follow me on social media. Because how else would he know it was my birthday? I reasoned.

"Why thank you sir!" I tried to mask the excitement in my voice. Cause I had no reason to get excited about this man telling me happy birthday.

"You're quite welcome," he replied. "What's on the agenda for today? Other than the dirty thirty shindig at Blaze tonight?"

"Keeping up with me, I see," I laughed. "I'm getting all beautified now, then on to get a pedicure before I rest up for tonight."

"Good. Sounds like you have time to let me take you to lunch."

I went silent, unsure of how to answer. Sure, I loved to be spoiled any day, but especially on my birthday but was he flirting with me? I'm sure this wasn't going to be a business lunch. "Umm…I'm not sure about that. I have a busy day. And a lot to do. And ummm…"

"I've been thinking," Dre began completely unbothered by my barrage of excuses. "I believe your apprehensions for holding off on our deal is because you don't know me. I want to take you to lunch to change that. I want you to be comfortable with the person you will be doing business with."

He was absolutely right. I didn't know him from Adam's housecat and I wasn't sure if I could trust him. But there was also Nick…would this be like cheating? I knew he wouldn't like it, but it was technically a business lunch. Even if we wouldn't be discussing business.

"I'm not sure, Andre-"

"Dre," he interrupted. "Please call me Dre."

"Sorry, Dre. But I'm not sure about that. You're right that I don't know you, but I don't know if I will have time today."

"I think you should make the time, Monica. Because right now, you are sitting on a very lucrative business. With the right investment, you could double what you're making now."

I sat silently while I considered what he was telling me. No one in their right mind would turn down what he was offering. Everyone that I have run his proposal by said it was a damn good deal, but something was still not clicking for me. And it was probably what he said: I didn't know him. I decided to throw caution to the wind and take him up on his lunch offer.

"Okay. You're right. I don't know you and that is probably my apprehension. We can go to lunch, but I am not sure what time. What's your availability?"

"I'm free when you're free, Monica. Just call me when you're ready. And tell me where you want to go."

"Okay, I'll let you know."

We hung up and for some reason I felt giddy. *Chill out, Mo this is not a date*, I scolded myself.

A few hours later, Dre and I were being seated at Maggiano's Little Italy. After getting my hair done, I got a pedicure and went home to change. Sure, I could have met him as I was, but I wanted to look a little more put together. After all, he was trying to invest in my business, so I needed to maintain his interest in Blaze.

"You look great, Monica." Dre told me as we were seated. I'm sure I looked decent. I didn't want to look like I spent a lot of time getting ready, so I had on a different sundress, a black one so that my purple hair would pop. I wasn't into makeup, but I loved mascara. I finished off my simple look with lip gloss on my full lips.

"Thank you. You look good yourself," I complimented. He was casual today in a green Polo shirt and khaki pants. He smelled good as hell, too.

Before we could get into small talk, our server came to take our drink orders. I wanted wine, but I had to drive back to my condo to get ready for my party tonight. I settled on water. Once we were alone again, Dre jumped right in.

"So...tell me about yourself."

"What do you want to know?" I inquired.

"Everything."

I raised my eyebrow which caused him to laugh heartily. "Okay, okay. Everything you want me to know. I don't need to know about the dead bodies you've hidden in the basement of Blaze. I'm not trying to be an accessory to no murder rap."

It was my turn to laugh and then I made the mistake of looking at him and them damn eyes got me. I quickly recovered and concentrated on my nails. "Well, I was born and raised in Americus. I attended college at Georgia Southern and I have an MBA from Clark Atlanta. I am the oldest of three. Well…I was the oldest of three. My brother passed away last year in January." Whenever I mentioned my brother, I avoided eye contact with people. I hated seeing that look on their faces.

"I'm sorry to hear that. Were you guys close?"

"Yes. Very. My brother was my best friend. It's strange to talk about him in the past tense. I'm still not used to it."

"Damn. Well, we don't have to talk about that. Tell me something else about you…something that's not going to make you cry."

I smiled, grateful for him recognizing I didn't want to talk about Jay. We continued talking and I found myself telling him all about my life from Midori to my fear of thunder and lightning. It was when I was halfway through my shrimp scampi that I realized I was doing all the talking.

"Enough about me," I said. "Tell me about you."

"Well, I was born in Hawkinsville and I've been in Atlanta for years. I have a younger sister, Amerie ,and she is my baby. My primary business is real estate. When I got into real estate a few years ago, that really opened my eyes to things. I saw that before, I wasn't really living. I was spending money as soon as I got it on dumb shit. Cars, clothes, jewelry. Things that won't give me a return on my investment. I wised up when I got into real estate. I buy and sell homes and flip some for profit."

I was quite impressed with his life right now. Not too many black men knew that the life these rappers portrayed in their videos wasn't real. Buying the latest car might get you street cred but it won't grow your portfolio. He wasn't that old, but he got it. "Do you have any kids?"

There was an empty look on his face before he answered. "Nah. I wanted some but...I'm not sure if I will." His pause let me know there was something not being said. But that was too much for a first date.

Wait...what? Date? This is not a date! I reminded myself.

I pushed that thought out of my mind and continued to enjoy his company. We spent the rest of our lunch talking like two old friends, and I continued to lose the battle of not looking into his eyes. It was almost like he was drawing me in.

We finished our lunch, but our conversation still lingered. He sprinkled his philosophies about life and business throughout and I knew I was going to do business with him. He had his head on straight, he knew what he was talking about, and he was about making money. The more we talked, the more I realized he had a little hood in him and he hadn't been a businessman all his life. When I noticed the time, I knew I had to go; it was going on 4 pm. I had plenty of time to get home and rest before heading to Blaze. I wanted to try to be there around 8, which meant I could take a two-hour nap.

"I really need to get out of here. I need to rest before my party. I have a busy weekend," I announced.

"What else do you have planned?" he inquired as we exited the restaurant.

"My boyfriend and I are going to New Orleans tomorrow." I may have been crazy, but I thought I saw his demeanor change when I mentioned Nick.

"Yeah ,you do have a busy weekend. I hope you enjoy it." He recovered but his eyes registered something different. I gave up trying to fight the beauty of his eyes and just allowed myself to stare into them. Something about him seemed different, so very different from Nick. Personally, I knew that I didn't know everything I needed to know about him. But from a business perspective, he won me over.

He walked me to my car and thanked me for joining him for lunch. "No problem. Since you treated me, why don't you come by Blaze tonight? My party is going to be a lot of fun!"

Dre smiled at me and told me he'd check his schedule and he would come if he could. I'm not sure why that made me happy, but it did.

* * *

By 9 pm, my party was in full swing and I was having a blast. It's funny that when I was in college, I would get pissy drunk on my birthdays and barely remember anything that went on. Now, I could have a great time without alcohol. I gave away the drinks people bought for me and I only drank one glass of wine the entire night. I wanted to remember 30. I'd been getting ready for 30 for months; I bought the black and grey jumper I was wearing on clearance at the end of last summer. I also didn't want to be drunk if Dre showed up. Why I was checking for Dre when my man was by my side was beyond me.

Around 10:30pm, my birthday cake which was made out of cupcakes was rolled out and everyone gathered to sing happy birthday. Before I could blow out my candles, I locked eyes with Dre. I wasn't sure when he snuck in, but I was secretly glad to see him. I blew out all thirty of my candles to the applause of my staff and customers. Someone started yelling out speech and Tyrin ran up to me with a microphone.

"I want to thank everyone for coming to celebrate dirty thirty with me! Especially all of my customers. A lot of you have been loyal for years and I thank you for continuing to support Blaze. To my staff…thank you for all of your hard work. You guys make work a breeze. Most of the time. To my best friend Lani…girl I love you and I thank you for being in my life. I don't know what I would do without you. And to my King…thank you for all you do. You sacrifice for me, you put up with my hours, and you continue to support me. I love you baby."

Everyone ahhhhed and Nick beamed with pride. I caught a glimpse of Dre and his face was stoic but when he noticed me, he shook his head and smiled.

"Alright everyone, enough of that mushy stuff…let's get back to the party! And ya'll come get some of these cupcakes. I love them, but my thighs don't!"

There was laughter as I handed the mic back to Tyrin who turned the music back on. The sounds of *It takes two* by Rob Base began and almost everyone in the building started rapping. A few women were hitting all the old school dances and then a soul train began. I was thrust into it and I did the running man down the line. It was even more impressive that I was able to do that with 5-inch heels on. That little stunt took all my breath and I had to sit down. As soon as I sat at the bar, Dre was by my side.

"You're smart, business minded, sexy and can dance…you're a winner all around!" he told me. I blushed, and I wished I could blame my reaction on the alcohol, but I wasn't anywhere close to drunk. Dre and I made small talk for a little while before Keyalani walked up to me.

"Girl, where you find all these fine men at? I done came up tonight, girl!" she slurred. She took one look at Dre and set her sights on him. "And I'm about to come up one mo' gin…hey there how you doing?"

"Damn, Lani are you drunk?" I was embarrassed and pissed off. We were too old to get wasted like this. "Give me your keys so I can make sure to call you an Uber before you leave."

She didn't give me her keys but instead, she tried to talk to Dre through me. He didn't seem to mind and laughed at Lani's drunken conversation. I scanned the crowd looking for Nick and saw him staring at me. I wonder how long he was looking at me talking to Dre.

He started walking over towards us and I was glad that Lani was talking to Dre.

"Nick, help me get her keys. I don't want her to try to drive home," I said as soon as he was close.

"Who is this?" Nick asked completely ignoring me.

Dre stood and stuck out his hand for Nick to shake. "Andre Restin. I'm looking to invest in Blaze."

"Nick, I told you about the investor. Now will you help me with Lani?" I asked trying desperately to avoid the subject. I didn't want Dre to say anything about our lunch date today because I didn't tell Nick I was going.

Dre didn't seem fazed by Nick's inquisition. Reluctantly, Nick shook Dre's hand. "Great party, Monica. Nice to meet you Nick and Lani."

He left the end of the bar I was sitting at and called to Nashonna. I saw him go into his pocket and pull out some money and hand it to her. Peaches stopped what she was doing and walked over to them and it looked like they were having words before she walked away from him. I raised my eyebrows wondering how Peaches knew him. Nashonna ran from around the bar to the DJ booth and snatched the mic from Tyrin.

"Aye ya'll," she yelled into the mic. "For the next 15 minutes all drinks are courtesy of this dude right here!" Nashonna pointed in Dre's direction, but he was already gone. "Damn where he go? Whatever, ya'll come get these drinks!"

Nashonna gave the mic back to Tyrin and hurried back to the bar. No one rushed the bar because grown folks don't get excited by free drinks but Peaches and Nashonna stayed busy for the rest of the night.

I finally got Lani's keys from her and started to call her an Uber. One of my regular customers lived in the same neighborhood as Lani and offered to take her home which made me feel better. I told my customer that next time she came in, everything was on the house. As soon as Lani was gone, I went to my office to text Dre.

> Me: *Thanks for sending my customers into a frenzy lol. And thanks for coming (smiley face emoji). Send over the paperwork on Tuesday...let's take Blaze to the next level*
>
> Dre: *Will do! Enjoy the rest of your weekend. We will touch bases when you get back*
>
> Me: *I will thanks! (smiley face emoji)*

I put my phone away content that I was making major moves for my business. I went back to my party and danced and laughed until my feet were screaming at me. It was going on 1am and I needed to get out of there to get ready to head to New Orleans. I was pretty sure Nick booked that early ass flight to try to get me to leave Blaze early. I had time to take a quick nap, shower, and change before we would have to get ready to head to the airport. I understood that early morning flights were cheaper, but a 7 am flight was ridiculous.

Nick and I were cutting it close at the airport. Luckily security wasn't too bad, and we made it to our gate 20 minutes before boarding. I got settled in my window seat and put in my earbuds. I switched my phone to airplane mode and went to my music library. I hit shuffle to avoid having to make a decision about what I wanted to hear. I was going to sleep this whole flight and most of the morning when we got to New Orleans.

Nick pulled my earbud out just as my first song came on. "Mo, what do you really know about that guy?'

"What guy?" I played dumb. I was too tired to think quick on my feet.

He shot me a look that begged me not to play the I-don't-know-him game. "This investor. He seems too friendly to be about business."

"Nick, you're worrying about nothing. I know enough to know this will be a great opportunity for my business."

"Yeah, well I don't trust him."

I sighed heavily. "Nick, trust me. I've done my research on him and he's legit. But I don't want to talk about business right now. It's still my birthday, and I want to enjoy it."

"We will, baby, don't worry about that. But be careful with him."

I leaned over and gave Nick a kiss. I knew I should have told him I would be signing a contract with Dre on Tuesday but for some reason, I couldn't. I just prayed it wouldn't come back to bite me in the ass.

Chapter Five

My weekend in New Orleans was just what the doctor ordered. From the food to the alcohol to the sex to Bourbon Street...Nick and I had a blast. I was having so much fun that I only checked on Blaze once. I knew it was in capable hands, so I just enjoyed my getaway with my man. He tried to slide in comments about marriage and moving in but I didn't give it any energy.

When we got back in on Monday, Nick begged me to stay with him, but I told him to come home with me. We'd been staying at his place because of Midori but I just wanted to sleep in my bed. Thankfully, Midori wasn't home, so we were able to make love without worrying about her hearing us.

Going to Blaze the next morning was refreshing. I liked my mini vacation, but I was glad to be back at work. I went to my office to find my desk almost the way I left it, minus the stack of paperwork I needed to get through. But there was also an envelope with my name on it. I opened it up and was surprised to see the contract from Dre. I couldn't contain the grin on my face. I wanted to sign it immediately, but I needed my lawyer/friend Chelsey to look over it first. I called her and asked if I could stop by her office that morning to make sure everything was legit. Chelsey told me to come on by because she had a busy morning.

I high tailed it to her office, stopping to get coffee on my way. I made it Chelsey's office in thirty minutes because I was desperate to get the ball rolling on this. Chelsey gave me the all clear with the contract and I signed it right there in her office. I called Dre when I was leaving hoping he'd meet me to come get it.

"Well, the birthday girl has returned," he greeted on the second ring.

"I have and found the present you left for me," I laughed. "It's signed and ready for you. Do you want me to meet you?"

"Word? Cool! I have a few things to do this morning, how about I come by Blaze around lunch. We can start making moves today."

"You move fast. I like it," I noted. "I'll be there, so I'll see you later."

We hung up and I cruised back to Blaze excited for what was about to happen with my business. I turned up my music and jammed out to Jill Scott's "A long walk". I was so happy that I was going to be able to do more with Blaze. Things were going great with Nick. When Midori got out of the apartment, she was good. My parents were in good health. My life was really at an awesome place right now. My ringing phone interrupted my moment of serenity and thinking about my awesomeness. I was surprised it was Nick but then again, I wasn't; he wasn't going back to work until Wednesday.

"Hey King. What are you up to?"

"Mo, when's the last time you talked to your sister?"

"I'm fine, thanks for asking." I replied sarcastically.

"Answer the question."

"Damn what's wrong with you? I don't know. Before we left I guess." He wasn't going to ruin my mood. Not when this day started off so awesome. "Why are you asking me about Midori anyway?"

"She didn't know I was in the house and I overheard her talking on the phone. She was pretty upset, Mo. She said she didn't know what she did to you to make you hate her. She thought living with you would make you guys closer. She said she made this post about you on Facebook for your birthday and you didn't even acknowledge it. Or tell her happy birthday. That's why."

"She's a lie! I did tell her happy birthday!" That's the only thing I could address but even that...I wasn't sure it was true. I tried to think back to my birthday, well our birthday. There was so much going on that day. She was there that morning and...damn. I told her I was going to get my hair done. That was it. I had a million and one notifications, so I don't remember seeing her post.

"Whatever, Mo. She's having a hard time and you're so busy with that club that you don't even notice."

"You act like you're not demanding some of that time, too." That wasn't the way I wanted to handle the situation. I was thinking about the relationship I've had with her and it wasn't great. But Midori was spoiled and entitled. I was ten years old when she was born; I was fine with just having a brother but then came Midori.

"I can't believe you've been treating her like this. Talk to your sister. Something isn't right." Nick hung up on me and I was confused by his behavior. He didn't have any brothers or sisters, and I think he resented being an only child. At least that's what I wanted to think. Because the alternative was that I fucked up with my sister bad.

Because I have always loved my birthday, Midori and I never celebrated our day together. That was my preference because I didn't want to share my day with her. Besides, what kind of party celebration can I have with someone who is ten years younger than me? I'm sure we made our parents life hell with these two birthday celebrations but for ten years, I was accustomed to having my own. That mentality continued and now my sister was feeling some kind of way about that.

I made it back to the office and pulled up Midori's Facebook page. If I didn't already feel like crap, that did it for me.

> *One of the best things about my birthday is that I get to share it with this amazing woman. My sister Mo Mack has been one of the most influential people in my life. She fusses at me all the damn time, but she pushes me, she encourages me, and she is helping me to be better. For 20 years I've had someone in my corner. Thank you for everything Mo! Happy birthday to us! I love you to the moon and back.*

Along with this post, Midori shared a picture of us that I hadn't seen in years. She was probably about 3 or 4 which made me 13 or 14. I remember that I was having a sleepover that evening so Midori's party was during the day. She had on a pink and white dress, a dress that she practically lived in. My mama used to have to hide that dress because she wanted to wear it every day. I remember my daddy snapping this picture while Midori and I walked hand in hand towards her party. It looked like we were in deep conversation about the meaning of life, but I was asking her what kind of ice cream she wanted. She looked pensive mulling over her options of chocolate or strawberry.

The picture reminded me of how our relationship used to be. It hadn't always been like it is now. Even though Jay and I were close, Midori used to love me to death. But the older she got, her attitude became worse and our relationship changed. Not to mention she was 8 when I left to go to college. When she was 14 or 15, she started feeling herself. She realized she was beautiful and it went to her head. I hated coming home to deal with her. I never knew what mood I was going to get. Some days she was quiet and stayed to herself. Other days, she was moody and irritable.

When Jay died, I think she took it the hardest. We had to give her melatonin to make her go to sleep. The day of his funeral, she was a zombie. I didn't approve of her smoking weed but she needed it that day. I had to take care of her and my parents leaving no time for me to have my own moment of grief over losing my best friend. It was only a few months ago that she blamed me for him dying; if she still felt that way then her post for my birthday was full of shit.

"Ahem."

I damn near dropped my phone, startled by whoever was standing at my office door. I was surprised, happy and annoyed to see Andre standing there. I glanced at my phone and saw that is was already lunch time.

"Andre, I mean Dre," I corrected myself. "How are you? I have the contract right here."

I got up to give him the envelope and knocked over the stack of papers onto the floor. I huffed as I bent down to pick them up only to hit my head on the side of my desk. "Shit!"

"Are you alright?" Dre queried, alarmed. He came to help me sit down again before gathering the papers I knocked down.

"Yeah, I'm good. Here's the contract. Signed and ready to go," I answered dryly. My whole mood was changed from earlier.

"What's wrong?"

I sighed deeply. "Nothing. Just life. So where do we start?"

"Nowhere," he responded sitting in a chair facing me. "Not until you tell me what's wrong."

I stared at him, and I was immediately sucked into the appeal of his eyes. Before I knew it, my whole dilemma with Midori was spilling out of my mouth. He listened intensely, his eyes rarely leaving me.

"Whoa, that's heavy shit. What are you going to do?"

His question solicited another deep sigh from me. "I'm not sure. Talk to her I guess. As soon as I figure out what to say."

"Well, you didn't ask my opinion but I'm gonna give it to you."

I laughed at him, grateful to be feeling something other than the ambiguity my sister had created. On one hand I was upset with myself for forgetting to tell my sister happy birthday and for making her feel like I hate her. Then again, I was also still pissed that she blamed me for my brother dying.

"You're the big sister," Dre began. "She looks up to you, naturally. Yes, she's gonna fuck up and piss you off but she has to learn. Making her get a job and go to school is a good idea but she also needs to learn to stand on her own two feet. Let her fall. Let her make mistakes. Let her hit rock bottom. She will learn to become more resilient."

I heard what he said, and it definitely made sense. This was the first time Midori had to actually put forth effort into something. My parents, well, everyone in our family, spoiled her. She's the baby. My daddy gave her money every week while Jay and I had to earn money from our parents. Granted, they were financially well off by the time she was older and able to provide for her with no problems. I think they are realizing now that they should have made her work like Jay and I did.

"I hear what you're saying, Dre but my sister is a piece of work. I'm going to talk to her, though."

"I'm just saying. You've already lost one sibling. The only thing worse than losing another one is losing her while she's still alive."

His comment really hit me hard and my heart thudded in my chest. I knew I needed to try to make things right with my sister. I haven't been the best sister I could be to her.

"Now that that's out of the way, let's talk business," Dre ordered. "These are my suggestions. You don't have to take them but in order for us to make a profit, we are going to have to make some changes."

"What kind of changes?" There was a panic in my voice as I feared he was about to take over my business. "Cause, I didn't sign on to be taken out of my own business."

Dre's face became stoic, as if I offended him. "Monica, listen. The sooner you stop doubting me and insinuating shit, the faster we can get this done. I've told you a million and one times, I'm trying to make money. I don't want to run this place; I want this place to run so that I can turn a profit. If you don't want the same thing, you can walk away now, and our contract will be null and void."

His tone surprised me, and I stumbled to get a coherent sentence out. "Okay. I'm sorry. Continue." I pulled out my legal pad and favorite purple pen and prepared to write.

"First, we need to purchase the space next door. It's a little high for my tastes but I'm sure I can get the price down. The good thing is no one wants to put a business next to a bar and lounge. We also need to do some renovations to the existing space. We need more TVs, the bathrooms need revamping and we need to make the bar area more functional. Not to mention we need to make some changes to the kitchen. Which brings me to my next point; you need a chef. The guys you have back there are fine, but your menu is limited to simple bar food. To compete with these other places, we need a chef that can crank out good, affordable, quality food."

I jotted down his suggestions and I agreed with them. These were some of the same suggestions I had; I just didn't have the money to bring them to fruition.

"Do you have a chef in mind?" Dre asked.

"Not off the top of my head. I'm sure it won't be hard to find one though."

"A friend of mine, Swan, cooks in the cafeteria at Grady. Amazing chef, just stuck cooking what they tell him to. He's cooked a few meals for me before and I'm sure you'd be satisfied. I can set up a meeting, so you can meet with him if you like."

"Yeah, that's cool. I don't know anyone personally, so I can meet with him to see if he'd be a good fit."

"Alright, I'll set that up." Dre pulled out his phone and made a call to Swan. He agreed to come in a few hours so we could meet. He was so excited for the potential of being able to run a kitchen. He sounded eager and that made me even more comfortable with him running the kitchen at Blaze. "Let's go look at the space next door and then in here too so we can get a visual of what we are working with."

"Sure. Let's go."

Dre and I spent the next three hours talking, planning, and number crunching. He had some really good ideas and some that showed his inexperience in the bar and lounge business. But he was open to my suggestions and didn't pretend to know it all. I was grateful for that. He even included Peaches to get her input on what would make the bar more functional. Even though we were only in the planning phase, Dre was proving to be just what Blaze needed.

When Swan arrived, I was pleasantly surprised by him. He was huge! He was every bit of 6 feet tall and had muscles everywhere. He looked more like a security guard than a chef. But after five minutes of talking to him, I was in love. He was like a big teddy bear, funny and he had such a reverence for food. He talked about food like how a man would talk about the woman he loved or a car he was into. But the kicker was actually tasting his food. He brought some ingredients to make a quick burger and I don't know what he did to it, but it was so good. Quan and Tank had come in to prep for the night and they were impressed, too. I was relieved they weren't intimidated or fearful of losing their jobs. Instead, they sat around and talked with Swan and showed him around the kitchen. Quan and Tank could cook but neither of them were leaders. So, Swan would be the perfect person to push them to do more than cook wings and spinach dip. I hadn't officially hired Swan yet, but he was in the kitchen helping the guys prep and giving them tips.

We left them in the kitchen and continued walking around Blaze. "Are you married to the décor in here?"

"Huh?" Because of Nick's insistence, just hearing 'married' threw me off.

"The pictures. How attached are you to them?"

"Oh. Very. My boyfriend painted them. I didn't want generic, stock pictures so he commissioned all of the pieces." Again, Dre's face changed when I mentioned my boyfriend. He tried to recover but I caught the change in his demeanor.

"Okay then. They are nice. I'm thinking if we change anything, we need to make them our focus. But we need to reach out to some designers and contractors. I can set up some consultations so we can talk numbers and make a decision hopefully by next week."

"Okay. How long do you estimate that it will take to make these changes?" Dre was suggesting taking out walls, remolding bathrooms, revamping the kitchen, creating a true DJ booth/stage for Karaoke/spoken word/open mic and making the bar bigger. And that was just in the existing part of Blaze. The space next door would require a complete revamping to make it a semi-secluded VIP area. I couldn't imagine that being an easy job. Or a quick one.

"You're probably going to have to close for about a month or two." He noted the shock on my face and laughed at me. "But just think, when you are prepared to open back up, you can have a re-grand opening. You will certainly make back the money with the changes, especially with the food."

He was making sense, but I couldn't pay my people if we weren't open. I'd have to make sure to give them a heads up, so they could file for unemployment when we weren't open. But I did want to somehow pay Swan, Quan, and Tank because I needed them to work together to make sure they were ready for when we re-opened.

I didn't realize that Dre had been at Blaze practically all day until our happy hour crowd started to file in. I settled down in my desk prepared to tackle the paperwork that piled up from my mini vacay when Dre asked what I was doing.

"I need to get this stuff finished up before it gets too crowded in here."

He looked at me and raised his eyebrow. "Don't you have something more pressing to do?"

Damn. Midori. I had forgotten all about her. Accidentally, on purpose I suppose. I wasn't in the mood to handle this, but I'd let it fester for too long. All the production I felt earlier was gone and now I was back to the reality of having to talk to my sister. I shot her a text to see if she was home and she was. I exhaled and gathered my things to go home to talk to her.

Dre picked up on my silence and stopped me before I could leave. "Family shit is never easy. But you have to deal with it before it takes you out of the game of running your business. We've got a lot to do over the next few weeks and you need to be on your A game if we're going to make Blaze great."

I smiled at him and thanked him for listening to me today. "Let me get out of here so I can go talk to Midori. Thanks again."

"No problem, Monica. Call me or text me if you need to talk afterward." The sincerity in his voice was apparent but I pushed the thought out of my mind. *Maybe he's just a friendly guy,* I reasoned.

"We've spent enough time together today to where you can call me Mo. Monica is for people that don't really know me. And I've shared a lot with you today." I laughed nervously because talking to him was easy. I could easily see myself getting caught up with developing a friendship that went beyond Blaze business.

Dre walked me out and I made my way to my condo. The entire drive home, I thought about him. The way he spoke, how he was sure of himself but not cocky, how he looked at me, his ideas, his drive, his willingness to admit he was wrong, and his eyes. He was completely different from Nick. Speaking of my boyfriend, I hadn't heard from him since he called me about Midori. But because I spent all afternoon with Dre, I hadn't thought about Nick at all.

* * *

I ordered a pizza from Pizza Hut and while I waited for it to arrive, I went into my sister's room to talk to her.

"So Nick overheard you talking today. He called to tell me that you think I hate you. Why do you think that?" I decided I was going to be honest with her and not sugarcoat anything.

She stared at me for a minute. It looked like she was contemplating whether she was going to tell me to fuck off or if she was going to be honest with me. "You act like you do."

"Well, I don't." I was usually assured in my words, but this was a hard conversation and I really wasn't sure what to say. "Why do you think that?"

Midori sat up and I could tell she'd been crying because her eyes were a little puffy and slightly red. "You've always hated me. Since the day I was born. You've always treated me like I fucked up your life. All my friends that have sisters talk about how close they are and all the stuff they do together. And you never wanted to do any of that with me."

"You are ten years younger than me. We can't do a lot of the same things," I reasoned.

"So, because I'm 20 and you're 30, we can't go shopping together? We can't go out to eat? We can't hang out? We can't talk?"

She had me there. Midori and I didn't have a close relationship but that was partially because I always had my brother. "We talk. I work a lot of hours, so my time is limited. I have to ration out time for Nick."

"Those are excuses, Mo. I'm not begging you to treat me like your sister, a real sister. You obviously don't want that. I just thought that since Jay died…"

She paused, and her eyes darted around. *What is wrong with her? She must be damn drunk!* I deduced. I had seen the evidence of my sister drinking around the apartment, but I didn't think much of it. I was getting wasted on weekends in college, so I really didn't think much about her drinking here and there. "Since Jay died, what?"

"I thought that we'd get closer. But it seems you hate me more now. I'm sure you wished it was me that died instead of him. Cause then you'd still have your favorite."

Tears fell from my sister's eyes and I was too embarrassed to speak. I had to admit that my sister was not always my favorite person, but maybe I'd been too hard on her. All this time, all of her life and all she was trying to do was get me to love her. But her attitude was a force to be reckoned with.

"I can take responsibility for what I have done but can you? You haven't always been the easiest person to get along with."

Midori started fidgeting with her comforter to avoid looking at me. "You'd be a bitch too if you had to deal with the shit I had to deal with."

I rolled my eyes accidently on purpose. Now I knew she was just making stuff up. "Midori, you are twenty. What shit have you had to deal with?"

She finally tore her eyes away from her comforter and gawked at me. The sorrow she just showed me was now replaced by anger. "I've grown up in you and Jay's shadow. No one knew me. I was always Mo's little sister or Jesse's baby girl. No one took me seriously because they thought I was moody. I have no friends because girls thought I was stuck up and guys just wanted to fuck me. Every relationship I've ever had has ended with me getting hurt and I don't understand what's so wrong with me that I can't keep a man."

I listened to Midori rant, but I didn't know what to say. I had no idea she was going through this. And looking at her, you'd think she didn't have a care in the world. She was beautiful, and her body was amazing. I was certain part of her issues was the way she shut down and shut people out.

Since my last comment seemed to make her upset, I opted to keep quiet. But she continued her slurred rant. "No one likes me. No one cares about me. Everyone uses me for what I have, and I get nothing in return. The one person in my family that loved me is dead and now I have nothing!"

Midori was raising her voice and she had a distant look in her eyes. Dre's words were playing in my head: *you've already lost one sibling. The only thing worse than losing another one, is losing her while she's still alive.*

My sister started pacing like she couldn't be still. She was making me nervous, so I reached for her shoulder to try to calm her down. As soon as I touched her, she reared back and slapped the shit out of me. My head flew to the side and there was a stinging pain on the left side of my face. I could taste blood in my mouth. I tried to gather myself because my first instinct was to beat her ass, but I had to remember she was drunk.

I held the side of my face and tried to think of the best thing for me to do. Midori started walking around again, muttering things under her breath. I knew I couldn't handle her alone, so I went to go call Nick so he could help me with her. I've never had to deal with a drunk Midori before and if she hit me again, I was going to hurt her.

"Nick, can you come over here, please? Something is wrong with Midori," I pleaded.

"Something like what?" he groaned. "I have a lot I need to get done tonight. I'm sure you can handle it."

"We were talking then she hit me. She's drunk and I just need help with her. Just come over here, please!"

The panic in my voice must have alarmed him because he told me he was on his way.

I went to my bathroom to look at my face and there was a slight bruise where Midori hit me. I couldn't find it in myself to be mad at her because I could tell that she was really hurting. I also couldn't be upset because I was part of the reason she was hurting. Once she sobered up, I was going to spend time with her and try to make things right.

I left my bathroom to see if she had calmed down any. I knocked on her door, but she didn't answer. I turned the knob, but it was locked. I was getting flustered because she was making me do too much, but I just went to find the tool I kept over my door. I unlocked the door, but I didn't see her.

"Midori, where are you?" I walked around her bed and jumped when I saw her on the ground. She was on the floor bleeding from her wrists. "Oh no. No. No. No. Midori, NO!!"

I ran to her, but in my panic, I had no idea what to do. I finally grabbed two t-shirts from her drawer and pressed it against her wrists to try to stop her from bleeding. She tried to push me off of her, but she was too weak.

"Let me go, Mo! Let me go!" she cried. Her face was streaked with tears.

I used all my strength to keep the shirts on her wrists, but I was struggling bad. "Calm down, baby. It's going to be okay. We're going to get you help!"

I heard Nick knocking on my door and I panicked because I had no idea what I needed to do. I needed Nick's help so I let Midori go and ran to unlock the door.

"What is so important that I had to come over-"

When he saw the blood on me, he understood it was serious. I was already running back to the room where Midori was.

"What the hell happened?" he yelled at me while pulling out his phone to call 911. After giving them all the information, he came to put pressure on her left wrist, so I could focus on the right. Every time she closed her eyes, I started screaming and shaking her.

"Midori! Don't you dare die! Don't you dare! I can't lose you, too!"

* * *

Hours later, Nick, my parents, and myself were sitting in the waiting room of Grady praying my sister was okay. Nick called Keyalani on the way and she made it there just after we did. Being surrounded by my family and friends made this terrible situation a little better. It took the paramedics about ten minutes to get to my condo, but those ten minutes felt like an eternity. Nick and I stopped the bleeding, but she lost so much blood. By the time the paramedics got to my condo, I was damn near hyperventilating because Midori lost consciousness.

At the hospital, my mind was running in a million different directions. Whatever was going on with her, I was having a hard time wrapping my head around it. My parents asked me a million times what happened, but I was just as confused as to why Midori tried to take her life. Finally, the ER doctor and another doctor emerged, and we hopped up to see if she was okay.

"Mr. and Mrs. Mack? Hey, I'm Dr. Adams. Midori is stable now. Her cuts required stitches, and we had to call psych in to evaluate her. I'm going to let Dr. Coleman explain the rest of it."

"Mr. and Mrs. Mack. As Dr. Adams said, I'm Dr. Coleman and due to her suicide attempt we had to admit her to our crisis stabilization unit for observation."

"What do you mean suicide attempt? You think she tried to do this on purpose?" my mama asked clutching her chest.

"Mrs. Mack, Midori slit both of her wrists. And we also found evidence that this was not her first time," Dr. Coleman stated.

I cocked my head to the side and looked at this doctor as if he lost his damn mind. "What do you mean this isn't her first time? I think I would have noticed if my sister tried to kill herself before!"

"There were healed scars on her wrists as well as cuts on her thighs. I am quite sure she hid them well so that you wouldn't see them." The doctor spoke so calmly while my mama began to cry hard. "It's too soon to tell her true intentions because she was intoxicated but we take these attempts serious, regardless of intentions. So, she will be admitted to our crisis stabilization unit. A nurse will be out in a second to explain the process and to make sure we have good contact info for you. This is just the beginning; Midori has a long, uphill battle and she will need your support."

The doctors left us in the waiting room with more questions than answers. I needed to go to sleep; I was drained. Nick offered to get my parents a hotel room because my place was out of the question, not with Midori's blood all over the floor in her room. Nick drove my parents to a hotel, got them checked in, and then took me to his place. He ran me a bath and helped me get in the tub. I sat in the tub until the water got cold. I was too exhausted to even bathe so he came in the bathroom to wash me. He got me out of the tub, put lotion on my body, and helped me into bed.

"Baby, will you get my phone?" I asked. My voice was almost a whisper.

"Whatever it is, I'm sure it can wait until tomorrow."

"I just need to let Peaches know I won't be in tomorrow. A quick text."

Reluctantly, he handed me my phone and I saw that I had a text from Dre asking how my conversation went with Midori. I contemplated if I should text him back and finally decided to let him know it didn't go well and I would talk to him about it tomorrow because I was staying with my boyfriend tonight. He sent back a thumbs up emoji.

I texted Peaches and told her about Midori and told her I wouldn't be in tomorrow. She told me not to worry about Blaze; she would hold it down until Midori was good. At least I didn't have to worry about that. I also texted Keyalani to thank her for coming to the hospital with me. She promised to check on me the next day.

Nick climbed in the bed next to me and pulled me close to him. Just being in his arms was refreshing. Today started out so awesome and it ended with my sister trying to die.

"You wanna talk about it?" Nick asked gingerly.

I didn't want to, but my words just started spilling out. "I just don't understand," I admitted. "How did I miss all of this? How did I not see how much she was hurting?"

"Don't do this, Mo. The doctor told you she was hiding it."

"But I should have known something wasn't right."

Nick breathed heavily and wrapped his arms around me tighter. "Baby, you're not her babysitter. After this, she needs to go back home. Especially if you're going to be at work so much."

He was trying to help but his comment seemed accusing. He didn't come right out and say it, but it sounded like he was insinuating that my business was partly to blame. I didn't have the energy to fuss with him tonight. I just let it go. I planned on calling Dre tomorrow to get the ball rolling on the renovations.

I wasn't too sure Midori going back home was in her best interest. Not saying my parents weren't capable but she could get more help in Atlanta than she could in Americus. If Blaze was closed for renovations, I could really be there for my sister. The way I was supposed to be since the day she was born.

Chapter Six

"Mo, I thought you had to deal with Midori? What are you doing here?" I walked into Blaze the next day, surprising Peaches.

"Yeah, they wouldn't let us see her today, so I couldn't just sit around doing nothing," I informed her. "Dre is on his way here with a contractor."

"So, what happened with your sister?" Peaches asked.

I told her the story and she didn't even try to hide her shock. "You don't hear about black folks trying to kill themselves. That's white people shit."

"I thought so, too. But I googled it and a lot of black people suffer with depression and other shit that would lead them to suicide. We don't get help for our problems. We're told to pray or that only white people can go to therapy. We suffer with mental health problems, but we don't believe in getting help. It's not something we deal with."

Peaches raised her eyebrow at me and a few hours ago, I was filled with doubt, too. I spent my morning Googling suicide and cutting and was surprised about all the information out there, especially when it came to black people. Other than not having access to mental health treatment, being religious prevented a lot of people from getting the help they desperately needed. Since God and I weren't on speaking terms right now, I knew Midori had to stay in Atlanta to get help. My mama and daddy would just take her church and that wasn't going to cut it. I found a website, therapyforblackgirls.com, that had a directory with black female therapists in Georgia. There were a number in Atlanta and I found one that I really liked.

Everything I read indicated that Midori was depressed. The more I read, the more upset I became because I didn't notice this in her. She's always been a moody child but when Jayshawn died, she was even worse. We all chalked it up to her grieving. When she came to his gravesite on the anniversary of his death, she said she blamed me; I wondered how long she'd been carrying that around. If she blamed me for his death, I could also take the blame for her suicide attempt. And that made me feel like shit.

Peaches and I made small talk until Dre and the contractor, Walter, arrived. We walked around, explaining our vision. Walter made suggestions and jotted down figures. After we talked about everything, he gave us his estimate. I gawked but Dre didn't seem phased.

"We're still meeting with a few other contractors and then Ms. Mack will make a decision," Dre informed Walter. They shook hands and Walter left.

Dre and I went to my office to go over the estimate. "That's a lot of money, Dre."

"It is, but I think we can recoup that within a few months of the grand opening. Remember we are adding a full menu. I also have some associates that will pay to have a private party here. I think it's worth it."

I didn't even hesitate. "Okay. Let's do it."

"Just like that?" he asked puzzled. "You don't want to meet with the other contractors?"

"Time isn't a luxury I have right now. I have a situation with Midori that is going to take up my time. If you think Walter can handle the job, let's just book him and get started in the next two weeks. I need to time to draft separation notices for unemployment and to let my customers know."

"What's up with your sister, anyway?"

I sighed and gave him the abbreviated version of Midori's situation. "Damn, Mo, I'm sorry. Yeah, Walter is legit. He's done work for houses I've flipped so I know he's about business and won't screw us over. Let's get the ball rolling with him so you can be there for your sister. Or we can wait. Your choice."

"No, let's do it. I can't see her for a few days, so I have time to get things going."

"Alright. I'll give him a call and get with you later in the week," Dre said calmly. "Take care of your sister. And yourself."

"I will. Thank you."

Dre's eyes lingered on me and that sincerity I saw before was still there but...it seemed more intense. I didn't want to fight looking at him, so I didn't. "Would you like to go to lunch?"

His request caught me off guard, but I didn't hesitate to tell him yes. I needed this distraction. Nick left me to go to work and being alone with my thoughts was not a good look for me right now. I got my purse and we headed out the door.

We ended up at Nina's. Because I'd been here before with Nick, I let Nina know that Dre and I were having a business lunch and we needed a semi-private table. She hooked us up near the back of the restaurant so we wouldn't be disturbed. Dre even pulled out some paperwork, so we could play the part. But I didn't want to talk about business. I didn't want to talk at all.

Dre and I ate our lunch mostly in silence. The chatter of patrons around us was calming enough for me. Dre's ringing phone interrupted our quiet lunch.

"Hey, baby girl. What are you up to?"

Dre continued to have his conversation and I assumed he was talking to his sister. He put her on speaker and I heard her raving about the trip she was taking to New York next week. Dre was engrossed in his phone and it seemed he was barely listening to her. He took her off speaker and told her he sent her some money for her trip. He also gave her instructions about traveling and making sure to stay with her group. He finally ended the phone call by telling her he was proud of her and to be careful in New York.

"Well, aren't you just a sweet big brother?"

"I gotta look out for my baby," he said. "She's in grad school earning her doctorate in psychology. She was selected to attend a conference in New York to help with her research. She didn't want to go, but I convinced her to take the trip because it would be great for her dissertation."

Hearing his sister was going into psychology definitely piqued my interest because of my sister's recent situation. "What's her dissertation on?"

He looked at me pensively. "I'm not sure the exact title but she's researching something about black men and mental health. The prevalence of mental health in the prison system. The outcomes of black kids not having access to mental health. Something along those lines."

"Wow. I just googled something similar this morning. I didn't realize how many black people suffer with mental health issues. We're told to pray about it and then it will be better. But I don't see how that's helping us."

"I don't think prayer alone is enough. Therapy is definitely needed, too."

"I see that," I admitted. "But I'm going to have a hard time convincing my parents of that."

Dre put his fork down and looked at me from across the table. "Mo, I wish I had something to say that would make this better but from what you told me, this is going to be an uphill battle. Because your brother's death is still relatively new, they are going to fight you on keeping her here. But I think if you tell them you are taking time off from Blaze to take care of her, they will be okay."

I wanted to agree with him, but he didn't know my parents. My daddy was going to be the hardest one to convince. Midori was definitely a daddy's girl. He spoiled that girl like nobody's business.

Dre and I finished our lunch and even threw some Blaze business in the conversation as well. He told me he'd handle some of the decision making while I was out but would run the important things by me. I told him I needed menu ideas from Swan by the end of the week, so we could do a cost analysis of ingredients. Swan preferred fresh ingredients, nothing boxed and organic as much as possible. It sounded expensive but judging from his burger the other day, it was certainly worth the money.

After lunch, we walked back to Blaze. Talking with Dre was easy, and I enjoyed his conversation. We made it back to my office and he told me he had to go. I put my phone down on my desk so I could walk him out. As soon as I turned around, Dre was standing really close to me. Before I could back away, Dre leaned down to kiss me.

I tried to push him off of me, at least in my mind I did. Instead, I found myself slipping my tongue in his mouth. His kiss was tender and intoxicating. I finally came to my senses and pulled away from him. With my breathing ragged, I stared at him, trying to find the words to ask him why he kissed me. But as if my body had a mind of its own, I was kissing him again. This kiss wasn't as gentle, this kiss was eager. This kiss made me imagine this talented tongue in other places on my body. This time he pulled away first causing me to whimper.

"You don't know how long I've wanted to do that," he whispered.

I didn't have any words for him. I just wanted to kiss him again. So, I did. His hands cupped my face as he moved his tongue expertly in my mouth. The throbbing between my legs was overriding my sensibilities. I knew I had no business kissing this man, but I didn't want to stop.

A glass crashing to the ground and Peaches cursing loudly caused us both to jump back like she was in the room with us instead of at the bar. Dre stared at me with those gorgeous eyes and the lust that occupied his gaze was more than apparent.

"I…ummm…I…I need to…ummm…" I tried to form words, but I couldn't. All I could think about was kissing Dre and the way he made my body feel.

"I have to go, but I'll check on you later, okay Mo?"

I nodded my head and before he left he gave me a quick peck. I sat at my desk with my head in my hands. *What the hell was I getting into?* I asked myself.

There was a knock on my door and I jumped at the sound. "Girl," Keyalani called to me. "I've been calling you! Who was that guy that just left?" she obviously didn't remember him from my birthday party.

"Who?" I knew I had the deer in headlights look and even if I wanted to hide this from Lani, I couldn't. She had some weird 6th sense about shit like this.

"Don't play dumb with me," my best friend replied while making herself comfortable in the chair opposite of me. She looked at me and without saying a word forced me to spill my guts about Dre.

"Mo, seriously? I mean no judgment, but you barely know this guy. Is he worth losing your relationship with Nick over?"

"Please stop over exaggerating. It's not that serious, okay?"

"You can lie to me, but don't lie to yourself," she countered. "All I'm saying is dude is fine, but Nick wants to marry you. Don't throw that away."

"Ugh, Lani! I'm not doing anything. The kiss was a mistake, I know that. But it's not going to happen again. We work together and that's it. That's all it's going to be. It's just…different. When I talk to Dre, I don't have to talk about moving in and marriage. He understands why I go so hard for my business."

"I'm not the one you need to convince," Lani said snidely. I threw a pen at her and she smacked it down before it hit her. "Oh, but see if he has a brother, homeboy, or cousin before you chump him off."

* * *

After three days, we were finally allowed to see Midori. I was nervous as hell because I didn't know what to expect. When people thought about psychiatric units, they thought straitjackets and incoherent ramblings. I didn't want to see my sister looking crazy. But after seeing her bleeding from her wrists, I guess seeing her alive was better than how she would come out of those doors. My parents and I were seated in a room at the hospital awaiting Midori and her therapist. When they walked into the room, I was relieved that she looked pretty normal, aside from the bandages on her wrists.

My mama and daddy hugged Midori and I saw my daddy wiping away tears. "Midori, what happened? What's wrong?" our father inquired. It pained him to see Midori like this; his hurt was written all over his face.

Everyone sat down, and my daddy waited for Midori to answer. "Baby, what happened? Why would you do this to yourself?"

"Umm…Mr. and Mrs. Mack," the woman with Midori interjected. "I know you have questions, but let's slow it down just a little bit."

My parents looked at the woman, neither of them wanting to follow directions. "My name is Dr. Patterson and I've been working with Midori since she's been here. We've had a lot of really good conversations, but I don't think Midori is prepared to fully share everything today."

"Well, what the hell are we here for then?" my daddy spat. He rarely cursed and for him to be using profanity, I knew he had to be mad. It was then that I knew that me asking Midori to stay up here with me was going to be a knockdown, drag out fight.

Dr. Patterson flipped her long weave from her face. She didn't look like a doctor to me; she was a pretty brown skin woman with a beautiful Colgate smile. She didn't wear makeup, but I assumed she probably got dolled up outside of these walls. "Mr. Mack, we are here today to update you on a few things with Midori and to go over her treatment plan."

For the next ten minutes, my parents fussed with Dr. Patterson while Midori and I sat silently. The one time I caught her gaze, she looked at me pleadingly. She wanted me to interject.

"Daddy, let's just calm down," I interjected. "We need to listen to what Dr. Patterson has to say."

My daddy huffed as he got out of his seat. "Monica, I don't need to hear nothing from you! She was living with you! Why didn't you stop this?"

"Daddy," I started. I had to take a few breaths to stop the barrage of curse words that were threatening to come out of my mouth. "This isn't the time for the blame game but just know Midori's problems didn't start when she moved to Atlanta. Whatever is going on with her has been happening for a long time."

My daddy started to fuss again but Dr. Patterson interrupted him. "Mr. Mack,"

"Call me Jesse," he told the doctor.

"Okay, Jesse. Monica is right. We are not here to place blame on anyone. Today, I just simply want Midori's support system to be aware of our plan for her. Now, Mr.-I mean Jesse, I know that you guys don't live here so we will have to make some provisions to include you in therapy."

Now it was my mama's turn to speak up. "When you guys let her go, we will be taking her home to Americus."

"Mama, that's not a good idea. There aren't a lot of places she can get help in Americus. I've researched therapists in Atlanta and I've found a few that I think can help Midori," I stated. I pulled out the list I wrote down so I could get Dr. Patterson's opinion on who she could recommend. "Plus, Blaze is about to undergo some renovations, so I will have time to take her to appointments and be there for her."

My sister gave me a slight smile ,and I knew she was glad I was standing up for her. Hell, I owed her that much.

My daddy wasn't having it though. "Monica, if you think she is staying up here with you, you've lost your damn mind. Another one of my children will not die on your watch!"

"Jesse!" my mama exclaimed.

My daddy's words hit me like a ton of bricks. We stared at each other; his face laced with anger, mine riddled with agony. So, Midori was right; my parents blamed me for Jay dying and now they blamed me for Midori's suicide attempt. My chest got tight and breathing was becoming a chore. I couldn't handle this blame.

I jumped up from my seat abruptly causing my chair to fall backwards onto the linoleum floor with a clang. I couldn't stay in the same room with my daddy and be his whipping post. I walked quickly out the door, ignoring my mama calling after me. I practically ran out of the hospital and got into my car. I didn't want to go home so I went to the only other place I felt safe, Blaze.

I rushed in and was disappointed that Walter was there with his crew looking over stuff and planning how to proceed with my renovation. I went to my office and closed the door. I was sitting at my desk with my head in my hands trying to control my breathing, but I couldn't.

There was a soft knock on my door, but I couldn't tell whoever it was to go away. There was another knock and I said go away as loud as I could, but it was only a whisper. The door opened anyway, and Dre walked in. He took one look at my face and rushed over to me.

"Mo, what's wrong? What happened?"

And then it happened.

I began to cry. Not just tears but wailing. I cried for Jay. I cried for Midori. I cried because my parents thought everything was my fault. Everything I had held in for the last year was coming out. I was trying to breathe but the weight of my grief was crashing down on me, constricting my chest. Dre made me stand up and started speaking calmly. "Mo, just breathe. It's okay, just breathe."

Finally, I was able to catch my breath. But the tears wouldn't stop. Dre ran to my door and locked it and came back to hold me. I cried for what seemed like forever. When my tears finally subsided, my head was pounding and all I wanted to do was lie down.

"Come on. Let's get you out of here."

I didn't object to Dre leading me out of the door and into his car. I didn't ask where we were going, and I stared out the window the entire ride. We pulled up at what I assumed to be his house, which was in a nice little suburban neighborhood. I didn't even pay attention to where we were. He helped me out of the car, unlocked his front door, and let me in.

Dre walked me to his den and gestured for me to sit on his sofa. I dropped down like I weighed 400 pounds. His sofa was the color of chocolate and extremely comfortable. I propped my feet on his sofa leaning on the arm. I took in his house trying to get my mind off everything that happened today. The den was simple and looked like a bachelor pad. It looked like he went to a furniture store and bought the whole room.

"Can you tell me what happened?" he asked quietly. I opened my mouth to speak but my words came out jumbled because once again, I started to cry. I cried until I felt my eyes almost closing. I knew they were red and puffy by now. Dre pulled me into him and held me as I tried to gather myself enough to speak.

My brother had been dead for over a year and I never got a chance to grieve. Since he died, I'd been carrying a lot of shit around with me. I missed my brother. My sister was hurting, and I didn't see it. My parents blamed me for what happened to Jay and Midori. My boyfriend wanted to marry me and I was running away from him.

"Do you need anything?" he asked.

Dre's voice startled me because I was so lost in my thoughts that I forgot he was there. "Umm…just some water please."

Dre went to his kitchen and returned with a bottle of water. I sat up as he handed me the water. Everything was blurry so I just closed my eyes. Dre didn't say anything, but I could feel him watching me intently.

"Do you need to call someone?" he spoke calmly.

"Yes. No. I mean…not right now. I just need to get my mind together," I said hoarsely. "I didn't mean for you to see me like this."

"Nonsense. You're dealing with a lot. It's expected," he explained. "I'm here if you want to talk."

"They blame me."

"Who blames you for what?"

I wiped tears away as I told Dre about what happened at the hospital today. He listened, and his face didn't hold any judgment. Instead he looked like he wanted to rescue me from the mental hell I was in.

"Listen, Mo. People handle grief in different ways. I am sure your parents don't blame you; they are just having a hard time with everything. I know it's easier said than done, but you can't let that get to you."

Sensible Mo knew he was right, but grief-stricken Mo couldn't accept that as the truth.

"I'm sure your emotions got the best of you when your brother passed. It's natural, it's part of the process."

"This is the first time I've cried about it. I never had the chance to grieve. I had to be the strong one for my family."

Dre cut his eyes in my direction and he didn't even try to hide his shock. "What do you mean you haven't cried for your brother? Like recently or…"

"Ever," I admitted. "When it happened, I was in too much shock to cry. Then my parents and sister were just out of it. And his baby mama was inconsolable. Someone had to step up and make decisions."

"No one said it had to be you," Dre responded quickly.

"Well who else was going to do it then?" I snapped. I got off the sofa and stood in front of him. He had a lot of damn nerve to judge me when he had no idea what it was like for me and my family. "Stop acting like you know me or what my family went through! Who the hell are you to judge me?"

Dre stood and even though he was taller than me, I wasn't intimated by him standing over me. "Yo, Mo. Calm down. I'm not judging you or your family. All I'm saying is you heaped this responsibility on your head when you didn't have to. And now it's coming out."

"Whatever. I'm not about to do this with you. Take me home."

I turned to head to his front door, but Dre grabbed me and pulled me into him. Without warning, his lips were crashing into mine. This kiss wasn't sensual like it was in my office the other day. No, this kiss was frantic. Impatient. Desperate.

His kiss was taking all of my logic and I needed my clothes off. I broke our kiss to strip my clothes from my body. Following my lead, Dre did the same. He looked at me, wondering if I was going to change my mind. I answered him by closing the space between us and kissing him again. Dre pushed me to his sofa, forcing me to sit down. Once I was seated, his lips blazed a trail from my mouth to my neck to my breasts. With my nipple in his mouth, I exhaled sharply. He paid attention to both of my breasts, but I didn't care about foreplay.

Until his lips traveled further down my body.

I spread my legs in anticipation of his destination, my breathing ragged, my heart racing. As soon as his tongue landed on my clit, my back arched involuntarily. My low groan energized him, and Dre began to expertly lick me. I grabbed his head to keep him between my legs because I didn't need him to stop. Not yet.

"Please, Dre," I moaned. "Don't stop."

He obliged my request and slipped a finger inside of the wetness he created. I had no words, just moans of pleasure as he pushed my body to the brink of an orgasm.

"Dre! Oh my God! Dre!" I continued to moan his name as I released. Dre continued to lick and suck between my legs causing me to climax again. I pushed his head away unable to stand another release like that.

Dre stood up and left me withering on his sofa trying to recover from the way he devoured me. He returned to his sofa sheathed in latex. He kissed me again, and I adjusted my body so that he could climb on top of me. Dre continued to kiss me as if he needed to kiss me to live. As he slid inside of me, I broke our kiss to curse under my breath. He pushed himself deeper into me, only giving me a second to adjust to his size. He moved methodically trying to make sure I felt every single inch of him.

"More...deeper...more," I moaned. I needed more of him but the sofa was too constricting.

He pulled out of me and led me to the floor. Quickly, he was back inside of me. I wrapped my legs around his waist and pushed him in deeper. Dre and I found a rhythm and I held on to him as he reached my spot.

"Right there, Dre," I panted. "Don't stop! Right there!"

"Right there, baby? You gonna cum for me again?"

"Yes! Shit! Yes!"

"Give it to me then," Dre commanded.

On cue, I gave Dre what he was working so hard for. I let go and grabbed on to him as my body shook. Guttural sounds were all that could come out of my mouth. Dre pulled out of me much to my dismay. He sat down on the sofa and told me to come sit on him. I pulled myself together and climbed on him. My eyes rolled into the back of my head as he filled me up again. I began riding him slowly, allowing my body to adjust to the fullness of him but Dre wasn't satisfied with me being gentle.

"Ride this dick, Monica," he demanded while slapping my ass. He continued to spank me until I was riding him the way he wanted me to. His hands traveled up my body until he was pinching my nipple harshly. I moaned at the sensation of the pleasurable pain. Satisfied with my reaction, Dre's hand snaked into my locs and pulled. I wasn't used to this. I wasn't used to being commanded. I wasn't use to being handled like this. It was different but it was…so sexy.

He leaned back and pulled me close to him. I lifted myself up until he was almost out of me and then I slammed my ass back down. I continued my movements causing Dre to moan in my ear and squeeze my ass. I could tell he was getting ready to climax by the way he moved and groaned. I worked harder to get it out of him.

I leaned down to kiss him and was rewarded with feeling him throbbing inside of me. Hearing Dre moan out his pleasure and feeling him release inside of me set off another orgasm in me.

Dre and I tried to catch our breath and I smiled at him. He leaned up and kissed me again. "Damn, girl. You are something serious. You good?" Dre asked me while rubbing my thigh.

"I am," I responded. "Are you good?"

"I'm better than good. I'm great."

I giggled and returned his kiss. I felt like we just performed what Jill Scott was singing about on "Crown Royal". And for the first time, my mind flashed to Nick. I hadn't thought about him in hours. I climbed off Dre and sat down beside him. I closed my eyes and breathed in deeply, waiting for guilt to overtake me.

It never came.

Chapter Seven

Keyalani and I were meeting for lunch while Midori had a therapy appointment. As promised, I was taking care of my sister and making sure she was getting to her appointments, taking her meds, and adjusting to life after her suicide attempt.

My parents fought me tooth and nail. Only after Dr. Patterson confirmed that there were few, if any, therapists in Americus did they finally relent, but they called me multiple times a day to check on her. My daddy was close to moving to Atlanta, but my mama talked him out of it.

Lani finally arrived at Chipotle, but I didn't complain about her being late since I didn't have to work right now. Blaze was undergoing renovations and I hadn't gotten used to the place being closed. However, my days were spent with Midori.

"Hey, girl. Sorry, I'm late," Lani said while we stood in line to order our food.

"No problem. I have nothing but time," I replied.

"Oh yeah. How are the renovations going?"

"They are going. Dre's keeping everything in line, so I don't have to worry about much."

Lani gave me a side eye and I decided to ignore her for now and ordered my burrito bowl. I hadn't told her I'd slept with him yet, and I knew she was going to freak out. That was part of the reason we were meeting for lunch; I wanted to tell her, but it needed to be in public.

We got our food and settled down at a table. "How's Midori doing?"

I sighed heavily. Taking care of my sister wasn't as easy as I thought it was going to be. "It's okay. She's trying to be okay but it's a struggle."

"I bet it is."

"Yeah, our first family session is next week. I'm not really looking forward to that," I mulled. I only talked to my mama about Midori. I refused to talk to my daddy even though my mama tried to apologize for him. I wasn't prepared to forgive, and I damn sure wasn't going to forget.

"Yeah, but you guys need this. You have dealt with a lot," Lani said. "I think it's a good idea."

"Nick does too," I began but paused to eat some of my lunch. "He also suggested we go to couples' therapy." Lani raised her eyebrow at me and I knew I had to tell her. Somehow. "He said I've been distant, but he doesn't understand I've been dealing with a lot with Midori."

"I'm sure he just wants to know why you're against moving in with him. Or getting married."

I really didn't want to get into this conversation with her because I was getting it damn near every day with Nick. He found ways to bring up moving in and marriage. We had a huge argument the night I slept with Dre because he called me a million times. I told him about what happened when we went to see Midori and how I finally cried for Jay, but he didn't seem concerned about that. He berated me for not picking up the phone. I know I was dead ass wrong for the whole lie I was disguising as a truth, but...I told myself that even if I wasn't with Dre that night, I wouldn't have talked to Nick. Or anyone for that matter.

"What's so hard to understand that I don't want to get married right now? I'm not saying ever, just not right now."

"Nothing is wrong with it, Mo," my friend told me. "It just seems you are holding out for some reason. Or someone."

"I'm not holding out for anyone. Just because I slept with Dre doesn't mean I'm holding back with Nick. I was apprehensive before that happened and-"

"What the hell! You did what?" Lani groaned. "Mo!"

Damn, I didn't mean for it to slip out like that, but it was out there now. I told Lani about that day and how I finally cried for Jayshawn and how that led to me busting it down with Dre. "I'm not making excuses, Lani. I wasn't vulnerable, and I knew what I was doing. But I don't feel a tinge of guilt. None at all. What's wrong with me?"

Lani sat silently eating her lunch. I knew she was pissed at me because here I was, turning down marriage with a great guy when her love life was in the toilet. I sighed heavily and ate my lunch as well.

"So, what are you going to do?" Lani asked as nonchalantly as she could. I knew she was anything but.

"What do you mean? There is nothing for me to do," I replied matter of factly.

"You're just going to continue to sleep with both of them? Aren't you too old to be thotting it out like that?"

I smirked but her face registered nothing but seriousness. "I'm not sleeping with both of them. That was a one-time thing with Dre and it's not going to happen again."

Even when I said it out loud, I didn't believe myself. I thought about that day with Dre and it caused butterflies in my stomach. When I saw him at Blaze the day after, he cornered me in my office and kissed me. Had it not been for Walter and his crew coming in, I would have bent over my desk for him.

"Well, just be careful. Nothing good can come from this. Especially when you have a man like Nick in your life."

I could tell Lani was disappointed. Even her reaction didn't make me feel bad for cheating on Nick, but I did feel bad for how it was making her feel. "Lani, look. I know you're not happy with me right now, but I promise you don't have to worry about me. I made a mistake with Dre and he knows nothing more will come from it. We are business partners, nothing more than that."

Lani remained silent, so I knew there was nothing I could say to make her feel better. So, I needed to change the subject. "How's school going?"

"It's fine," she replied shortly. Lani had never been mad at me like this and I really didn't know what to say or do. I knew she wouldn't be thrilled but I didn't expect her to be like this. Rather than subject her to dealing with me for her lunch break, I told her I needed to go pick up Midori from therapy. She barely looked up at me when I left. If more women had friends like Keyalani, they wouldn't cheat. Because my friend being mad at me didn't sit well with me.

I made my way back to the office to pick up Midori. She came storming out as soon as I sat down in the waiting room. Her therapist was coming out after her.

"Midori, I understand this is difficult, but we will pick this up next week," Dr. Madison called out.

"Leave me alone!" Midori screamed. Thankfully there was only one other person in the waiting room and she looked completely unbothered.

"Midori, calm down," I intervened. I remembered a session Midori and I had with Dr. Madison and she explained that using phrases like 'calm down' could further agitate Midori. "I'm sorry. Don't calm down. What happened?"

"I just need to go," she told me. She didn't look at me and continued out the door.

I looked apologizingly at Dr. Madison, but she seemed used to it. "Do you want to schedule her next appointment?"

"Yes, that's fine," I answered quietly. "Is she going to be okay?"

"Of course. She just needs to process today's session. How about next Tuesday at 10:30?"

"Okay," I replied absently.

"Monica, don't worry," Dr. Madison replied when she noticed my blank stare. "Remember we talked about the highs and the lows. This is a low. Give her space, allow her to talk if she wants, but don't push. Maybe you can come to that session?"

"Okay," I reluctantly agreed. The last session I attended was tough because Midori brought up how I was president of the shitty sister association. It wasn't easy to face how bad I messed up and how I was a contributor to her pain. But I agreed to be there for her so I just had to power through it.

My sister's depression was hard for me to wrap my head around because I didn't really understand it. Depressed people had a myriad of problems and Midori's problems didn't seem...credible. Sure, I understood the death of Jay; that was hard for me as well. But for someone as beautiful as my sister, I couldn't understand why she had such low self-esteem. Dr. Madison explained that she just didn't see herself as everyone else did. And getting her to that point would take time.

I took the appointment card and headed to my car where Midori was sitting in the front seat sulking. I desperately wanted to tell her to snap out of it, but depression wasn't something someone could just get over. So, I decided to take a different approach.

"You wanna go get pedicures?" I asked tentatively.

"Whatever," she mumbled.

We drove in silence to our destination. Because of the time of day, it wasn't that crowded, and we were served immediately. We picked out our colors and sat down in our chairs. My nail tech had my water just the way I liked it and her hands on my legs and feet felt amazing. I glanced at Midori and she was staring off into nothing. Dr. Madison told me that sometimes silence was okay, but it really bothered me.

Before I could find some random thing to say to Midori, my phone chimed with a text from Dre. I opened it to find two pictures of tile for the ladies' bathroom. Neither of them were what I picked. I was about to call Dre, but he called me first.

"Mo, I know this isn't what you picked, but that one is on back order and we don't have time to wait for it.

These two are comparable options. Which one do you like?"

I looked at the options again and then looked at Midori. There was no way she was that engrossed in the plants in the nail salon. "Hey Dre, let me call you right back." I hung up before he could object.

"Hey, Midori, which one of these do you like?" I showed her the two options for tile. "This is for the ladies' bathroom. It's not what I picked, but what I want is on back order."

Midori took my phone and seemed to study the two options. She paid more attention to it than I anticipated.

"It's kind of hard to tell without seeing the entire space. The first one might be fine, but I think it might be too big for the bathroom. The smaller ones will probably look better."

I was shocked and impressed by her observation. "When we leave here, we can go by there, so you can see."

"Okay, cool."

She wasn't as nonchalant as she'd been, and I was grateful for her change in demeanor. We finished our pedicures and headed over to Blaze. We stepped over boxes and other materials to make our way to the bathroom. I saw Dre at the bar talking to Peaches and something about her face perplexed me. She looked...upset. That was truly Peaches but this seemed different. Dre was here quite often, and he'd gotten to know most of the crew, but it seemed like they were having a personal conversation.

Dre saw me and hopped up, looking almost relieved to be getting away from Peaches which further perplexed me. I raised my eyebrows, but he ignored me and walked to the bathroom where Walter and some of his crew were.

"Hey guys. Sorry for the delay but can't rush pedicures," I joked to kill the vibe I was getting from Dre talking to Peaches. *Was I jealous?* I pushed the thought out of my mind and made introductions, but Midori wasn't interested in that. She was busy studying the tile.

"Definitely this one," she stated pointing to the smaller one in the picture. "The smaller one will make the space bigger. I would probably go with something lighter if it's available. You don't want the bathroom to be too dark."

"Hmm…that's a good idea," I admitted. "Do you have any other suggestions?"

Midori looked around the space and seemed to mentally design it. "Definitely need a full-length mirror, good lighting, and seating. At least a bench. If you're going to keep the same theme from inside the bar, I'd do some pictures of female athletes. You know, Serena Williams, Gabby Douglas, some WNBA players. Or even some pink Georgia or women love sports kind of stuff. Who did you get to do the art out there?"

"Nick did it. I can get him to do it. Or he can ask some of the kids he's worked with." At the mention of Nick's name, Dre seemed perturbed that I mentioned him. I chose to ignore that as well. Mostly because this was the most Midori had spoken in weeks.

"Okay. Good. I'd do something similar in the men's bathroom as far as the art work."

I brought Midori out into the bar area and she made suggestions for the space that neither Dre and I thought of. Even Walter was impressed. We finished up by altering some of the plans we had based on Midori's suggestions. Midori and I prepared to leave, but Dre was motioning towards my office. I shook my head.

"Hey Mo, can I run something by you?" he finally said out loud.

I rolled my eyes at him and stifled a smile. "I can't. I have to get my sister home. I'll call you later though."

I turned to walk out the door but not before I caught Peaches looking in our direction. Then it dawned on me that she had no reason to be here during the renovations. "Peaches what are you doing here?"

"Sl-I mean he asked me to come because vendors were coming in throughout the day. Is that a problem?" Her voice was laced with irritation.

"No, not at all. I just wondered why you were here." I was too thrown off to address her tone. "I'll see you guys later." Midori and I left, heading to my condo.

"What was that about?" Midori asked. I was so lost in my thoughts that her question almost startled me.

"I'm not sure," I responded.

"What's up with you and that guy? He's trying to holla?"

"You can say that," I admitted but I wasn't going to tell her all of my business. "But he's the investor that's making all the renovations possible. It's nothing but business."

"Does he know that? Cause he seems interested in more than just your business."

I glanced at Midori and caught the smirk on her face. I was relieved to see something other than the scowl she permanently wore. "Girl, please. I got a man!"

"Haven't seen much of your man. I see why now," Midori chuckled.

I playful hit her but I couldn't dismiss what she said. Nick hadn't been around as much, and I was using her as an excuse. I told Nick I had to take care of my sister which stopped me from coming over to his place as often. He was frustrated and it irritated me that he didn't understand that I had to be there for Midori. No, she didn't need a baby sitter, but right now I wasn't comfortable leaving her home alone.

The other reason I hadn't seen Nick was because of Dre. When Nick pissed me off, I called Dre. I knew I was playing a dangerous game, but Dre understood what I was dealing with when it came to Midori. He didn't push me and he didn't bombard me with questions. He didn't even pressure me to have sex again. I was sure he thought about it because Lord knows I had, but Dre was proving to be an awesome friend and I really needed that right now. Especially since Lani was barely speaking to me these days.

I continued to tell my sister that I wasn't interested in Dre like that and the more I said it, the less convinced she was. Having conversations with her like this made me happy and let me know that my sister was going to be okay.

We arrived home but before we could get out of the car, my stomach growled loudly. I hadn't eaten much with Lani and now I was suffering for it. Midori's counseling sessions always had me on edge because I didn't know how she was going to come out. "You wanna go get something to eat?"

"Sure."

I was in the mood for a burger, so I headed to The Varsity. We parked and headed inside. We ordered our meals and settled down near the back of the restaurant. I remembered hearing about The Varsity growing up and I loved living in the vicinity of this Atlanta landmark. I was not an Atlanta native and I would never consider it my hometown, but Atlanta definitely had my heart. The traffic was a nightmare, but I could deal with that better than one-way streets in Americus. Living in the city wasn't for everyone, but it was for me.

"So, Midori," I asked wiping my mouth after taking a huge bite of my chili cheese burger. "Where did all this design knowledge come from?"

"I've always liked stuff like that. I've designed a lot of spaces. Homes, offices, things like that. Mostly in my head, but there is a computer program that allows me to bring some of this stuff to life. It's just a hobby really."

Midori was right; decorating was always her thing. I remember my mama would leave putting up the Christmas tree to Midori because no matter what my mama did, Midori would always come back and change it. She changed her room constantly and always watched those home improvement shows. So how did I not notice she was that good at it?

"Have you considered making this a career?" I inquired.

Midori stared at me as if I spoke a foreign language. "What do you mean a career?"

"Interior design," I informed her. "When we get home, we can look up some options. Dre flips houses so I can ask him who he uses to stage his houses."

"Hmmm…finding a way to bring him into it, huh?" she smirked. I could tell she was enjoying messing with me about Dre and if this is what it took to get her smiling then she could go on all day.

"Anyways, part of the reason you are," I paused to try to find the right word. "Sad, may be because you're not doing something that you enjoy. We pushed college, but the Art Institute is a good option as well, especially if this is something you like."

Midori averted her eyes at the mention of her situation. We hadn't had a real conversation about it since it happened. I still didn't know why or what she was really depressed about.

"I don't think I can do that," she almost whispered.

"Why not?"

"I don't think I'm that good," she admitted with tears threatening to fall from her eyes.

I handed her a napkin so she could wipe her eyes. My sister's self-esteem was shot to hell. She didn't believe in herself at all and it was disheartening to hear. "Midori, you are that good. I am going to use all of the ideas you pitched today. Matter of fact, I'm going to do you one better; I'm going to hire you to design the addition that will be the VIP/private party space."

My sister looked at me and the panic on her face would make someone think I asked her to turn into George O'Malley and perform surgery in an elevator. "No. I can't. I don't want to mess anything up. It's too important to you. You need to hire a professional."

"Look at me," I insisted. "I know that you have a hard time thinking about yourself in a positive light, but I need you to understand that you are capable, very much so, of doing this. You will not mess it up because if you have questions, you will come to me. I want you to do this so you can see if this is something you can see yourself doing long term."

"Mo, I don't know," she began but I interrupted her.

"I'm not going to push you, but I really want you to think about it. If you want to do this, come up with your designs, let me see them, and we will go from there. Just from what you came up with today, I know you can make that area really pop."

Midori wiped her eyes again and whispered, "Thank you."

"No problem."

"I mean for everything. For trying to help me. I know I haven't been the easiest person to get along with and I'm sorry for that. Just know that I am really trying. I know that you guys want to know why, and I really don't have an answer. It's like," she paused to try figure out what to say. "It's like I have conflicting voices in my head. Sometimes they tell me that everyone will be better off if I'm dead. Every time I try to do something good, I hear something tell me that I'm not good enough. It seems like I have more bad things happen to me than good."

I sat silently for a minute taking in what Midori said. I didn't really understand why she felt like this, and I probably never would. But hearing some of what was going on with her was refreshing-even if it was a tough conversation.

"I'm not gonna lie. I don't a hundred percent under-stand but I'm here to help you in any way you need. I know I haven't been the best sister and I've been very selfish, so I have to take some responsibility for how you're feeling. We aren't going to fix this overnight, but I want to be a better sister to you."

Midori started crying again and I got up to hug her. Of all the places to have a heart to heart, we had ours in The Varsity. Some people looked at us but didn't dare interrupt our moment. For the first time in a long time, I felt a peace I didn't know was possible.

Chapter Eight

Craziness is trying to re-open a bar that's been closed for a few months. The renovations took a little longer than anticipated and Midori needed a little more time to bring her vision to life. We were having our soft opening tonight and our grand opening would be in two weeks. Nervous was an understatement.

Spending this amount of money needed to produce a profit. My loyal fans had expressed how excited they were to come back to Blaze and I hoped all the time we took off paid off. We now had a full menu and I felt like it was going to be a hit. From pasta to steaks to vegetarian dishes, Swan was about the business of producing quality food. In the short amount of time I'd known him, I was not only impressed with his food, but his personality. If Lani was talking to me, I'd introduce them. It was so weird that the two constants in my life, Nick and Lani weren't as sure anymore and they had been replaced by Dre and my sister.

Nick and I were still fighting about me moving in and I was definitely over that argument. With Midori working on designing Blaze, she had less time to think about how inept she was. She was really shining in her ideas and even more so with executing them. I was proud of her and I though she was proud of herself. Because she was doing okay, I was trying to spend more time with Nick, but I also tried to avoid him because every single conversation surrounded why I wouldn't move in. It was so draining. And when I told him so, he asked me who was stopping me from moving in. I blamed it on Midori. While that wasn't the complete truth, it was definitely wasn't the only reason why.

I tried not to sleep with Dre any more, but I couldn't stop. Dre was a triple threat: he didn't pressure me, he was a great friend, and his sex was spectacular. We did more than just have sex. We had lunch dates; we were able to talk about any and everything. Because it wasn't just about sex, I couldn't deny that I had feelings for him, even if it was just relief to be able to be with a man and not talk about living together and getting married.

My biggest concern about Dre was his interaction with Peaches. On more than one occasion, I saw what seemed to be intense conversations and they both swore it was just a professional disagreement. I didn't believe that for a minute, but I brushed it off because I really didn't have a leg to stand on. Even when I came in today, Dre and Peaches were coming from the back where we kept the liquor. She had a scowl on her face and he looked perturbed. I slipped into my office, not allowing them to know what I'd just seen.

I waited a few minutes and then went to the bar. Dre was nowhere to be found. I sat down at the bar and looked at Peaches. She still looked upset and I knew there was something going on with her and Dre. I had to check my jealously because I had a man, no matter how strained the relationship was.

"What's up with you and Dre?" I asked.

"What do you mean?" she feigned innocent and did a piss poor job of it. I looked at her and tilted my head. "Nothing. I just don't agree with everything he says."

"I don't care if you date him, Peaches. Just remember he's an investor and we need his funds," I semi-lied. It was true that we needed him financially, but I really needed to be having this conversation with myself.

"Don't worry about that. He's not my type," Peaches replied dismissively. I didn't believe her but pushing the issue would be suspect, so I let it go. I headed back to my office to finish up the final business before the soft opening tonight.

I headed home to get ready. I really hated that Midori couldn't come see the final product tonight, but I didn't want to take a chance with someone from the state checking IDs. I let her walk through yesterday and take a lot of pictures. She did an amazing job. So much so that she was applying to the Art Institute.

On my way home, I called Lani and invited her to come out to the soft opening. I was surprised she agreed. I knew I'd be busy, but I had to make time for my friend tonight. We hadn't really talked since that day we ate lunch and I missed my friend. Through conversation at work, I knew Swan was single and I planned on introducing Lani and Swan to each other. Nick was supposed to be coming too, and I really didn't know how I was going to handle being in the same room with him and Dre.

At home, Midori was sitting on the sofa with her friend KJ. She met him at Nina's about a month ago and they have been almost inseparable. He was a student at Clayton State and working at Nina's part-time for extra money. He was a respectable young man and called me ma'am. I always had to tell him I wasn't old enough to be a ma'am, and his response was he couldn't help it; that's the way he was raised.

"Hey, sis. Hey, KJ. What are ya'll up to?" I asked. I didn't really have time for small talk, but I was learning to make time for my sister.

"Nothing. We are going to the movies later. Probably get something to eat," Midori informed me.

"Okay, well it will be late when I get in so ya'll have fun." I left them sitting on the sofa, but Midori followed me to my room.

"Mo, help me," she said in a panic.

Her tone made me nervous and dread consumed me. I prayed she wasn't pregnant. Or that KJ was beating her or something like that. "What's the matter?"

"I think tonight is going to be the night that KJ and I...well you know..." she stammered. "I'm so nervous."

I breathed a sigh of relief, but I was also perplexed. I assumed they had already done the do but I was proud of my sister for not giving it up so easily. "What are you nervous about?"

"Dr. Madison said that in order to get something different, I had to do something different. So, I let KJ know I wasn't having sex anytime soon. We've talked about it and he said he's not going to pressure me but...I really like him. I think it's time."

"Midori, if you have doubts, then you're not ready. Dr. Madison is absolutely right that you have to do something different. Don't rush it, when it's time, it will happen."

"I mean, but how do you know?"

I laughed much to Midori's irritation. "I can't really explain it but sex has consequences...physically, mentally, emotionally. When emotions get involved, the consequences seem minimal but you have to think about this stuff ahead of time. KJ has shown you nothing but respect and I'd like to think that he will still be the same after you have sex. But if you have the slightest doubt, don't do it. You don't need to add regret to your life."

Midori sat pensively, taking in what I said. I loved where we were now; it was a far cry from the place we were a few months ago. She trusted me to give her advice and I gave her freedom to design my bar. Dre encouraged me to go home and be with Midori. Even my parents were impressed with our relationship. The only person who didn't seem to care was Nick. When I chose to spend time with her instead of him, it was a problem.

"I think I'm gonna wait," she finally announced.

"Okay, sis. I'm glad you are taking the time to think about your decisions. Dr. Madison is really doing a great job. I may need to go see her myself."

"Yeah, because I don't know how you have juggled both Nick and Dre," she stated with confusion.

I rolled my eyes at her. "Bye, Midori. I have to get ready to go. I am not juggling them. Nick is my man."

"Umm...okay. If that's what we are going with," she winked at me. I tried to swat at her and she ran from my room screaming. I had a mind to chase after her, but I didn't want to embarrass her in front of her company. I closed my door and got ready for work.

* * *

A few hours later, Blaze was in full swing. I was doing my usual mingling with my customers and riding the high of hearing their praise for the renovations. I knew that the time we spent closed was definitely worth it. I brought Nick around with me so I could introduce him as the artist. He smiled politely but I could tell he wasn't happy that Blaze was re-opened. I think he secretly wanted it to fail so that I wouldn't have my business. I couldn't prove it, but I felt it in my gut.

Even Lani seemed to be having a good time. When she got in, I took her to the kitchen to introduce her to Swan and they spoke briefly because Swan was working hard to keep up with the food demand. Even though Swan was busy, I could tell he found my friend attractive because he was flirting shamelessly. And she was eating it up. I was hoping that helping her love life would get me back into her good graces.

I was sitting at the bar talking to some patrons and stuffing my face with Swan's spinach dip and absorbing the crowd. I couldn't put my finger on what was different about it, but it was so good. Peaches was good and busy, so she wasn't paying me any attention. That's the way it had been for the past few weeks, so I didn't really take that to heart. I was chit chatting with some people about the changes to Blaze when the music was turned down. Then I heard Dre coming over the microphone.

"Good evening everybody! How ya'll doing?" Dre called. His question was met with a resounding 'good' from the crowd. "Ya'll having a good time? We want to thank you for your patience while we got things together, but Mo wanted to give you guys a party experience for the grown and sexy...The Mo Mack Experience! I think she did an outstanding job. What do ya'll think?"

Claps and cheers from the crowd gave me a glimmer of hope that all this was worth it. Dre continued. "Ya'll, Mo has worked really hard for you guys and we hope you come back in two weeks for the grand opening."

Another loud shout caused me to blush. "I just wanted to shout out the talented, hardworking, beautiful, smart, feisty woman that made all of this possible. Ya'll have a great night and for the next 20 minutes, drinks are on this guy." He pointed to Tyrin and the crowd laughed at Tyrin's bewildered expression. I know I paid him well but not well enough to cover drinks for the crowd and pay bills. "Just kidding, man. All drinks on me. Enjoy ya'll!"

Dre and Tyrin dapped each other up and Tyrin took the mic from Dre. "Ya'll heard the man, go let Ms. Peaches hook you up with the drinks! I'm kind of partial to the liquid marijuana myself. Not on the clock though. Ms. Mo will fire my ass if I'm drunk," Tyrin announced to the crowd. He got the music crunk again, not to club levels but loud enough to where you could be in your zone when your jam came on.

I smiled proudly at what my bar had become. It was great before but now…it was going to take me places I could never dream. And I had Dre to thank for it.

I was basking in my happy place when Nick grabbed me by the arm and led me to the hall by my office. He tried to open the door, but it was locked so he pushed me into the wall next to it.

"OWWW, Nick!" I screeched. "What the hell?" I snatched my arm from him and rubbed the spot he held entirely too tight.

"Mo, who the hell is this guy? And don't lie to me," Nick bellowed ignoring my question.

"Who are you talking about? Dre? You already know who he is!" I insisted. Nick glared at me, unwilling to accept what I was telling him.

"He's too friendly with you Mo, and I don't like it. You need to find a way to pay him back, so he can get the hell on."

"First of all," I began. "Please don't come to my job and act stupid. That's so fucking childish. Second of all, you don't tell me how to run my business!" I was livid at Nick for coming to Blaze and showing his ass. Out of the corner of my eye, I saw Dre standing at the end of the hallway. He looked ready to pounce if things went south between Nick and I.

"Is he the reason you won't move in with me? Are you fucking him, Mo? Is that what's going on here?" Nick was raising his voice and truthfully, it scared me. He never talked to me like this before.

"Nick, will you please calm down. Stop asking me dumb ass questions. I have told you a million and one times, Dre is my business partner, nothing more, nothing less. Stop being so damn insecure! And the fact that you continue to ask me to move in with you when you know Midori is going through her shit is selfish as hell!"

"I can't win for losing," Nick said with anger dripping from his lips. "First, I had to fight off your ex who left your stubborn ass. Then I have to compete with your dead brother, now I have to deal with your sister that tried to kill herself because she can't get her way."

Hearing Nick's words should have made me angry, but instead they just made me cry. As the first tears began to fall, I got upset with myself for being so damn emotional. I tried to walk past Nick, but he grabbed my arm again.

"Mo, wait. I'm sorry. I didn't mean that. I'm just so…I think I'm losing you." His voice trailed off and I saw the hurt in his eyes.

"Let's just talk later," I stated flatly. "I have to go."

Nick reluctantly let me go and I went to the bathroom to get myself together. I was thankful I didn't overdo it with the make up today because my tears would have ruined my face. I got a paper towel and wiped my face off. I felt horrible for lying to Nick, but I was also frustrated that he was being so pushy.

I left the bathroom and headed to the kitchen so I could hide out for a little while longer. Swan, Tank, and Quan were busy cranking out food. They were busy but they all looked happy and in their element. When we were deciding the menu, I suggested that we cut off food orders at 10, they all looked at me like I lost my mind.

"Why give the Waffle House that money? When folks are done partying, they want to eat. Might as well do it where they are," Swan told me, and he promptly added a few breakfast dishes to our weekend menu.

"Hiding out?" Dre asked startling me. I didn't even see him.

"Kind of."

"Well, let me get out of your way. Seeing as to how we aren't anything but business partners. Nothing more, nothing less." I looked at him perplexed until I remembered he was standing in the hall when Nick and I were arguing.

"Dre," I started but he cut me off.

"Nah, it's cool. I know where I stand."

Dre left me standing in the kitchen looking a damn fool. I found myself heading back to the bathroom trying to figure out what the hell just happened. I was staring at myself in the mirror when Lani emerged from one of the stalls. I could tell she was a little tipsy.

"Swan is pretty cool, Mo. What do you know about him? And I'm sorry I've been distant. I don't have to agree with what you do but you are still my girl and I'm sorry. Wait, what's wrong?"

"Lani, I don't know what the hell is wrong with me. It's like...I finally got Blaze on the up and up and Midori and I are doing great. But now both Nick and Dre are pissed at me. It's like I can't just be happy all around. I don't want to have to choose between my family, my love life, and my business."

"Slow down. What happened?"

I sat down on the bench and silently thanked Midori for this great idea. This is exactly what this bench was needed for in the ladies' room. I recounted tonight's events with Nick and with Dre and waited for her to unleash on me.

"Do you have feelings for Dre?" she asked even though I'm pretty sure she already knew the answer. I sighed heavily because I didn't want to answer that. Lani took my silence as a yes. "You have a decision to make. It's not fair to keep stringing them both along."

"I know, but Dre's reaction really caught me off guard. I mean, he knows I have a man. Why would he assume this was more than just sex?" Even saying it out loud, I didn't believe me. By not admitting it, meant it wasn't true. It wasn't the best logic, but that's what I needed to tell myself to justify why I really loved being with him.

"Just talk to him, Mo. And Nick, too. You know I'm partial to Nick but what he said was definitely out of line. I just don't want you to get hurt or to hurt anyone."

"I promise I'm not. This thing with Dre just snuck up on me and I really needed the distraction from Nick, my parents, and Midori. Not a great excuse, I know, but when I'm with him, I'm just. I don't know. He makes me feel like I don't have to be the boss. I don't have to be in charge. I can just let my guard down and be free. I don't feel like that with Nick. I never have."

"I understand, boo, but you do have to consider the history you have with Nick. He was there for you when Jay died. And with Midori. Nick has his flaws, as does Dre, but you have history with Nick and I don't think you should just throw it away."

"Lani, I'm not trying to throw anything away. I'm not sure what I'm doing," I admitted.

"Whatever you decide, I'm here. And I won't judge you."

Lani and I hugged and we both wiped away tears. I missed my friend and I was so glad she was back in my life. I really needed someone to vent to.

"Thanks, Lani. I love you girl." I stood up and once again got a paper towel to wipe my face. "Let me get back to hosting."

"No problem, honey. I love you, too," Lani responded. "Now tell me about your chef!"

I talked Swan up before we headed back out to the party area. She asked me to give him her number.

Finally, at almost 3am, everyone was gone. Peaches and some of the other staff stayed to help clean up before taking off. I was too tired to run the numbers, but I knew we made a good bit of money tonight. I knew my grand opening would be crazy. I was gathering my belongings to go home when I heard a light knock on my door. I hollered at the intrusion because I thought everyone was gone. I was surprised to see Dre standing there. I thought he left hours ago.

"Damn it, Dre! You scared the shit out of me!"

He laughed lightly and folded his arms across his chest. "I'm sorry, I didn't mean to."

I leaned on the edge of my desk trying to catch my breath. "What are you still doing here?"

"I came to talk to you," he responded.

I dropped my purse on my desk and tried to gather my thoughts. "Listen, Dre. What you heard earlier was-"

"You trying to cover your ass, I got that," Dre chided.

"That's not fair. You knew I had a man so where is this coming from?"

"You're right, I knew but that didn't stop me from having feelings for you." His admission made my heart beat hard in my chest. I wasn't sure what to say so he continued. "I apologize for my behavior earlier. It wasn't fair for me to take my frustrations out on you. I am not trying to pressure you into anything. I'm just simply letting you know that I see you as more than just a business partner and a friend. But if I have to be just that, then I will."

"Dre...I'm not trying to hurt anyone. You or him, but right now, I don't know what I want or how I should feel or-"

Out of nowhere, Dre's lips were pressed up against mine. Kissing this man was so sensual and so erotic that I could feel my juices beginning to flow as his tongue danced with mine. We kissed softly at first, but suddenly our passions erupted.

Dre broke our kiss to pick me up and sit me on my desk. His lips briefly returned to mine before traveling down my neck. He paused long enough to take off my fitted Blaze tee. He admired my breasts sitting in my purple lace bra before nibbling at my nipple. The sensation of his teeth against the lace was pure bliss. I whimpered as he danced back and forth between each nipple, leaving wet stains at the center of my bra.

Dre stood up and pulled me up with him. Without speaking, he unbuttoned my pants and pulled my underwear quickly. I helped him get my clothes off and he placed me on the desk again. He wasted no time dropping to his knees and kissing me between my legs. I let out a low, guttural moan at the sensation of his tongue.

Dre licked and sucked on me as I tried frantically to find something to grab on to. He was trying his best to bring me to orgasm and I was getting really close to giving him what he wanted. We had been together enough times that he knew when my body was going to release. As he sensed it getting close, he concentrated on sucking on my clit while slipping two fingers inside of me. My eyes rolled into the back of my head as he was rewarded with my juices. I could barely catch my breath before Dre was pulling me up and pushing me onto my stomach on my desk. I heard his pants being unzipped and a condom wrapper being opened.

Quickly, Dre pushed himself into me. I knocked over my pen holder at the sudden intrusion. I grabbed on to the edge of my desk as he pounded me senseless. He and I had no words. This was something desperate, something primal. In this moment, nothing else existed except this passion. One of Dre's hands left my hips and grabbed a handful of my dreads. He pulled my head back until my back was against his chest. His other hand pinched my nipple, while his other hand still gripped my hair.

Dre's rhythm told me he was going to cum soon. He felt so good inside of me that I didn't want him to stop, but I also loved feeling his release. Dre tightened his grip on my hair and pushed in deeper. He gave me his all with a throaty moan in my ear.

Breathing hard and satisfied, Dre stumbled back into a chair. I stood up to face Dre, my thoughts racing. I needed to say something. I needed to tell him this needed to stop because juggling them both was too hard. I needed to tell him he wasn't alone in his feelings. I needed to tell him that being with him was what my body needed. I needed to tell him...

"You don't have to say anything," Dre said, almost reading my mind. "Just know I'm not going away so easy."

Chapter Nine

I woke up the next day on a high. The soft opening went great. Keyalani and Swan hit it off. Dre took me down through there. I needed more so I went home with him instead of going home. He took me to breakfast before making me cum two more times. This was as close to heaven as I was gonna get. I left Dre's house in Stone Mountain and headed back to my place in midtown. Today was an unseasonably cool day for October, especially in Georgia. In October, it could still feel like 145 degrees.

I stopped to get lunch for Midori and KJ if he was there. I walked in the house and they were cuddled on the couch. "Hey ya'll. I got you guys some Burger King."

They got up and came to the kitchen to get their food and I headed to my room. Midori followed me to my room. "Where you been?"

"Why?"

"Cause, Nick came over here looking for you. I didn't know what to tell him," she quipped. She was thoroughly entertained by the look on my face.

Nick had called me a number of times, but I didn't answer. I was enjoying my time with Dre. I knew I should have told him something, but I was still mad at him. And I also knew I was using that as an excuse and an adult would handle their relationship problems by talking. So I was being very immature right now and I needed to be doing better. I just wasn't going to do it right now.

"Anyway, how was your night?" I asked changing the subject. *Did I just ask my sister if she slept with her boyfriend to avoid talking about my shamble of a love life?* I asked myself.

She smiled slyly and, although I really didn't want to hear it, I tried to prepare myself for her story. "Nothing happened last night but I think it will happen tonight." She left my room and I assumed she was heading to her room. She came back about a minute later and handed me a card.

The front was some cheesy dollar store card with flowers and hearts on it. But the inside was a handwritten poem:

The greatest manifestation of love

I shared my vision
And saw you
Through my eyes
The beauty
The confidence
The energy
The power
I found
Tucked behind your fear
I pulled it out
By simply
Loving you

"Oh my God! Where did he get this? This is too sweet!" I gushed. I wasn't really jealous because Dre kept a smile on my face and Nick still had my heart, but no man had ever given me a card with poetry in it.

Midori beamed with pride. "He wrote it. He writes poetry. He wrote this for me."

My sister was smiling. Smiling big. Her smile and the look in her eyes was happiness. Pure happiness. So of course, I was worried. "I'm happy for you, sis. I really am. But..." I needed to choose my words carefully because I didn't want to upset her. "Does he know?"

"Yes, he does. We talked about it and he's been supportive. He asks me about sessions and he's offered to take me if I need him to. Especially since Blaze has opened again. He asks a lot of questions and he makes me think about things differently. Mo, we haven't even had sex yet and he's...like this. It scares me, but I've never felt like this with anyone before."

"If this is how you feel, go with it. You don't get a chance like this," I reasoned. "Just be careful and don't get caught up in your feelings. If something feels off, trust it. And as always, I'm here."

Midori gave me a quick hug and ran back out to her company. I went to take a shower and changed in to some lounging clothes. I knew I probably needed to go to Blaze tonight but I was tired. I would probably take the night off because I needed to recoup from my night.

I was stretched out in the bed when my phone flashed with Nick's name. I knew I needed to answer but I really didn't want to. Against my better judgment, I answered. "Hello?"

"Mo, I'm sorry. What I said was out of line. I spoke out of my anger and I know I'm being selfish but I'm sorry."

His apology caught me off guard because I was anticipating having to fight him. "I hear you."

My attitude didn't push him away and he continued. "We've been really distant lately and I want to make it up to you. I miss you, Mo."

Now he was just tugging at my heart strings. I wanted to still be mad. Because so long as I was mad, I wouldn't feel guilty about my dealings with Dre. "I miss you, too. You can come over."

"Get dressed," he demanded. "We're going on a date."

Nick didn't give me time to protest because he hung up. If I fought him on this, I would give him reasons to be suspicious, so I got up and got dressed. Nick made it to my house thirty minutes later and told me to change my shoes because we would be doing a lot of walking. Reluctantly, I went to put on my white and Carolina blue Jordan's and changed my shirt so that I would be matching.

"Midori, Nick and I are going out. We will be back," I called.

"No, we won't. You kids have fun," Nick countered. He pulled his wallet out of his back pocket and peeled off $40. He handed it to KJ. "Take her out tonight. We will be back tomorrow."

I didn't have time to protest because Nick was whisking me out of the door. "Where are we going?"

"Don't worry about that. Just know that when you're with me, you're going to be good."

We drove to downtown Atlanta and walked to the Georgia Aquarium. I'd lived in Atlanta for years but never took the time to visit a lot of the places tourists hit up when they come to the city. I thought it was strange to be tourists in our own town, but I knew Nick really wanted to be with me, so I just went with it.

Nick and I spent our afternoon at the Aquarium and I had to admit, I was pleasantly surprised at how awesome the place was. We walked, talked, and took in all the exhibits. I made it a point to check out more of Atlanta's spots because I really had a good time.

We left the Aquarium and grabbed burgers from Johnny Rockets and ate in Centennial Park. We people watched and enjoyed the cool Atlanta evening. We finished our food and headed back to Nick's car. Back at his apartment, he told me to go take a shower and relax so he could get our dessert together.

Even though I hadn't been there in what seemed like forever, I still had some clothes stashed at Nick's. I took a shower, lotioned my skin, and put on my yoga pants and tank top. I found Nick sitting in his living room with two pieces of cheesecake.

"Ohhhh my goodness! I hadn't had this in a while!" I gushed. I grabbed my fork and dug right in to my red velvet cheesecake from the Cheesecake Factory. Nick knew this was my favorite dessert in the world. "Thank you!"

I devoured my cheesecake and some of Nick's before I settled back into the couch. I put my feet up and Nick grabbed my feet and put them on his lap. He handed me the remote to his TV and began to massage my feet. I went to his DVR to see what movies I had saved and settled on *The Fifth Element*. It was one of my favorite movies and Nick couldn't understand why. He always despised when I watched this movie, but I absolutely loved it.

Twenty minutes into the movie, the movie was watching me. I vaguely remember him leading me to the bed. I woke up the next morning feeling more relaxed than I had in what seemed like forever. Nick was already up, and I went to the kitchen to find him.

"Good morning, baby," he sang while pouring me a cup of coffee.

"Good morning, King. Thank you." I went to his fridge and pulled out my French vanilla coffee creamer and added a few spoons of sugar. Nick always complained that he could never buy me coffee because I never seemed to take it the same way. Some mornings I felt like I needed a lot of sugar and some days I didn't. Just depended on how I felt that day.

"So, I want to apologize again," Nick began. He was leaning against his sink looking at me.

"Nick, it's okay. It's not a big deal. It's over with."

"Not just about what I said," Nick began. He walked towards me and pulled me into his arms. "Well, it is what I've said and done for the past few months. I've been unreasonable and I'm sorry."

I didn't know what to say. It was so much easier to handle Nick and Dre when Nick was being demanding and unreasonable.

"This doesn't mean what I want has changed. I still want you to move in, and I still want to talk about getting married. But this means I will not pressure you. I realized that I was driving you away and I don't want to be without you."

The guilt that had been non-existent was now threatening to take me out. I never expected this to happen. Nick is stubborn. He was supposed to keep pushing me which would allow me to justify my fling with Dre. Now…I was going to have to do something about Dre.

"Nick, I appreciate you being patient. I don't want to be without you either." I meant what I said. My relationship with Nick was good when he wasn't pushing me to give up my life. But things with Dre were…different.

"I want things to be different with us, Mo. I just need to know if you're going to put in the effort with me."

"Of course I will, King." Even though I said it out loud, I wondered if I really meant it.

Nick leaned down to kiss me. It seemed like it had been forever since he kissed me. It was nothing like kissing Dre. Nick was soft and sensual, definitely more apt to making love to me. He broke our kiss and led me to his bedroom where he took my body to ecstasy.

"I love you, Monica," Nick whispered after I was settled in his arms.

"I love you, too." I knew I had to end things with Dre. I just hoped it wouldn't hurt our business relationship.

* * *

For the next few days, I didn't had time to talk to Dre. Between Blaze, Nick, and because I really didn't want to, I was avoiding him. Apparently, he was busy too because our only conversations had been via text and about Blaze. He told me he was going out of town for a few days which was good because Nick had really been great. Maybe it was reverse psychology, but with the way he has been treating me and being supportive of Blaze, I thought more and more about him.

I was at Blaze working on the schedule and trying to come up with my next big event. With Thanksgiving around the corner, I did know I wanted to do something to give back. I really did not want to go home because I wasn't up for seeing my daddy yet, so I figured I'd be here. I was sure Nick and I would do something.

I was brainstorming ideas for a food drive or feeding a family or two events. I wanted to get some ideas on paper to run them by Nick, Dre, and Peaches to see what we could do. I was deep in thought when my phone buzzed with a notification from Facebook. I saw it was from my Blaze account. Being a business owner meant social media was a big deal. I didn't particularly care to post that often, but this is how we connected with our customers. I was going to wait until I finished up with this, but more notifications popped up. I grabbed my phone to see what the buzz was.

I opened the app to find Blaze tagged in a post. This wasn't unusual because my customers were loyal and loved to post about us, especially after the renovations. But this post wasn't a good one. There was a picture of a very unappealing omelet and I had to read the caption at least three times to try to wrap my head around this.

> *Lisa Smith*
>
> *This is why I don't support black owned business. Went to @BlazeATL last night and I*

won't be back. The place was ok, nothing to rave about. I had to send my breakfast back three times because the idiots couldn't understand a simple instruction. Spoke to the manager and she was dismissive. The music was crappy, the food sucked, everyone was rude. I won't spend my money here again.

I left my office to go look for Peaches and Swan to find out what this post was about. Surely, they had to have the wrong place. Peaches wasn't at the bar, so I went to the kitchen. I found them in the kitchen laughing and talking.

"Hey guys, have you seen this?" I showed them the post on my phone.

Peaches looked first, and her face scrunched up in confusion. When Swan saw it, he immediately went into cursing.

"What the hell is this? I didn't cook this! I wouldn't send no food out that looked like shit!"

"I don't know!" I exhaled perplexed. Peaches was quiet while Swan studied the picture.

"Wait," Swan boomed. "Hold up. They said they were here yesterday? We didn't even serve breakfast yesterday. Yesterday was Wednesday. And look at the plate…that's not ours."

I got my phone and looked at the plate. He was right; it wasn't our dinnerware. Now I was even more confused.

"So, someone just made this up?" Peaches finally asked.

"That's what it looks like," Swan answered for me.

I started to make a comment on the picture, but I realized I didn't have to. My loyal customers already had my back. There were at least 50 comments calling bullshit on the post. I went to the page of the woman that posted it, but her page was private and I couldn't see anything.

I left them in the kitchen and went to go comment on the post.

> *Hey Lisa, here at Blaze we pride ourselves on being able to provide our customers with an exciting party experience. This includes entertainment, food and an environment for the grown and sexy...The Mo Mack Experience. If you had a negative experience, please contact me so I can get to the bottom of what happened. ~Mo Mack*

I went back to see if she commented but after about 20 minutes, the post and the page was gone. *What the hell is going on?*

* * *

I was meeting Dre at the Cheesecake Factory for lunch so we could go over this private party we were hosting this weekend. He wanted to come to Blaze, but I knew that would give us the opportunity to have sex and I couldn't do that with him anymore.

After we ordered our meals, we jumped right into business. Dre convinced me to host a private party for basketball star Justin Dawson. He was a phenom from Hampton University. Justin was a small-town kid from Rochelle, Georgia. He earned a scholarship to Hampton and shocked the world when he was drafted to the NBA last year. Basketball players from HBCUs rarely got drafted and Justin was giving the institution of Historically Black Colleges and Universities hope.

Even though he made money, more money than anyone in his family has ever seen, Justin didn't ball out. The most money he spent was paying off his mama's house. Dre knew Justin's family and raved about how good off a kid he was. His father passed away when he was six and his mama worked two and three jobs to pay for basketball camps and AAU teams. And Justin was a mama's boy that lived for his mama's approval. And Mama Dawson did not play about her son. She made sure he had a financial advisor who stressed the importance of saving to have money after the NBA. She didn't let people borrow money from him. She shut down the family's expectations that Justin should take care of them. She talked to him about living the way that she raised him. I hadn't even met her, and I loved Justin's mama.

Justin, along with his girlfriend's sister, planned this weekend in Atlanta for the proposal. His girlfriend Stephanie thought they were coming to Atlanta to celebrate Justin's birthday. They were high school sweethearts and from what I saw of her social media, Stephanie was very down to earth. She wasn't flashy. No long weave. No face beat to the gawds. No expensive clothes. She looked like a typical 21-year-old college student (she attended Hampton), despite having a boyfriend in the NBA. It didn't take a lot of convincing because from what I read about Justin and Stephanie, I was happy to be a part of this. Dre and I went through the details to make sure everything would go off without a hitch. I was really excited to be in on the surprise for his girlfriend.

"Just make sure Swan looks over everything before it leaves the kitchen. Having someone like Justin in the building is major and we don't need any more situations."

I told Dre about the post the other day, and I was glad I had a screenshot. He was just as perplexed as me. That was a made-up situation. We didn't need anything to pop off when we had a celebrity in the building. Blaze would be open to the public, but his event would be in the VIP area and was invitation only.

"That still baffles me. I don't know the woman and the page is gone now. I don't bother anyone, so I don't understand why anyone would make something like this up." Our server brought our meals and refilled our drinks. Every time I came to the Cheesecake Factory, I vowed to try something different, but I was stuck on the Jamaican black pepper shrimp. Dre's chicken Madeira looked really good too. I wanted to ask him for some but that would be too much like a date.

"What baffles me is why you've been avoiding me," Dre said after taking a bite of his food.

His statement caught me off guard. Even though I planned on talking to him, I didn't want it to be in the middle of lunch. "About that…Things are going well between Nick and I, so we are going to have to stop. This is going to have to be a strictly business relationship."

I made the mistake of looking at him and I almost lost my resolve. Before, his eyes held curiosity. Now, because I knew the passion he was capable of, looking at him reminded me of all the ways he made my body explode.

"And you avoided me because…?"

"I wasn't sure how you were going to take it," I admitted.

I didn't know how to read his face. He seemed upset and simultaneously unbothered. "What you thought I was gonna do? Cry and beg you to leave your boyfriend? I'm not that kind of guy."

"No, I didn't think that. I just thought…nothing. Don't worry about it. I'm glad that's out of the way."

"Cool."

We finished our lunch, almost in silence and I desperately wanted to know what he was thinking. I wasn't expecting his nonchalance. It wasn't that long ago that he admitted he had feelings for me and now he didn't care if we talked or not. I wasn't in a position to ask him why he didn't feel the same because it wasn't fair. I was glad that things were improving with Nick and I, but I was also feeling some type of way that I was losing Dre.

* * *

Getting ready for Justin's surprise engagement party was more stressful than I anticipated. Justin wasn't the type of celebrity that asked for ridiculous things. He was fine with our menu but asked for a special wine that Stephanie liked. I caught hell trying to get bottles of Red Electra. I'd never had it, but Justin said Stephanie didn't drink much and this was pretty much all she liked.

By the time Friday night rolled around, I was a nervous wreck. I needed everything to go right with this event. Nick told me everything would be fine, and I was surprised at how supportive he was being. Even after he did all he could to relax me, I was still uptight. I decided to call Dre. He didn't sound happy to hear from me.

"Hey. Do you have a second?"

"Not really," he said. "What's up?"

I knew I didn't have a right to demand that he treat me how he used to, but I hated this dryness. "I'm just nervous about tonight," I said.

"Why? What's wrong? Did something happen?"

"No, this is just a big deal." There was an awkward silence, and I thought Dre hung up on me. "Hello?"

"You called me because you're insecure?" he sighed heavily into the phone. "Where is this coming from? When we started working together, you were confident about your business. What happened?"

I hated his tone with me. "Damn, Dre. I'm not allowed to be nervous because Justin Dawson will be at Blaze tonight?"

"You've planned. You've prepped. You've done everything you needed to do to prepare for this night. I thought this is what you wanted."

"It is. It's just...you know what never mind. I don't even know why I called you." I wasn't used to the way he was treating me, and I was over it.

"Whatever, Mo. You're thinking too much. Stop doubting yourself. I'll see you later." Dre hung up, causing me to rub my temples. I didn't feel any better after talking to him. I did know that tonight had no room for error.

By 8:30pm, Justin's event was popping. About fifty of their friends and family were gathered in the private area of Blaze enjoying drinks, food, and mood music while all of my other patrons were in the front partying as usual. Because the back area was semi-secluded, no one knew a celebrity was in the building. I was glad Midori insisted on a separate entrance for this space. Everything was going as planned and in 30 minutes, Justin would propose.

I met them when they arrived, and they were even more adorable in person. Stephanie seemed virtually unimpressed that her man was a superstar; to her, he was the man she'd been with since they were in the 10th grade. I could tell that Justin was raised by an older woman because he called everyone ma'am, held doors open, and pulled out chairs for Stephanie. He was a gentleman, something that was rare for guys his age.

I was chilling at the bar when Stephanie approached me. "Ms. Monica?"

I went into a panic because Justin was going to propose in a few minutes. "Hey Stephanie, what's up?"

"I just wanted to know if I could make a toast to Justin when we sing happy birthday. I know sometimes these things need to be cleared but…I wasn't sure if I was going to do it."

She was so sweet and innocent that it made me smile. I was also relieved that it wasn't anything more serious. "Of course, you can! I'll slip you the mic right after you guys sing." I was lying of course but I had to play it off.

"Thank you so much! I can't wait to surprise him!" Stephanie gushed. She went into her purse and pulled out an ultra sound. *Oh Lord, they were both in for surprises tonight.*

"Oh, my goodness! Congratulations!" I reached out to hug the young lady, genuinely happy for her and her soon-to-be fiancé. Tonight, was truly going to be special.

Stephanie made her way back to the VIP area just in time for Justin's proposal. I had moved Tyrin to the VIP section for the proposal, and on Justin's cue Tyrin began to play "Who Knows" by Musiq because it was Stephanie's favorite song. Tyrin handed Justin the mic and Swan rolled out birthday cake that was really a congratulations cake.

"Hey everyone. Steph and I want to thank all of you for coming out to celebrate with us. Hey baby, come up here with me." Stephanie looked perplexed because she was trying to figure out how she was going to tell him her news if he had the mic in his hand. "I know it's my birthday, the big 22, and I know I am blessed for where I am in my life right now. I think I did alright for a kid from Rochelle."

A few of his friends clapped at the mention of his hometown and Justin continued. "There is only one thing I can think of that can make this night better." Justin turned to Stephanie and looked at her intensely. "Steph, this night is supposed to be about me, but I'm making it about you. I love you with all of my heart. I've loved you since I was in 9th grade, even though you wouldn't give me no play then."

The crowd chuckled, and Steph rolled her eyes and hit him playfully. I could tell she had no clue what was about to happen. "Steph, you make me happy. I couldn't ask for a better person to go through this journey with. You keep me grounded, you look out for me, and I know you aren't after my money." Again, he got laughter from the crowd. "You asked me what I wanted for my birthday and I told you I had everything I wanted. But I lied. What I want for my birthday is for you to say yes."

Justin put down the mic, pulled the ring box from his pocket, and got down on one knee. Stephanie started crying and covered her face. "Stephanie Jenae Marcus, will you marry me?"

Stephanie couldn't even speak so she just nodded her head to cheers from the crowd. Justin placed the ring on her finger and stood up to hug and kiss her. I wiped away my own tears because these kids were just too sweet. Stephanie was on a high that she almost forgot her news. She motioned for him to give her the mic.

"Oh my goodness! Baby, you got me!" she laughed. "I thought I was going to surprise you, but you got me." Stephanie's sister handed her a wrapped gift box and she gave it to Justin. Now, it was his turn to be confused. He tore into the gift like a kid on Christmas, not caring at how pretty it was wrapped. He opened the box and pulled out a shirt. When he read it, he looked at Stephanie and then back at the shirt. He then dropped his head and wiped away tears of his own.

"Happy birthday, Daddy!" Stephanie called into the mic, reading what was on the shirt she got him.

There was another loud cheer from their family and friends and I was pretty much a bucket of tears. With all of the people in the crowd, I spotted Dre. As soon as we locked eyes, I looked away. With the proposal and baby announcement, I wasn't emotionally prepared to deal with Dre, too. Instead, I went to my office to call Nick. He didn't answer, which didn't surprise me because he had an idea for a new piece that he was working on when I left. When he painted, he was in a zone and didn't answer.

I sat in my office for a second before deciding to go back out to the party. I was rounding the corner when I heard Peaches yelling. When I got closer, I heard Peaches yell, "What the hell are you waiting for? Make it happen!"

By the time I got to her, she hung up her phone and shoved it back into her pocket. "What's wrong, Peaches?"

She jumped, indicating I startled her. "Huh? Oh, nothing. Just handling business with my landlord."

I studied her face and knew she was lying. I had no idea why she would lie to me but that's just the feeling I got. I was about to ask her again when I heard Tyrin calling me over the mic. "Yo Mo! You need to come out here!"

Both Peaches and I took off towards the main area of Blaze where two guys were going at it. My security jumped in and separated the guys before the fight got out of hand. They weren't anywhere near Justin and Stephanie and I hoped and prayed they didn't see this.

"What happened?" I shouted. My security staff was escorting the two men out of the building. They kept the guys separated until the police arrived. Outside, I got the 411 on the situation. Apparently, someone from the main area found out Justin was in the back and people tried to bombard the private area to get Justin's autograph. After getting an autograph, one guy kept talking to Justin. As politely as possible, Justin told the guy he was trying to chill with his lady. Justin's cousin tried to get the guy to go away and it lead to it an exchange of words. Then it just escalated from there. There wasn't a real big scuffle, and no one was hurt, but a fight could be detrimental to my business. I'd had some drunk people here and there, but fights were few and far between. A jealous girlfriend, a guy that had one too many drinks, but nothing serious. Besides, I paid my security well to handle situations before they popped off.

I made my way to Justin and Stephanie and Dre was talking to them. They were cool and Justin said he didn't know why his cousin didn't let my people handle it.

"Justin, I am so sorry! My security should have been closer to handle this."

"It's cool Ms. Monica. Rodney always feels like he has to take up for me. He's been doing that since we were kids."

"Do you guys need anything? Stephanie, are you good?" I waited with bated breath hoping they wouldn't storm out.

"Yes ma'am. We're good. Thank you so much for tonight," Stephanie said.

Looking at the newly engaged, first time parents, I could tell that Blaze could have burned down and they would have been unbothered. They were riding the high of the night.

Now I needed to find out who let it be known that Justin was here. I gave specific instructions to my staff that no one from the main area was to know what was going on in VIP. I had special servers for the area, so they had no reason to interact with my other patrons. Someone had leaked the information and I wanted to know who.

Chapter Ten

After I left Blaze that night, I didn't want to go home; I needed to be with Nick. Honestly, I wanted Dre to talk to me, but he really was over me. I couldn't figure out if I really had feelings for him or if I was just pressed about his rejection. It was easier to assume the latter because the former would complicate my entire life.

I walked into Nick's place and heard the sound of "Spottieottiedopaliscious" by Outkast blasting from his speakers. That meant he was still at work. I watched Nick for a few minutes because I didn't want to disturb his groove. He didn't seem to hear the music; his entire focus was on the abstract painting he was working on. Seeing him in his element always made me smile. And now that he was understanding that Blaze was my element, I felt that we were in a really good place right now.

"Hey King," I said once the song faded out.

Nick whirled around, surprised to see me. "Hey yourself. Didn't expect to see you tonight."

"Long night. I didn't want to sleep alone," I admitted.

Nick smiled and came over to kiss me. "I'm almost finished with this. I'll be in the bed in a little bit."

"No rush, baby. I'm going to take a shower."

I left Nick to finish his painting and I went to the bathroom to wash off the night. I was still worried about Blaze getting negative publicity because of the fight. As promised, Nick made it to bed before I drifted to sleep.

He climbed into bed and pulled me into him. "Did you finish your painting?"

"I'm not sure. It doesn't feel finished," he said while caressing my breasts through his t-shirt I was using as a night shirt. "But I wanted to come taste you."

His words caused a flood between my legs and I was glad I didn't bother putting on panties. He moved to allow me to roll over on my back. I was dead tired, but his tongue was sure to give me the relaxation I needed to end this night properly.

"Can I taste you, baby?" Nick didn't wait for me to answer before he positioned himself between my legs and devoured me. I spread my legs for him and moaned as he licked and sucked my body until I released for him. He didn't stop until I had two more orgasms and didn't even try to have sex with me. I wanted to satisfy him, but I was dead tired. I was sleep before I knew it.

I woke up the next morning relaxed. I wanted to lie in bed all day, watch Netflix, and eat chicken wings. I wondered if Nick would be cool with that. He wasn't in the bed. I grabbed my phone and had a text from him saying he went to go get us some lunch; it was after 1 pm.

I texted him back to tell him what I wanted to do today, and he agreed we could make it a lazy day. Then I called Midori to see how she was doing since I hadn't been home in a few days.

"Hey sis. What are you doing?" I asked while going to brush my teeth.

"Hey sis. Nothing. Just cleaning up. Where are you?"

"I'm at Nick's. Is KJ there?"

"No, he had to go to work. He might be back later", she said.

"You're okay?" I asked.

Midori snorted into the phone. "Yes, Monica, I'm fine. We've been together for a few days. I just wanted to be alone. I'm probably going to get a pedicure later."

"I can come home if you want me to. I don't know if I'm going to Blaze tonight." Hearing that she wanted to be alone concerned me, but I didn't want to come right out and ask her if she had intentions of hurting herself. Her depression still didn't make sense to me and even though she was fine right now, that didn't mean she wasn't depressed.

"No. Mo, I promise I'm fine. I have some projects I need to catch up on. I'm not hurt, sad, depressed, or anything. I just need to recharge," she announced. "But speaking of Blaze, what happened there last night?"

I assumed Justin's proposal made it to social media even though we didn't advertise it because it was a surprise. "We had a private party. Why?"

"Oooooooh," she groaned. "I'm guessing you haven't seen the video."

My heart thudded in my chest at her tone. "What video, Midori?"

"Hold on, let me DM it to you."

The ten seconds it took her to send me the video felt like ten hours. When I got the DM, I quickly opened it. My mouth dropped when the thirty second video played. The video was obviously altered because none of the events of the night went this way.

In the video, Justin's proposal was interrupted by the fight. The video then jumped back to him when he shed a few tears when Steph told him she was pregnant. Whoever made this video made it seem like his proposal was interrupted and he was upset over it. Then the video jumped back to when the guys were pulled outside.

Someone literally took the time to put together a video to make the fight seem worse than what it was. I just couldn't figure out why. And the caption perplexed me even more.

Lisa Smith

@BlazeATL is a premier party spot? Please!! This is what happens when a super star is in the building. Justin Dawson's proposal was ruined by the Mo Mack Experience! How do ya'll still support her?

"Midori, let me call you back." I hung up on her and immediately called Dre. He answered on the first ring.

"I was just about to call you," he began foregoing pleasantries. "I just saw the video. Justin actually called me about it."

"Dre, what the hell is going on?"

"I have no idea. I wish I knew. But it doesn't make much sense."

"What do you mean?"

"Think about it. The stuff being posted can be proven to be fake. It seems like they would do something that can cause a little more damage."

I was silent for a few seconds as I thought about what he said, and he was right. One upload of a video from last night can disprove this. I clicked on the comments and most of them talked about the proposal, but a few tried to place blame on me. I clicked on those profiles and they all looked fake. "You're right but...why target me anyway? Why are they trying to bring Blaze down?"

"What's that the young folks say? If you ain't got no haters, you ain't poppin'? I think this qualifies as you poppin' because you certainly have a hater."

I appreciated Dre trying to lighten the mood, but I was just so out done with why anyone would want to bring me down. "I guess but I wish she would just go away."

Dre chuckled and told me that even though Justin wanted to keep his personal life private, he would upload the video of his proposal to social media so that everyone would know the real story. Because the video was making its way around to celebrity blogs and pages, he wanted to clear the air.

"No. Tell him not to worry about me. He doesn't have to do that. Tell him just to enjoy his fiancé and future baller."

"I'll let him know." Dre paused for a second before continuing. "How are you doing otherwise?"

The sincerity in his voice let me know he still cared for me. "I'm okay. How about you?"

"I'm straight. How is your sister?"

"She's good. She's doing much better. Thank you for asking about her."

There was an awkward silence as I tried to come up with other pointless small talk. I wanted to keep him on the phone while he was being cordial to me again.

"Well, I'll talk to you later," Dre informed me.

"WAIT!" I yelled but I didn't mean to. I caught myself off guard with that. I really didn't have anything to say so there was another pause of silence.

"Yes, Mo?"

"Ummm…nothing. Don't worry about it. I'll talk to you later." I hung up before I further embarrassed myself. I was struggling to wrap my head around why I was acting like this. Especially since things were turning around for Nick and I. Before, Dre was a breath of fresh air. I could talk to him about Blaze and anything else and there was no pressure to discuss anything of deep substance, even though we did. He understood me. My drive. My fears. My passion. Why Blaze was my priority. That was enough to thoroughly enjoy conversations with Dre.

Not to mention the sex was mind blowing. With Nick, it was gentle. Passionate. Delicate. We made love. I loved that about him because he took his time with my body. But with Dre? It was the complete opposite. Dre had my pleasure in mind, but it wasn't sensual. It was frenzied. It was almost porn like. He appealed to a side of me that I hadn't been able to tap into. Dre brought it out and now…I needed it. I almost craved it. But it was over now, and I had to let it go.

Thoughts of Dre and that forged video had ruined my day and Netflix and chill was out, so I texted Nick and told him I had a situation that needed me at Blaze. He was disappointed but said he understood. I got dressed and headed out.

I busied myself with Blaze, so I didn't have to think about Dre or the video. I began to finalize my plans for what I wanted to do for Thanksgiving. I made up my mind that I wasn't going home for the holidays, so I needed to make sure my time was going to be spent productively. I didn't know what the kitchen staff had planned but I really wanted to feed the homeless or some needy families. I heard Swan come in because of the music playing in the kitchen. He was partial to 90's R&B, so the sounds of Mint Condition came through his portable speaker.

I made my way to the kitchen to run my idea by him. "Hey Swan! What's up?"

Swan turned his music down a notch but continued to prep. "Hey, Mo. Nothing much."

I made small talk mostly about Lani. I wanted to see where his head was at. His coy smile let me know he'd been talking to my friend and he felt the same way she did. "So, I have a question," I began, changing the subject to my real purpose for coming in there to talk to him. "And this is not a demand, this is a question. How would you feel about feeding the homeless or some needy families for Thanksgiving?"

Swan stopped for a second before smiling at me. "It is ironic that you asked me that. My family usually does a big thing, but my mama and her sisters are beefing, so we have no plans. I'm game. Does my family count as a needy family? I have some cousins that will probably starve to death."

I laughed at him and shook my head. "I don't want to take you away from your family, so you can decline."

"No, it's cool. I'm down. Do you have a family in mind?"

"I don't. We can search around. I know some people at the Department of Family and Children Services, so I can reach out to them."

"If you can't find someone, my dad's church wants to do some outreach like this. We can partner with them or contribute in some way."

"Do they do this yearly?"

"No, from what I've gathered they want to start. I can talk to my dad today and get back with you."

I was starting to get excited. "Good! I'm thinking I'm going to ask our customers to contribute somehow. I guess we need to find out what we're going to do before we get into all that. Thank you, Swan!"

"Not a problem. I'll let you know when I talk to my pops."

I left the kitchen and went back to my office to jot down my ideas. The more I wrote, the more excited I became. Swan came to my office to let me know his dad and pastor wanted to meet to discuss my plans. I didn't think the pastor would be comfortable coming to Blaze, so I decided to meet with them at his church. Pastor Billings had some time this afternoon, so I got my notepad, grabbed my bag, and headed to the address he gave me.

The church was unassuming, and I don't know why I expected some huge mega church. I walked in and was greeted by Pastor Billings. I expected a church secretary or armed guards or something.

"Ms. Mack?"

"Yes, sir Pastor Billings. Nice to meet you!" We shook hands and he led me to his office, which again surprised me. It was simple. An Ikea desk. Some pictures of his family. Some other knick knacks. Unless I knew he was a pastor, I wouldn't have guessed this was his occupation.

"Thanks for coming down so fast. It's amazing how God works things out!"

Pastor Billings comment brought me back to reality. It'd been over a year since I had a conversation with God. I hadn't communicated with him since my brother died. I actually hadn't thought about God in a long time and it didn't even dawn on me that the conversation of God would come up today. I just wanted to do something good.

"Yes, you're right," I agreed with as much enthusiasm as I could muster. *This was going to take a lot of fakeness to get through this,* I warned myself.

Pastor Billings and I spent the next hour formulating a plan. He was so easy to talk to that he didn't put me in the mind of being a pastor. He was just a man that wanted to help as many people as he could. He wasn't pushing Jesus down my throat and he didn't seem put off by the fact that I owned a night club. As we were ending our meeting, I decided to let him know.

"I'm glad I met you Pastor Billings. I don't think I've met a pastor quite like you," I told him.

He raised his eyebrow and gave me a quizzical look. "I'm not sure if that's a good thing or a bad thing," he said.

I laughed at his expression before I continued. "I mean…most pastors I know would have declined to work with me because of my occupation. And I'm not involved in any church. Truth be told, I haven't been on speaking terms with God for a while."

I really don't know why I said all of that. I was shocked those words fell out of my mouth. I closed my eyes and prepared for the dousing of holy oil and the laying of hands. Instead, Pastor Billings leaned back in his chair and crossed his hands.

"Is that something you want to talk about?"

"No," I said quickly. "I don't know. I'm not really sure what I can say."

Again, Pastor Billings was silent for a second and I worried I offended him. "Well, I'm not going to force you to talk to me. I know we just met. But what I will tell you is this. My church is small because I'm not a traditional kind of guy. I believe in God and I was called to do this work but it's not my job to beat anyone over the head with Bible verses and judgment. All I am required to do is live my life and show kindness to everyone. In doing that, I hope that someone wants to get to know Jesus for themselves."

Out of nowhere, I began to cry. It caught me off guard and I felt foolish for crying in this man's office. I only came here to discuss feeding people for Thanksgiving. Pastor Billings got up and handed me a tissue.

"Ms. Mack, I'm sorry. I didn't mean to make you upset."

"It's not that. I guess I just have some unresolved issues I need to work through."

"As a pastor, I do offer some counseling. And you don't have to worry, I won't brow beat you with the Bible."

I laughed a little and began to calm down. He really made feel at ease. "I may have to take you up on that. My sister sees a therapist, and I thought I had a handle on my life but maybe I don't."

"No pressure, Ms. Mack. When you are ready, I'll be here. But just know that the longer you put it off, the more layers you add to your problems."

I stood and shook his hand. I made the decision to try to visit his church because I really got a good vibe from him. We spent all that time talking and I didn't feel at all like I was drowning in religion. "Thank you, Pastor Billings. I really appreciate it. I will call you this week to schedule a session with you. And I'm really looking forward to our holiday event."

"I am as well. And I am grateful Swan was able to put us in contact with each other. I think this will be a mutual benefit for us and all the people we will help."

I smiled at him and basked in his calming presence. Maybe this is what it felt like to be genuinely cared for without the expectation of anything in return. I left his office carrying a bag of mixed emotions. I was ecstatic to be able to give back to my community. I wouldn't go as far as saying I would be philanthropist of the year, but I really loved the idea of being able to use what I had to help someone else. On the other hand, Pastor Billings opened up a can of worms. I had a lot of things that I needed to address. I'd pushed pieces of my life under a rug, never to be seen or heard from.

I made it back to Blaze and I sat down at my desk to decompress. I went to the bar and poured me a shot of Vodka. That one didn't do much, so I took another one. If I wanted to function at a seemingly normal level, I couldn't take one more. I went back to my office and tried to steady myself. I took a few deep breaths and pulled out my pad. I started to scribble out my ideas for how I was going to advertise and get my patrons to contribute.

I was on a roll and deep in my thoughts that I didn't notice Dre standing there watching me. "Busy little worker bee."

I jumped at the sound of his voice. "Oh, hey. I didn't see you."

I couldn't pretend that everything was okay, and I know he saw that on my face. "What's wrong?"

I opened my mouth, but nothing would come out. There was a time when looking at him would cause my guts to spill unwilling from my mouth. But we weren't there anymore. "Nothing. Just have a lot to work on." I knew he didn't understand the double meaning behind my words, but I left it alone. I didn't have the energy to do this.

"I know things aren't the same between us but I would like to think that we are friends. You know you can talk to me."

"We used to be able to talk. Not so much anymore."

Dre leaned against my office door and stared at me pensively. Those eyes, those eyes caused my heart to beat a little deeper. "Yeah, I guess we kind of messed that up. But, at least Blaze is making money."

I laughed at his attempt to lighten the mood. But it was everything we weren't saying that was causing the confusion. I opted not to entertain him and decided to talk about Blaze business. "Hey, let me run this idea by you."

Dre came in my office, sat down across from me, and waited for me to speak. I told him about my idea to feed people during the holidays and how we were going to partner with Pastor Billings.

"Wow, Mo. That's a really good idea. Awesome way to give back to the community. I love it. My sister won't be in town so I have no Thanksgiving plans…count me in."

Dre's approval made me happier than it should have. I was also ecstatic that he was going to be a part of it. I made a mental note to ask Nick if he wanted to help as well.

"Great! I'm gonna get with the girl that makes my fliers and get her to make me one for this. I just need a way to sign up volunteers."

"You can create a Google form to keep track of people. That way you can get their contact info and then send out email blasts updating them on the time-line."

"I've never used a Google form before. Is it difficult?"

"Not at all. It can be a little tricky, but I can show you. It's really not that difficult."

He stood up and came around my desk. I got up and allowed him to sit in my chair. He pulled up Google forms and we spent the next ten minutes creating a form that would allow customers to sign up to volunteer.

"Wonder how I've never heard of this. This is so convenient. I need to take advantage of this."

"Technology constantly evolves so they come up with new things all the time. I've found this one to be very helpful."

Dre stood up to allow me to sit back at my desk but instead of him moving backwards, he came towards me. Being in such close proximity to him gave me butterflies as I thought about all the times he ravaged my body. I wanted to take a step back, but my feet were planted in this spot. Subconsciously I needed him to touch me, kiss me, show me some kind of affection. The look in my eyes gave him the okay and he leaned down to kiss me.

Because of the moment, I expected a soft and sensual kiss. But in true Dre form, his lips on mine felt like fire. It wasn't gentle. He wasn't trying to show me he was passionate. He wanted me to need him, to crave him. Just as I was about to allow him to have his way with me, he pulled away. I whimpered when his lips were no longer on mine.

"Did you hear that?" he asked looking around my office.

My eyes were closed, and I was not aware of anything but the feeling this man gave me. "Huh? Hear what?"

"I thought I heard something."

"It was probably the guys in the kitchen."

I tried to get him to kiss me again, but he seemed to be weirded out. "I need to go. Can I call you later?"

I wanted to protest but I was the one that broke things off; I didn't need to lead him on. "Y-Yeah. That's fine."

Dre gave me one more quick peck before he left my office. I sat down at my desk and absently rubbed my fingers across my lips. *I really needed to get this guy out of my system.* I grabbed my phone and searched my contacts for Gabby to get her to do my flier.

I talked to Gabby for a few minutes and my excitement for Thanksgiving came back. She told me she would have the flier ready by tomorrow so I could go ahead and start posting it. I thanked her and headed to the kitchen to talk to Swan and Peaches.

"Hey ya'll. What's up?" I announced when I walked into the kitchen. Swan greeted me immediately, but Peaches seemed standoffish. Her behavior as of late had been very strange and I just hadn't had the time to address it.

Since Swan was already privy to my plans, I filled Peaches in. I did have to update Swan on my meeting with Pastor Billings and I thanked him for making the connection.

"So, I can't spend time with my family for Thanksgiving?" Peaches inquired with her hand on her hip.

"Damn girl. You must can't hear. Ms. Mo said it wasn't mandatory," Swan chided in his jovial tone.

Peaches rolled her eyes at him before setting her gaze on me. "I have plans."

I raised my eyebrow and wondered where this attitude was coming from. This was more than just her rough edges; she seemed genuinely perturbed with me. "That's fine Peaches. It's completely optional. I'm just trying to get an estimate of who will be available. I know your family gets together on the holidays."

Peaches popped her lips and left the kitchen. I gave Swan a puzzled look and he just shrugged his shoulders. I followed Peaches to the bar and sat down. "Peaches, what's wrong?"

"Why something gotta be wrong?"

"Because you're popping off at the mouth with me, and I haven't done anything to you."

She looked at me and I think my tone caught her off guard. Immediately her face softened. "I'm sorry, Mo. You're right. Just stressed about stuff. I don't mean to take it out on you."

"Well, what's wrong?"

Peaches paused before speaking. She looked as if she was trying to decide if she wanted to tell me. "We're going to have to put my grandma in a nursing home and my family is tripping."

I knew Peaches was close to her grandma, but I had no idea she was having problems. "Damn, Peaches. I'm sorry to hear that. What do you need me to do?"

"Nothing. We're trying to talk about it, but it hasn't been going well." She busied herself with things around the bar, so she could avoid eye contact.

"Why didn't you tell me what you were dealing with? You could have taken some time off. Come in later or whatever."

"I don't know. I was just trying to deal with it. She has Alzheimer's and it hasn't been easy. She barely remembers me."

"I can't say I know what you're going through, but you know I can't help you if you don't tell me you have a problem. Just let me know if you need some time."

"I know. But you had your own stuff going on. Your sister's shit alone is stressful. Not to mention all this stuff going on with Dre."

I raised my eyebrow at her. I tried to be careful, but I was sure she noticed the way we interacted. Her tone also insinuated that she was a little jealous. "What do you mean?"

"Oh nothing. Just the way you guys are working to-gether more and what you're doing with the place."

I gave her a fake smile because I knew that's not what she meant. "Okay. Just let me know if you need a few days off."

She didn't get to respond because our happy hour crowd began to pile in. I left her at the bar and begin to mingle with people. I dismissed her accusations and settled in to work the crowd.

* * *

I left Blaze relatively early for a Friday night and went home. Even though I really wanted to see Nick, I did need to go check on Midori. I called him to let him know I was going home and he said he'd come over to my place.

I got home, and Midori was preparing to go to bed. KJ wasn't there and I wondered why I hadn't seen as much of him. "Hey sis. Where is KJ?"

She sighed heavily. "He had to work late. He's work-ing a lot of overtime to save money to move."

"Girl, ain't nothing wrong with a working man!"

"I know. I just miss him."

I smiled at my sister and her forlorn puppy dog eyes. I was grateful her biggest concern right now was miss-ing her man who was at work. Since her suicide attempt, she had gone to therapy religiously. I could see the difference it was making in her life and in our rela-tionship.

"You'll be okay. Is he coming over when he gets off?"

"Yes."

"Okay. Well, Nick should be here soon," I started to leave her room and remembered I need to see if she was going to Americus for Thanksgiving. "Oh, are you going home next week?"

"Nope. KJ invited me to his mama's house. But mama mentioned something about going to Auntie Dee's house."

"Okay, good. I'm doing an event with a church here to feed families for Thanksgiving and I didn't want to go home."

"Don't worry. I don't think they were expecting us."

Since her situation, my parents had almost smothered Midori to the point that she stopped talking to them. They called and texted constantly. My mama sent her bible verses and videos about God and prayer on Facebook. At the insistence of her therapist, she told my parents to chill out.

My parents meant well, and they definitely wouldn't be able to handle losing another child, but they were clueless about mental illness. Old school and set in their ways, they thought all Midori needed to do was come home and go to church and she would magically be cured. We had so many conversations about why therapy was important, but they weren't convinced.

We had small talk for a few more minutes before I went to my bedroom to prepare for Nick to come over. I laid across my bed and scrolled through social media before I promptly fell asleep. I'm guessing Midori let Nick in because I remember him putting me under the covers and holding me.

The next morning, I woke up feeling refreshed. I didn't realize how tired I was but that was really good sleep. I grabbed my cell phone and saw it was after 11. I didn't have a particularly busy day, but I did want to get with Gabby for the flier and start promoting our Thanksgiving event.

Until I heard my toilet flush, I forgot Nick was even here. He walked back into my bedroom and sat down on my bed.

"Good morning, baby."

"Good morning, King. Sorry I fell asleep last night. I really wanted to run my idea by you."

"It's cool, Mo. What's up?"

I gave him the run down and unlike Dre, he didn't seem too thrilled. "You're really not going home for Thanksgiving?"

"Nah."

"Is your sister going home?"

"Nope. She told me my parents are probably going to my aunt's house in Alabama."

Nick sat quietly for a minute and I was puzzled that he wasn't excited by my plans to feed families next week. "You're really going to work on Thanksgiving."

It wasn't a question; it was a statement spoken of disbelief. "It's not really work. I'm giving back. If I'm going to be here, I want to do something worthwhile with my time."

"Well, I guess we'll be here then." He wasn't exactly thrilled but at least he was planning to help. "You want some lunch?"

"Yes, please. But I have no groceries so are we going to get something?"

"Yeah."

I got up to take a shower, so I could prepare for our date. I figured once I told Nick about meeting Pastor Billings, he would be more on board. If not for the community service, but also because I was planning to talk to Pastor Billings and get some help.

When I got out of the shower, Nick was sitting on my bed staring at his phone. I went on about my business of getting ready and he was just sitting there. "Are you going to start getting ready?"

"What the hell is this?" He got up and shoved his phone in my face. I moved and tried to see what he was talking about. I pulled the phone away and stared at the screen. My heart dropped to the floor.

Someone emailed Nick a picture of Dre and me kissing in my office the other day. The day he said he said he heard something. But it wasn't just that picture. There were more. Pictures of us at lunch. Pictures of my car parked at his house. Pictures of me leaving his house. Pictures of us laughing at Blaze. I looked at who sent it and when I saw the name Lisa Smith, I almost screamed. But that was the least of my worries.

"Answer me, Monica. What the hell is that?"

I didn't realize I hadn't spoken since he shoved his phone in my face. I didn't know what to say. I had nothing to say. I didn't know how to explain this away. So, I remained quiet and tears welled up in my eyes.

Nick jumped up and started pacing. He came close to me and I flinched. "You told me not to worry about him and now I see why. How long has this been going on?"

I didn't trust myself to speak. "HOW LONG?" He raised his voice and pounded his fist on my dresser causing some of my perfume to fall on the ground.

Hearing the commotion, Midori knocked on my door. "Is everything okay?"

"Ask your stupid ass sister. Fuck you, Mo."

With that, he put on his shoes and stormed past Midori, bumping into her in the process. "Excuse you, asshole!"

"Watch your mouth, little girl. This ain't got shit to do with you!"

I knew I needed to stop this, but my words were stuck in my throat. I felt like I was in a haze. I was standing outside of my life looking at me fail miserably. My subconscious was screaming at me to say something but nothing came out of my mouth.

"I wouldn't give a damn if this had something to do with Jesus, you ain't finna talk to me or my sister like that!"

Nick glared at Midori and I think he realized his fight wasn't with her and directed his sights on me. "I've done nothing but treat you like you needed to be treated. And at every turn, you fought me. From your ex to your brother and your sister, everything stopped you from moving in with me. And now I see the real reason why."

I sat down on my bed, still trying to wrap my head around what happened. I couldn't understand it. I had no idea who this Lisa Smith person was, but she was hell bent on ruining me. She started with Blaze; now she wanted my love life to fail. I put my head in my hands and just like I did with Jay, I couldn't cry. I sat perfectly still trying to figure out why this was happening. Midori came to sit beside me. She laid her head on my shoulder, probably relieved that for once, I was the one that had the fucked up life.

Chapter Eleven

After Nick left and Midori and I sat in silence for a minute, I jumped up and headed out of my condo. I had no idea where I was going but I ended up at Keyalani's house. I met her on her way out and when she saw me, she stopped dead in her tracks.

"Lani, I fucked up. Bad." I blurted out. There was no time for pleasantries.

"Mo, what happened? I was on my way to meet Swan for lunch," she responded.

I turned to walk away because I didn't want to ruin her date with Swan. They'd been seeing a lot of each other and the last thing I wanted was to mess up another relationship.

"Mo! Wait! Where are you going? What happened?" Keyalani called out.

I stopped and turned around. "Don't worry about it. Go have your date. I'll work it out."

"Monica Elyse Mack. Tell me what happened."

I finally relented and went inside her apartment. I kicked off my shoes and made myself comfortable in her oversized chair. I always picked this chair when I was at her house because it always sucked me in and made me relaxed. Immediately, the chair worked its magic on me and I started spilling my guts.

"Wow. I'm so sorry this is happening to you but what are you gonna do, Mo? Are you going to call Nick?"

I sighed heavily. I was hoping to ease this uncomfortableness, but no amount of deep breathing was going to get rid of this. Not so easily anyway. "Call him for what? There is nothing to say."

"Explain yourself. Try to convince him to give you another chance," Lani answered.

"Nah. It's over. How can I explain kissing another man? How can I explain any of that? I can't because I don't know why I got involved with Dre."

"First, you need to figure out what you want. You do owe Nick an apology and then you need to just go from there. People rebound from this stuff all the time. It doesn't have to be over."

"But, Lani, what if it needs to be over? I mean I know Nick is a good guy, but he never approved of my job. He didn't understand it. He didn't get me."

"That's true. But that doesn't mean he can't learn to try. Just think about it. If the negatives outweigh the positives, then let it go. But if you can find more good things about Nick than bad, you deserve to fight for him."

What she said made sense. It's something I should have done a long time ago. Without putting much thought into it, I felt the negatives were far greater. We fought over such major things and there wasn't an easy out. If I truly felt like this, I should have said so without involving another man.

While I mulled over life, Lani announced she was ordering lunch from a restaurant not too far from her place. She also called Swan and he was more than gracious with her having to reschedule. I still felt bad for showing up unannounced and ruining her plans, but she swore it was ok.

"He's going to cook me brunch tomorrow. Oh, and thank you for introducing me to him. He's really sweet," she gushed. The smile on her face was evident that she was happy. Maybe something good came out of something my dealings with Dre since it was apparent that my relationship suffered tremendously.

Lani's doorbell rang announcing our lunch arrived. I thought I wasn't hungry but the orange chicken and lo mein smelled amazing. We fixed our plates and ate in silence for a few minutes.

"Have you talked to Dre?" Lani interrupted our quiet moment.

"Naw, I don't want to involve him. It has nothing to do with him. It's about me and Nick."

Keyalani gave me a mean side eye but she tabled her judgment. "I agree but at least give him the heads up in case Nick decides to say something to him."

I hadn't thought about that, but I really didn't want to talk to Dre. I wasn't sure if I wanted to talk to Nick either. I realized I had no idea what I wanted to do. But Lani was right; I needed to give Dre a heads up.

I looked around for my phone, but couldn't find it. I finally located it in the chair cushions. I had a lot of missed calls and notifications, but I wasn't concerned about my phone because my life was taking an unexpected turn. I scrolled through my contacts and found Dre's number. I knew I needed to call him, but I found myself shooting him a text saying we needed to talk.

"Mo, I know you just didn't text him!"

"Lani...I-" My ringing phone cut me off and I rolled my eyes that Dre was calling me.

"Gone and handle your business. I'll be in my room." Lani left me sitting there to have this difficult conversation.

I started to ignore him, but I really couldn't because I told him we needed to talk. I finally answered. "Hello?"

"Hey, Mo. What's up?"

"Are you busy?" *Why am I making small talk?*

"Not really. What's up?"

I opened my mouth to speak but nothing wanted to come out. I didn't know what to say.

"Hello? Mo, what's up?" Dre said impatiently.

"Nick knows about us," I blurted out.

"What do you mean he knows about us? You told him? Why would you do that without talking to me first?" Hearing Dre's tone let me know he was perturbed.

"I didn't tell him. Someone emailed him pictures of us. A lot of pictures."

"Someone?"

"Yeah, this Lisa Smith person. She has it out for me, but I don't know why. First, she came after Blaze, now she's coming after my personal life. This shit is just...I don't understand."

Dre was quiet for awhile and truthfully, I didn't mind because I didn't want to talk. "Wait...are you okay? Where are you? What did he say?"

I scrunched up my face at all of his questions. "I'm okay. I'm at Lani's house. He just asked me how long. I couldn't answer him. He left."

"Have you talked to him?"

"Not since he left."

I heard Dre exhale loudly. "Monica, I'm sorry. I didn't mean for any of this to happen. I just…"

"Don't worry about it, Dre," I interrupted. "I don't blame you. I made the decision. Well I kind of made the decision."

"What do you mean you kind of made the decision?"

I leaned back in the chair and got comfortable. I looked up at the ceiling and tried to figure out the best way to explain what was on my mind. "After a while it wasn't a decision I was making consciously. To be with you, to want to be with you. Not just sexually. I really enjoyed talking to you. You understood me. And maybe that clouded my judgment about Nick. I wasn't fair to him. I didn't handle any of this right."

"Mo. Let's just take things a step at a time. What do you need from me?" The sincerity in his voice was undeniable. The calm in his voice was refreshing.

"I don't really know right now. I just need a minute to think. I just wanted to give you a heads up in case…you know in case he tried to come to you."

Dre chuckled. "Don't worry about me. I can handle me. What do you need? Are you going to be okay?"

"I think so. Just trying to process it all."

"If you need anything. To talk, to come over, anything; just let me know. I'm here for you."

Hearing Dre's words was a big comfort. And even though I knew I had no business doing so, I knew I would probably take him up on his offer.

* * *

A few days before Thanksgiving, I decided to give talking to Nick one more chance. He was ignoring my calls and texts and he blocked me on social media. I couldn't really say I wanted to work things out, but I did at least owe him an explanation. So today, I was taking a huge risk and going to his house. I still had his house key so I was just going to pop up. It was Sunday night and I knew he'd probably be home.

I heard his music before I got to his door and knew he was painting. I didn't want to interrupt but I needed to do this. I used my key and was surprised he hadn't had his locks changed. As I suspected, Nick was painting. I went to his sound bar and turned his music down. He turned around when he noticed the change in volume and his face registered anger. I knew he didn't want to see me but seeing it all over his face made me regret coming.

"What the hell are you doing here?" he barked.

"Can we talk?" I asked meekly.

"You couldn't move in with me because you were too busy fucking that nigga. Talk over. Nothing left to say."

"Nick, please. I know I can't really explain but can we just please talk?"

"What is there to say, Monica? I asked you to move in with me. I told you I needed you to be my wife. You declined. Because of him."

"It wasn't because of him," I admitted. "I was telling you no before I even met him."

Nick scoffed at me because he really didn't care to hear the truth. "Whatever, Monica. I don't want to talk to you. Get the hell out of my house. And give me my key."

I approached him cautiously, hoping that once he saw my eyes, he'd know I was truly sorry. "Nick, I want to apologize to you. I do not expect you to forgive me. I can't even get you to talk to me. I just want you to know I never meant for any of this to happen. I just dealt with my life in the best way I knew how and it wasn't the best way."

"Save me the 'my family is fucked up and my ex hurt me' song. I've heard it from day one. And I'm tired of it."

"Why didn't you ever listen to me?" I knew this was supposed to be my apology, but I needed to know why my apprehensions weren't valid to him.

Nick glared at me. "What?"

"I told you so many times that I wasn't ready. I told you I wanted to expand my business. I told you I wasn't over my ex. Or my brother dying. And you didn't listen. You continued to push."

As soon as Nick got in my face, I knew I should have kept my mouth closed. "Are you saying this is my fault?"

"No," I almost whispered. I was afraid with him so close to me like this. I could see the beads of sweat on his forehead and I saw the rapid rise and fall of his chest. I tried to step back but he stepped forward staying right in my face.

"I swear to God you have to be the most selfish person I know, and I hate I ever got involved with you. You cheated on me and I get blamed? I tried to be patient with you but you were being so fucking unreasonable."

I stepped back again because he was definitely scaring me. "Nick, I'm sorry. I'm not blaming you. I shouldn't have said that. I'm just gonna go."

I fumbled with my key ring and struggled to get my key off. He snatched my keys from me and took the key off before throwing my keys at me. "Get the hell out. And don't come back. Don't talk to me. Don't call me. Don't say shit to me!"

I turned to leave, completely unnerved. "Nick, I'm really sorry. I know you don't believe me, but I do love you."

Thinking I needed to let him know that, in case he was unsure, I turned to finally leave. I was defeated but I should have expected this. I only took one step before I felt his hands on my back pushing me with such a force that I went flying towards his front door. I ended up tripping over my feet and hitting the ground hard. I was trying to process what happened when Nick stood over me with a crazed look in his eyes. I began to cry out of fear. He grabbed me and drug me to his door. He opened it and literally threw me into the hallway. Once again, I went tumbling down to the ground, the wall catching my fall this time.

"Don't feed me that bullshit that you loved me! GET THE FUCK OUT OF MY HOUSE!" Nick screamed at me before slamming his door.

I sat on the floor trying to gather myself, but I was scared shitless. I got up as quick as I could to leave in case he came out again to do something worse to me. I made it to my car and with shaky hands started it. I drove in shock and silence, in complete disbelief that Nick behaved that way. I couldn't really blame him; I know I fucked up, but it scared me nonetheless.

Once I got home, I went straight to my room and got in the shower. My body was sore from falling but nothing hurt as much as my broken heart. I climbed into bed and as soon as my head hit the pillow, I felt the tears running into my ears.

Whether I wanted it to be over or not, Nick wouldn't have anything else to do with me.

* * *

I threw myself into the Thanksgiving prep to keep my mind off my encounter with Nick. I didn't tell anyone because I was embarrassed. I knew I hurt him bad and I deserved what he did. Actually, if he would have beaten me to a pulp, I would have understood. Nick loved me, and I broke his heart and his trust. I really wasn't shit for what I did to him.

Feeding hundreds of people was time consuming and Pastor Billings and his congregation were great and helpful. Swan led the charge with cooking along with a few other people. I had hundreds of volunteers that were donating hours, money, and even purchased food.

It was the day before Thanksgiving and my heart was brimming with pride. My Blaze patrons showed up and showed out for this event and I could hardly contain my happiness.

We were finishing up our prep while Pastor Billings gave the last round of instructions for our volunteers for tomorrow. Today was an extremely long day and I wanted nothing more than to take a long bath and drink a bottle of wine. Before I could run out of the building, Pastor Billings stopped me.

"Monica, I can't thank you enough for everything that's happening right now. Your people really showed up for this and it's going to be great."

"It was your people too, Pastor Billings. You have a lot of pull," I admitted. He was genuinely happy, and I was glad we could work together. I turned to walk away but he stopped me.

"Monica?"

"Yes, Pastor Billings?"

He pulled me to a corner of the kitchen so that no one else would overhear our conversation. "I know I said I wouldn't push, but you never called to make an appointment. I can tell something is bothering you."

I stared at Pastor Billings and wondered how he knew my life was in turmoil. My last interaction with Nick was still frightening to me. I hadn't exactly spoken to God in a long time, but he was still trying to talk to me. Apparently, my silence let Pastor Billings know he was right.

"Again, I'm not going to push. Just wanted to re-mind you that I'm available to talk to you. Whenever you're ready. You don't have to figure out anything on your own."

I wanted to open up to him, but I just wasn't ready right now. I was embarrassed; I was too old to go through this. "I appreciate you Pastor Billings, but I do not think I am quite ready for that yet."

Pastor Billings smiled, confusing the hell out of me. "I understand, Monica. It takes a lot to admit you need help. I just want you to know that I'm here whenever the time comes."

He left me standing in the corner feeling lost and confused. Not sure if it was pride or if I just wasn't prepared to deal with my bullshit but I wasn't ready to talk.

Instead of wanting to go home, I decided I didn't want to be alone. It wasn't the best strategy, but it would have to do tonight. I searched for my phone so I could call Dre.

* * *

Thirty minutes later, I was sitting on Dre's sofa drinking a glass of wine and eating cheesecake. Instead of talking about what was going on, we talked about everything else. Our conversation morphed from current politics to having the age old 'Tupac or Biggie' debate.

"Are you serious?" he queried. "You think Tupac is the better rapper? How?"

"Yes, I do! Sure, Biggie was more main stream and got more radio play, but I think Pac was deeper."

Our debate went on for a few minutes before he pulled up iTunes to play me some Biggie songs that I'd heard a million times.

"I'm not saying he isn't good. I really love his verse on 'Get Money'. It's classic storytelling. So much better than these damn mumble rappers out now. I'm just saying…I think Pac had more of a message. I actually don't even get why they were comparable; they were two different artists completely."

"Yeah, these mumble rappers couldn't hold a candle to either Biggie or Pac. But Biggie had flow and he had lyrics. I agree they can't be compared because Biggie was definitely better."

I grabbed his phone and searched for a Pac song to prove my point. My search was interrupted by his doorbell ringing. Dre gave me a perplexed look as if he was confused by his unannounced visitor. I put on my shoes, prepared to have to leave if necessary. I also didn't want it to look like this was anything but a business meeting, so I pulled out my pad I kept with me.

I overheard female voices and immediately went into a panic. *Damn, a girl and her friends. He didn't strike me as the type that would allow unannounced visitors and be happy about it.*

Dre and his guests emerged from the front door and made their way to the living room. I took one look at the woman standing in his living room and knew it was his mama. She didn't look like him, but she had a look in her eyes that screamed mama. And because the woman was obviously his mother, the other young woman had to be his sister.

"Mo, I mean, Monica, I'd like you to meet my mama April and my sister Amerie. Mama and Doll, this is Monica."

I got up from the sofa and stood to shake their hands. "Nice to meet you ladies."

They both shook my hand and smiled politely. It was obvious they weren't expecting him to have company which kind of relieved me. "Dre, we can finish this up tomorrow. I think everything is ready to go for tomorrow, so I'll see you in the morning. It was nice to meet you guys."

I gathered my things and prepared to leave when his mama interrupted me. "You don't have to go, honey. We just stopped by to feed my baby since he will be busy tomorrow. We're not interrupting your date."

"Mama, it's not a date!" Dre groaned. For the first time in the months I'd known him, Dre looked...vulnerable. I never pegged him for a mama's boy, but it was definitely coming out now.

"And hell ain't hot," April retorted. "Monica, you want to help me in the kitchen for a second?"

It was a question, but it was more like a command. I looked at Dre for confirmation, but his face had an 'I'm not about to argue with my mama' look. I followed April into the kitchen while Amerie and Dre sat down on the sofa.

April and Amerie had brought BBQ from This is it! I hadn't had their food in a minute and from what I remember, it was great. April and I fixed plates of ribs, mac and cheese, and collard greens. I went into Dre's fridge and pulled out his pitcher of tea before getting four cups out of his cabinets.

"You know your way around Dre's kitchen pretty well, Monica," April observed.

I stopped in my tracks, unaware of what I was doing. I didn't spend an exurbanite amount of time here but after our marathon sex sessions, I knew Dre always had sweet tea in his fridge and I knew where he kept his cups. I tried to think quickly but admitting the real reason was even worse than what she thought. I hung my head and tried to hide my embarrassment.

"It's okay, honey. Dre is a grown man, I don't judge who he has around."

I smiled as politely as I could. "Dre and I are business partners. I own a bar and lounge and he invested in me. I mean my business."

I was usually quicker on my feet, but I wasn't prepared to meet Dre's mama, much less having to explain my…whatever this was with her son.

"Sounds like my son. Always looking to make a buck," she chuckled. "He's been like this since he was a kid. That boy could sell snow to a penguin. I'm just glad he finally got some sense and started making money the legal way."

I cut my eyes at her and tried to figure out what she meant. April continued fixing plates. The plate she was piling food on obviously was for Dre. Unless she and Amerie had an appetite of a 400lb man. April continued talking never noticing my face.

"It was hard being without him for that long amount of time. It was real tough seeing my baby boy behind bars for seven years. But it honestly turned out to be the best thing for him. Everyone he ran with ended up dead or doing major time. His best friend is doing a life bid for murder right now. Getting locked up put his life in perspective. Dre was going down the same road as his dad and he needed a detour. Being away from his family really broke him down and he saw he needed to make a change. He never had a chance to really grieve his son. All because he made terrible decisions."

I tried to mask my emotions and obviously I did a good job because April didn't notice my deer in headlights look. "I'm just rambling. Let's go eat."

April nodded her head towards the two plates on the counter and I absently grabbed them and followed her in the living room. April handed Dre and Amerie their plates. She turned to me and got one of the plates from me. I sat in the chair, as far from Dre as I could. He looked at me puzzled but I kept my eyes in my food.

I felt stupid for allowing myself to get involved with a man that I didn't know anything about. I allowed myself to catch feelings for a man that I didn't even know went to jail. For seven years. And to grieve his son? Dre never told me he lost a kid. As much as I talked about my brother and my sister almost dying, I thought he would have brought it up. Come to think of it, Dre never really discussed his personal life outside of his mama, his sister, and where he was from. And I never asked.

Maybe I was selfish as Nick implied. Maybe I was just so happy to be able to talk about something other than marriage and moving in that I didn't even ask about him. We talked about a lot of things though, just nothing personal from his end.

"Earth to Monica," Dre called to me and snapped his fingers in my direction.

I was obviously lost in my thoughts that I didn't realize they tried to include me in their conversation.

They were all staring at me, waiting for me to answer "I'm sorry. What did you say?"

"I just asked if the food wasn't good. You haven't eaten a bite," April stated.

I looked down at my plate and sure enough I hadn't taken a single bite of my food. "Yes, No. I mean…I've just had a really long day."

Suddenly, the room was too small, and I felt like the walls were closing in around me. "I think I'm gonna go. Dre, I'll see you later. April and Amerie, it was nice to meet you."

I took my plate and headed towards the kitchen. I heard Dre follow me. "Are you okay? What's wrong?"

"Nothing. I'm just-"my phone buzzing took me off the hook. It was just a text message, but I pretended it was a call. I just needed to get out of the room to try to wrap my head around the fact that I really didn't know Dre at all. I motioned that I needed to take it and Dre returned to the living room. I stayed in there for a few seconds before I overheard them talking. I crept closer to ear hustle.

"She knows her way around your house pretty well, Dre," April commented causing Amerie to cackle loudly.

"We're just business partners. That's it," Dre countered.

"But it's cool, big bruh," Amerie said. "I like her better than your baby mama."

Baby mama? He told me he didn't have kids!

"I don't have a baby mama, Doll," Dre said.

Amerie popped her lips. "Whatever you want to call her. She was a nightmare after jail and AJ passing away."

"Doll, that's not fair. I can't imagine losing a child and becoming sterile is a tough pill to swallow. She was doing the best she could."

Amerie popped her lips. "Nah, mama. She was just mean. Before and after AJ and no matter how much we tried to welcome her. She acted like we did something to her."

"Seriously, Dre. Monica seems nice. Why is it just a business relationship? Wait...are you still talking to-"

"Mama, please, let it go," Dre begged.

I heard Amerie pop her lips again. "Yeah, Monica is nice. And pretty, too. I love her purple locs. I will never understand what you saw in Calandria."

My heart sank down to my toes and I felt like a complete idiot. I came around the corner, completely unashamed that I eavesdropped their entire conversation. I lost my ability to be able to be pleasant. "Really, Dre? Really?"

They all turned to look at me, surprised that I snuck up on them. When he saw me, Dre hopped up and approached me. "Wait, Mo. Let me explain. Please, I can explain," he pleaded.

"Yeah. Between the seven years you spent in fucking jail or the fact that you had a relationship and a whole baby with my bartender, I'd say you have a lot of explaining to do."

Chapter Twelve

I sat in the middle of my bed, unable to sleep. Unable to think. Unable to cry. Unable to process. Everything was a blur. I didn't want wine. Or a hot shower. Or ice cream. I didn't want anything. I take that back. I wanted answers. I needed answers, but I had no idea how to get them when I didn't want to talk to Dre.

He had called me fifty-leven times and I had ignored every phone call and every text he sent me. He showed up at my house and thank God that Midori wasn't there, so I didn't have to explain why my life was getting more fucked up by the second. I let him stand out there and knock for five minutes refusing to let him in.

How did I allow myself to get this point? Not only did I allow Dre into my bed, but I gave him access to my business. My most prized possessions. I let him in and now…

My ringing phone took me out of my thoughts. It was Dre again and I ignored him again and turned my phone off. I went to my bathroom and found my ZzzQuil. I hadn't taken any of it in a long time, but I desperately needed to sleep and the day had drained the hell out of me.

I woke up the next day and got ready to go to the church. Since we prepped most of everything last night, it made our day much easier to manage. I arrived at the church really early to be the contact point for our volunteers. Pastor Billings and I pulled up at the same time.

"Monica! Happy Thanksgiving! How are you?" he called. He was always in such good spirits.

I wasn't prepared to see him, so I had to pull some happiness out of thin air. "Same to you! I'm well."

He unlocked the door and allowed me to enter before him. Once inside, he looked at me and I tried to avoid eye contact because that would be a dead giveaway that I was faking it.

"What happened?"

His question caught me off guard because I didn't know how he knew. His simple question caused my dam to break and everything that happened since I saw him last burst from my mouth. When I finally finished bearing my soul, I had to admit I felt ten pounds lighter.

"Monica, first because of what happened with Nick, are you safe?" Pastor Billings asked.

"Yes. We haven't spoken since then and I highly doubt we will."

"Okay good. I see our volunteers are showing up, so we can't really have the conversation we need to have. But I want you to think about a few things today," Pastor Billings said while getting out of the way of the people coming in. "You said Nick called you selfish and this is the time for you to be. Whatever you are planning on doing has to be a selfish decision. You cannot think about Nick and you cannot think about Dre. You have to think about what you want."

His statements were simple and logical, but simultaneously difficult. Luckily, I was being pulled in a million different directions. Once the day got started, it was non-stop from start to finish. I had no idea how many people came through to be fed but I did know my feet were screaming at me by the time we ran out of food. I was so busy fixing plates and talking to people that I didn't take the first picture. Everyone that came to the church weren't exactly needy. There were a few people that just didn't want to be alone today, and we welcomed them with open arms. One young lady lost her mother a month ago and she couldn't bring herself to go be with the rest of her family; she was trying to process her mama being gone. Pastor Billings took her to his office to talk to her and pray for her. He also invited her to the church for their grief ministry.

A few homeless people came, and the church gave them each a bag of essentials and contact information for shelters and other programs that could help them. While I was extremely grateful to be able to be a part of this event, I realized this one day barely scratched the surface of what was needed. I really needed to figure out how I could do more on a consistent basis. Since Pastor Billings and I worked so well together, I figured we could come up with some outreach to tackle some of the issues we encountered today. When the last of the people left and all the volunteers were finished cleaning up, I went to find Pastor Billings to run my thoughts about a long-term project by him.

I found him in his office sitting at his desk. His eyes were closed, and I could see the tiredness all over his face. I almost didn't want to interrupt him. I decided I'd just tell him I was leaving and table the rest for one day next week. "Pastor Billings?"

He opened his eyes and gave me a tired smile. "Monica, I thought you had long gone. Thank you again for this, for your support and help. We really made a difference today, but I think this was just the tip of the iceberg."

"Funny you said that. I was just thinking about what else we could do to help people more than once a year."

"Great minds think alike!" He chuckled. "Speaking of minds…have you given thought to what I said?"

"I have but we can talk next week. I know you are tired. I'm beat myself."

"How about Monday at 10? Does that work for you?"

I wasn't prepared for him to give me a concrete date and time, and I was already trying to figure out a way out of it. "Yes. That should work."

"I'm here to help. I'll see you Monday. Enjoy the rest of your day."

"You do the same."

I was grateful I didn't have to talk to him today because I was drained. All I wanted to do now was soak in a tub and get in the bed. On my way home I called Midori and she was staying with KJ and going Black Friday shopping with his family tomorrow. Midori living with me was less of an issue now, but I was grateful to have my house to myself.

I walked into my condo and started stripping as soon as the door closed behind me. I went to my bathroom and ran a tub of scalding hot water. I threw in one of my Lush bath bombs, lit some candles, and turned on my Anthony Hamilton Pandora station. I slid in the tub and was immediately relaxed by the sounds of "Can't Let Go" coming through my wireless speaker.

I didn't want to think about anything, so I concentrated on singing, the hotness of the water, and anything else that caught my attention. Forcing myself to be oblivious to my problems was easy with the hot bath and candles. I stayed in the tub for close to an hour. My water wasn't hot anymore and I was a prune, but I felt awesome.

I got out and dried off, choosing to lather my skin with coconut oil. I tied up my hair and climbed into bed without clothes because I was comfortable as is. Against my better judgment, I got my phone to scroll social media. The first post I saw made me regret not going straight to sleep.

Lisa Smith

SMH anything for recognition, huh? This is the Mo Mack experience? If you have to advertise your good deeds, your motives are fucked up! I'm sure she got something out of this deal cause everyone knows Mo is all about the money!

Along with her post, there were pictures of me at the church today. Apparently, Lisa Smith stole them from some else's page because I didn't post a single picture today; I hadn't even taken any. I didn't mind anyone taking pics of me or even posting. I knew my intentions were pure. But this Lisa Smith person was really trying to defile my character and I had no idea why.

I took a screen shot and sent it to Dre. As soon as I sent it, I forgot I wasn't talking to him. He called me almost immediately. I reluctantly picked up.

"She's still at it I see," he said stoically. I knew his somberness wasn't over this post.

"Yeah. I don't have the energy to fight it today. I'm tired."

"How was Thanksgiving? Did ya'll feed a lot of people?"

"Yes, it was great. We ran out of food."

"Wow that's great. I'm glad it worked out. I'm proud of you, Mo." His voice was soft, and I knew he meant it. But that didn't mean I was about to let his lies go.

"Why didn't you tell me? Any of that? Are you still with Peaches? After all the time we spent together, you didn't think any of that was worth mentioning?"

Dre was quiet then he exhaled deeply as if what he was going to say was painful. "Monica, please believe I didn't expect any of this to happen. At all. No Peaches and I aren't together anymore, and we haven't been in years. I had no idea she worked at Blaze. We were together before I went to jail. She was running drugs for me because she was less of a suspect. She got caught and was prepared to do time for me because I'd already caught a drug charge. On one hand, I wanted to be selfish and let her take my charge but she was pregnant with our son. So I had to turn myself in. But I waited four days before I did. She was arraigned and everything. I know I wasn't shit for that. I felt like less than a man, but at the time I really wasn't a man.

"I went to jail for seven years for drugs. My mama told me she told you and she didn't know that you didn't know. I was one of the biggest drug dealers in the city. It's actually why I moved from Hawkinsville to Atlanta; there was much more money to be made here. A year before I got locked, my homie, who was more like a brother to me, caught a murder rap and is doing life. After that, I kind of got reckless. Started doing business with an undercover cop."

"Dre, why couldn't you tell me this? I told you all about my dead brother, my sister's suicide attempt, my rift with my parents, my problems with Nick. I told you a lot."

"I don't talk about this stuff. With anyone. It's not exactly a secret but I'm not proud of who I used to be. Do you know why my mama comes to Atlanta? Because I refuse to go back to Hawkinsville. People still remember me as Dre the dope dealer. Young boys in the game talk about my hay days. I don't like being the drug dealer they look up to. I took my family through hell. Peaches was going to have our kid in jail because of me. I missed so much of my sister's life. My mama had to deal with people giving her grief cause I turned out to be a felon."

I took in what he was saying and on one hand I got it; he didn't want to be known for who he used to be. But I couldn't understand why I wasn't worth sharing his life with, especially since I gave him a front row seat to the train wreck of my life.

"Dre, I get it. You have a troubled past. But that doesn't excuse you from telling me about you and Peaches."

"You're right. I was being selfish. I knew if you knew about Peaches and me especially with what I did, you would cut me off."

"Cut you off? Business or personal?"

"Both."

His assumption was right. I would have definitely cut him off with the quickness. I would have judged his decision to let Peaches do his time harshly. But that also meant Blaze would still be in the same condition it was in. "You're probably right, but you didn't give me the option of making that decision."

"You're right. Not my finest hour, that's for sure. So, what are you going to do?"

I hated he asked me that cause I really had no clue, just a thought that I wasn't even sure was feasible. "With Blaze it will be business as usual. We work well together, and you have delivered on your promise of taking Blaze to the next level. As far as everything else…there can't be anything else."

"You're right," was all he offered.

Making this a strictly business relationship was probably the best decision, but I had no idea how to make that happen. How can I just forget about the way he made my body feel? Or the friendship we developed? Honestly, if it wasn't for his past relationship with Peaches, Dre would be someone I could see myself being with. At least the Dre he showed me he was. I had to keep remembering I didn't know him.

"Are you planning anything for Christmas or New Year's at Blaze?" Dre asked changing the subject.

"Maybe a toy drive for Christmas. Definitely a New Year's Eve party. I haven't really planned anything out yet."

"Cool, cool. Let me know what you come up with and what you need me to do."

"I will. Thanks."

We sat silently on the phone for a few seconds, both of us probably ignoring what needed to be said. He finally said he needed to go and we got off the phone. I sank back into my bed and closed my eyes, thankful this day was over. I had a lot I needed to address, but right now all I wanted to do was go to sleep.

* * *

Friday afternoon I went to Blaze. Maybe it was everything that has taken place recently, but I was just not excited to be there. I'd never felt like this before. I went to the kitchen to thank Swan for his help yesterday and to talk to Tank and Quan for a few minutes before heading to my office.

I was trying to get my ideas out, but my mind was in a fog. I couldn't concentrate at all. I really needed to do something to de-stress. I pulled out my phone and scheduled a spa day for me and my sister at Jeju for tomorrow. I could have gone alone, and that was actually my preference, but one of her complaints was that we didn't do enough together. Spending time with my sister wasn't as bad as I thought it would be. It was crazy of me to assume that because of our age difference we couldn't do simple things like go eat or just hang out.

I texted Midori to let her know I had a spa day for us tomorrow and she was beyond excited. I went back to trying to get plans together for our next events, but I was still drawing a blank. Maybe I just needed to do something else to get my mind off my life.

I went to the main area to find a few customers in the building. After Black Friday shopping, this crowd was mostly women who wanted to relax after spending the morning catching deals. I mingled with a few people and I was back in my element. I spent about an hour out on the floor, ate some lunch, and had to run to my office to get my ideas out of my head.

I was deep in my groove when there was a knock on my door. I looked up and was surprised to see Peaches.

"Hey Peaches, what's up? How was your Thanksgiving?" I tried to sound as normal as possible but I'm sure I over did it.

She raised her eyebrows at my over enthusiastic response. "It was cool. Listen, I need to be off on Monday. I got shit to do."

"Okay, that's fine. Just make sure you let me know what needs to be ordered today."

"Alright."

She turned to walk out of my office, but I stopped her.

"Why didn't you tell me you had history with Dre? Especially the history that you guys had?" I asked. I looked at her and saw her face contort into anger.

"Cause it was none of your business."

"I realize that but what I meant was that I wouldn't want you to be uncomfortable. Had I known…"

"If you had known, what? You wouldn't have fucked my ex?"

I stared at her, confused by her hostility towards me. "Look Peaches. All I'm saying is I wish you would have told me you had history. I had him in here, in your space, and I had no idea you used to be with him. Or about your son. Or about you almost doing his time. I don't know the whole story. All I know is that you shouldn't have had to see him like this so often."

Peaches rolled her eyes at me. "I'm a grown ass woman. I don't need you to look out for me. I can handle myself. What happened with me and Dre was a long time ago. I've moved on. I don't care if you fuck him or not."

"Peaches...are you mad at me? Do you think I did this on purpose? Cause judging from your tone, you seem upset." I spoke calmly because I was perplexed more than I was mad. She was definitely tripping, and I didn't blame her; I just didn't want her to blame me. Hell, she didn't even tell me she was in a whole relationship with him.

Peaches laughed at me before turning to leave my office. "Upset? Dre's convict ass ain't no damn prize. Yes, I was going to do his time but that's because I was young, dumb, and in love with his stupid ass. I'm done with that life. I guarantee he's still moving major weight and just using your dumb ass as a front. Men like Dre don't change. Once a dope boy, always a dope boy." Peaches walked out of my office leaving me dumbfounded.

She came back a second later to finish up her rant. "And don't worry about Monday. I don't need it off anymore because I quit."

I sat at my desk stunned by what just happened and it became more than obvious that Peaches was nowhere near over Dre. And he put me in the middle of his bullshit to make a buck.

I grabbed my phone to call Dre and he didn't answer. I hung up and shot him a text asking him to come to Blaze ASAP. I tossed my phone on my desk and tried to make sense of what Peaches said. *What if Dre really hadn't changed?* I didn't even want to consider the possibility of what that could mean for my business. I groaned as all the negative thoughts rolled around in my head.

"Ms. Mo," Tank called from my doorway. "You know where Peaches is? We got folks at the bar."

Just that damn quick I forgot she quit. "Yeah she um...she's sick. Here I come."

"Ahight."

Tank and I walked out from the back, running into Dre in the process. "Hey Mo, What's up?"

Tank continued walking to the kitchen and I slowed down to tell Dre about what happened.

"Damn, she just walked out?" he questioned.

I kept walking towards the bar, not really having time to address him. I know I left him with more questions than answers. I hopped behind the bar and started filling orders.

"Hey, Dre will you go to my office and get my phone? I need to see if Nashonna can come in."

"Sure, no problem."

He brought back my phone and I shot Nashonna a text so that I could keep talking to my customers. She texted me back and told me she'd be there in a few minutes.

Dre sat patiently waiting for me until Nashonna arrived. I had such a good time behind the bar, I almost forgot that was where I started. When Nashonna got there, I told her to come find me when she got a break. I planned on promoting her to Peaches job.

I made rounds around Blaze to make sure everyone was okay and then Dre and I went to my office.

"I really don't appreciate you putting me in the middle of your shit with Peaches," I said as soon as my door was closed.

"What are you talking about? There is nothing between us."

I relayed my conversation with Peaches to Dre and his face scrunched up in confusion.

"Are you still selling drugs and using Blaze as a front? Cause I swear to God if any shit pops off…"

Dre stopped me before I could finish my threat. "Whoa, whoa, whoa. Not a chance. Losing seven years of my life was enough to get my attention."

"How can you afford what you're doing?" I knew that was a personal question, but I felt I had the right to ask it seeing as to how my business was at stake.

Dre leaned up in his chair and looked me directly in my eyes. I wanted to look away but his damn eyes were so captivating. "Hustling 101: Keep a stash for a rainy day. I had a good little nest egg in a savings account accruing interest. While I was locked up an old head schooled me on real estate and then I did my research. When I got out, I started working on my real estate license. The rest, as they say, is history. Don't worry, Mo. After I saw how I can make money without having to look over my shoulder, I have no desire to do anything else illegal. And I'd never put you in a position to get caught up. I made that mistake once. "

The way he spoke let me know it really meant that Peaches was definitely bitter. Maybe she had reason to be. But that didn't excuse the fact that neither of them told me about their relationship. "She's not over you, Dre."

"I don't know why she isn't. When I got out, she was one of the first people I hit up. She told me to go fuck myself. Over the years, I tried to reach out to her to apologize and every time she shut me down. So, I don't get why she is in her feelings."

Nothing was making sense and I had no idea who to trust in this situation. On one hand, Peaches came across as bitter, but she'd been with me for a minute. I think seeing Dre and assuming we slept together, cause I never would admit that I did to her, put her in her feelings. I could understand that. But Dre...we weren't sleeping together anymore and whether I believed him or not, I was bound to him by contract. If nothing else, we had to work together. There was no benefit to him lying to me.

"You put me in a bad spot with her and I don't appreciate it."

"Me?" Dre asked incredulously. "I asked her why she didn't tell you about us and she insisted I wasn't that important to her to mention it to you. So, it wasn't just me. I figured she didn't want to cause any issues on the business side. I have no idea why she didn't want you to know."

"Okay, well I guess it doesn't matter anymore," I announced. "I gotta go, Dre."

"Are you good? Do you need me to do any-thing...for Blaze?"

"No, I'll text you later this week. I have ideas for Christmas and New Year's and I need to see if they are feasible."

"Cool. I'll look forward to hearing from you."

"UN-FUCKING-BELIEVABLE!"

Both Dre and I jumped at the sound of Nick's voice. I didn't even hear him come up or see him standing in the hall.

"N-n-n-ick what are you doing here?" I stammered. Seeing him did something to me. I wasn't sure if I was happy to see him or if I could have done without seeing him again. That confusion really fucked with me.

"I came to give you the shit you left at my place, but I see you're busy," Nick spat. He threw down the box he was holding and left my office.

Knowing that was a piss poor excuse and perhaps maybe he wanted to try to work it out made my heart leap. Although I didn't know if I really wanted to work anything out. But I got up and went after him anyway. I saw him parked in front of Blaze on the street. I don't know how he always managed to snag such a good parking space when he came here. I caught him just before he made it to his car.

"Nick, wait!" I ran around his car and blocked him from getting to the driver's side. We stood in between the cars parallel parked on the road.

"Mo, get the hell out of my way. I see you've moved on," Nick warned.

"I haven't moved on. We were talking business. He is my business partner...you know that," I pleaded. "I've been trying to talk to you, to apologize."

"There is nothing to apologize for. You've made your decision about who you want. Move please."

I hung my head but refused to move. I inched closer to him not because I wanted to be closer to him but because cars were whizzing by. He took a step back as if being in the same space with me was causing him discomfort. "How can I make a decision when you refused to talk to me? You threw me out, literally. What do you want me to do? If we can just sit down and talk…can we just talk?"

Nick thought for a second and I thought his face was softening. I thought he was really letting go of his anger and we could finally have the conversation we should have had. In this moment, I felt there was a glimmer of hope.

Nick rubbed his hands across his face. His eyes were distant. They used to be hold passion. They used to be full of love. But looking in his eyes now…I knew I hurt him. Bad. I wondered if I could ever get the light back in his eyes.

"You know, Mo, I trusted myself with you. I gave you my heart and you played me. You strung me along. I asked you over and over again and you lied to me. I came here today because…I missed you but you, you're still with him!"

"I'm not with him, Nick. I promise. You can ask him yourself. I can't just not have him around, but I promise it's strictly business. Tell me what I have to do!"

Nick looked at me intensely and firmly said, "Quit Blaze."

I looked at him incredulously. "Are you serious? The only way we can talk or work on us is if I quit Blaze?"

"Your business has been in our way. The only way we can make this work is if you let this go," he said matter of factly.

"You're giving me an ultimatum? I had Blaze when I met you. Why do I have to give this up? I shouldn't have to choose between you and my job."

I don't know why I was surprised. Nick never supported me. He never understood what this business entailed, and he never tried. I knew then there was no hope for us.

"Mo, Blaze has caused all of the problems in our relationship and if we have a shot at making it, your job has to go. You can sell it and come out ten times richer than you are now. Then you can do other things."

"Other things like what Nick?" I questioned. "In all the time you have known me, when have I ever expressed having an interest in doing anything other than running Blaze?"

"You've limited yourself. No one just does one thing. I paint. I draw. I take pictures. I teach. You can find your niche in something else."

I stared at Nick and tried to figure out who this person was. I knew he never liked my job, but this was extreme. "I can't even believe this is coming out of your mouth."

Nick pushed past me and unlocked his door. "Well, I guess that's my answer. Bye, Monica."

I followed him and stood in his door, so he couldn't close it. "Nick come on now. Be realistic. That's not a real option."

"That's the only option for me. Now move," Nick stated. He pushed me away from his car to close his door.

I wasn't expecting his movement and I struggled to keep my balance to no avail. I stumbled backwards and into the road. No matter what I could have tried to do, I wouldn't have been able to stop the car coming towards me.

Chapter Thirteen

I was sitting in a room, I wasn't sure where. The walls were white, the curtains were white, the furniture was white…everything was so crisp and clean. Even I had on white. All around the room were pictures of my family. Like the one Midori and I took on her first birthday and my eleventh birthday. And the family picture we took at Easter when I was 15. And when Jay and my daddy escorted me during homecoming when I was crowned homecoming Queen.

I walked through the room, admiring the pictures and remembering my childhood. I couldn't really complain about how I grew up. My parents took really good care of my brother and I…we never knew my parents were struggling to pay bills or to put food on the table. All we knew was that dinner would be on the table every night; we never knew the struggle to get it there.

"Good times, huh sis?"

Jay was standing in the doorway looking at me look at all the pictures of our childhood.

"Yeah. Mama and daddy hid their struggle. It made us work harder. I wish Midori would have seen how hard it was for them," I replied unable to tear my eyes away from the pictures. All of the pictures had a story behind them and I was trying to remember each one.

"You're too hard on her. She's trying," Jay coaxed.

"I know. I was too hard. We're better now."

"Look what it took to get there, though. You almost lost another sibling," he accused.

I finally was able to look at my brother. He had on the same jeans and Mack family reunion t-shirt he had on when I saw him for the last time. He was the only thing that wasn't white in this room. "I miss you, Jay."

"I know, sis," Jay began. "But life happens. You have to learn to keep living."

"It's too hard to keep living without you," I cried.

"I get it. I would be the same way. But what about all the people that need you? What good are you to them if you stay stuck in hurt and unforgiveness? It's made you bitter and you're not that person. Life loves the lover of it…remember that, Mo. Go live your life."

"Mo…Mo…are you okay? How do you feel?"

My eyes fluttered and I everything around me was blurry. I blinked a few more times to adjust to the light in the room. I looked around and realized I was in a hospital. I groaned as I felt pain in my body. I felt like I got run over by a truck.

"Don't try to sit up. The doctor's said you just need to rest."

I looked at who was talking to me and it was Nick. "Why am I here? What happened? Everything hurts."

"Okay, baby. Let me get the doctor and see if they can give you something else for pain."

Nick left the room and no matter how I tried to get up, I couldn't. I started to panic but Nick was back in the room and by my side. I asked him again what happened.

He looked everywhere but at me. "You were hit by a car."

"What? How? Is my car totaled? Did I call…"

"No. Everything is alright. Don't worry about it. I took care of everything," Nick assured me.

A nurse came in and gave me some meds for the pain. I asked her what happened to me.

"Well darlin'," she began in a sweet southern drawl. "You were hit by a car and luckily this guy was there and was able to call 911 quickly. You had a few cracked ribs, a broken arm, and some cuts and bruises. It could have been worse, but the driver was looking for a spot to park in and not driving that fast. He said you came out of nowhere."

Before I could ask how I even got in the road, my parents and my sister came rushing into the room. My mama came right to my bedside and my daddy stood behind her. Midori stood at the foot of the bed.

"Monica, are you okay, baby? We've talked to the doctor. Do you need anything?" my mama rattled off.

"I'm okay, mama. I think. I just hurt a lot," I said quietly trying to calm her down. I'm sure I looked as bad as I felt but if I was calm, then she would be, too.

"Nick, thanks for staying with her. We really appreciate it," my daddy said while standing to shake Nick's hand. Nick returned the gesture, but his eyes shifted all over the room.

"So, you're not going to tell them what really happened?"

We all looked towards the door and saw Dre there.

"Who are you? And what do you mean what really happened?" my daddy questioned.

"Hey, man. This don't have anything to do with you," Nick said.

Dre chuckled a little and stepped closer into the room. "You're right. It doesn't but I think you owe it to Mo and her family to let them know you pushed her in the road."

The room got quiet and I began to recall everything that happened prior to me ending up here. Nick and I argued because he told me that in order for us to even talk, I had to quit Blaze. And he did push me, and I tripped. But it wasn't on purpose…right?

My daddy glared at Nick. "You said he did what? He pushed Monica into the road? On purpose?"

"Mr. Jesse, no. Not on purpose. And I didn't push her. I just tried to move her out of my way and she tripped into the road. It was an accident."

Out of nowhere, Midori was on Nick trying to beat his ass. Dre grabbed her by the waist and pulled her back, which was a struggle for him because she was swinging wildly. My mama screamed at Midori to stop and my daddy walked swiftly to where Nick was.

"Boy if you don't get your ass out of here I will beat the hell out of you! You've got some nerve!"

"Daddy!" I wanted to sit up, but I couldn't. "It really was an accident. At least I think it was. We were arguing, and he was mad, but I know he wouldn't have done that on purpose."

It wasn't until the words came out of my mouth that they probably didn't help as much as I needed them to. "Nick, just go. I know it wasn't on purpose, but you need to go."

"But, Mo- "Nick began.

"Boy get the hell out!" my daddy yelled.

Nick looked at me with somber eyes and when I refused to look at him, he hung his head in defeat and left.

With Nick out of the room, my mama asked me what happened, and I told them the story. The abbreviated version. I decided I needed to spare Dre the embarrassment of having my parents know that we had an all-out affair. Plus being judged for my decisions by my parents wasn't something I wanted to entertain today. Not when I was laid up in a hospital bed.

"Monica, you need to press charges against him and take out a restraining order. I'm not going to have this fool coming back and trying to finish the job," my daddy announced. Because I knew my daddy, I knew this was not really a request, but I wasn't going to do that.

"Daddy, it's not that serious. He's not a violent person. He doesn't mean to do things like this. I just keep making him mad and-"

"Wait," my mama interrupted. "What do you mean, you keep making him mad? Has something like this happened before?"

I avoided eye contact with everyone in the room and concentrated on the hideous pattern of the hospital gown. I never told anyone what happened that night he literally threw me out of his apartment. "No, mama. Nothing has happened before."

Even after the words left my mouth, I didn't believe me.

"Has he hit you before, Mo?" Dre asked me. The look on his face was a combination of anger and protection.

I sighed deeply and as much as I wanted to protect Nick, maybe I did need to take heed to what my daddy suggested. "No, he's never hit me. He threw me out of his apartment…literally pushed me out but he's never hit me. But it's my fault…I hurt him."

Dre looked at me and he understood what I meant. The anger left him, and his eyes still held the need to want to protect me. We couldn't say anything with my family in the room, but we both understood just being friends was going to be a difficult task.

Without warning, my daddy got up and left the room. My mama called after him, but he kept walking. Midori and Dre followed him. I couldn't imagine my daddy wanting to do any harm to Nick, but he was definitely upset. When they left the room, my mama probed me to tell her what really happened.

I broke down and let her know everything. From the fights Nick and I had, my involvement with Dre, what happened the night I went to Nick's apartment, and what happened today.

"Baby," my mama began. The tone she had was the one she used when she needed to dispense tough love. She'd spoken to me like this a number of times, so I knew what was coming next would probably hurt but it was necessary. "I can see why you are trying to justify what Nick did, but you can't make excuses for some else's behavior. It can start out simple enough and turn into, well, this."

I knew what she was saying was probably the truth but in the years I'd known Nick, he'd never done anything like this. Sure, he'd get mad but never like this. "But mama, I did this. I hurt him when I got involved with Dre."

"And you were dead wrong for that. But that doesn't give him the right to endanger your life. Baby, love doesn't give you ultimatums. Or put you in the hospital."

I sighed again, and my daddy, Dre, and Midori came back in the room. Midori and Dre looked amused, but my daddy was still pissed. "What happened?"

"Daddy almost got arrested!" Midori exclaimed.

"WHAT?" my mama and I asked in unison.

"Midori, don't be so dramatic. I did not almost get arrested. The security guard just told me I shouldn't threaten Nick in his presence."

"Daddy, what did you say to Nick?" I groaned.

"Mr. Jesse just let him know his daughter was not his punching bag. With a few choice words sprinkled in there," Dre stated causing Midori to cackle loudly.

Daddy was unphased. "I've called the police, so you can press charges and do the restraining order. And you're coming home to recover."

I rolled my eyes. As much as I wasn't happy with Nick right now, I did feel some of this was on me. I would not be taking his livelihood from him; I wasn't going to be that person. But I knew I had to give Jesse Mack something. He wasn't the type to be defied.

"Daddy, I am not going to press charges. We are over and I'm not trying to ruin his life. I will come home when I get out of here."

My daddy looked at me and I couldn't tell if he was angry with me or angry with Nick. Either way, I didn't like his scowl. "Okay, then."

He walked out again and this time, my mama followed him out. I sighed heavily and tried to stop the avalanche of emotions threatening to overtake me. More often than I wanted it to happen, I was being emotional and it was making me mad with myself for having this weakness.

"What's wrong, sis? Are you in pain?" Midori asked with concern.

Thankful she gave me the out; I admitted I was just sore and tired. She told me she was going to go find mama and daddy so that I could get some rest.

After she left, Dre asked," So tell me what's really wrong."

"I've made a complete mess of things! How is Blaze supposed to run without me? And oh God, Peaches quit! Shit! I can't go home. I'm going to have to- "

"Let me handle it. Between Nashonna and I, Blaze will be fine for a couple of days. Don't worry about Blaze; just get better."

If I'd never been grateful for having Dre around, I was now. He didn't know the ins and outs of Blaze, but he'd been around enough to know how to handle it. He walked over to me and kissed me on my forehead. The simple act was one of the most endearing things he'd ever done. I smiled involuntarily. Before he left, we locked eyes and I got weak. *Yeah, this just friends shit was for the birds.*

* * *

Being back in my parents' house was simultaneously a gift and a curse. My mama was waiting on me hand and foot, but she was smothering the shit out of me. I knew she meant well but every five minutes she was asking if I needed anything. I loved my mama but Jesus.

I did have to admit, it was great to be home and to be able to spend quality time with my parents. Since the incident with Midori, we spoke here and there but now we were able to talk. We were sitting in the living room watching Family Feud when my phone rang. It was Nashonna and I went into a panic.

"Shonna? What's wrong?" Before I left Atlanta, I made my mama take me to Blaze so I could give Nashonna a crash course on the behind the scenes at Blaze. I showed her how to make deposits, how to do the schedule and how to inventory to see what needed to be ordered. I let Swan order his own stuff to keep Nashonna from being overwhelmed. For the most part, she was doing the damn thing. I was impressed with how quickly she caught on.

"Nothing is wrong. Just giving you an update. Quan is out sick with the flu, but Tank and Swan said they could handle the kitchen without him. Taz has been late every day this week and I know I don't have the power to do anything to her, but you may need to call her. She's throwing everything off. I've had a few customers ask what you were planning for Christmas since you did the Thanksgiving dinner. I know you had some ideas but with the accident, I don't know how you want to handle this. In the very least, I'd say set up a toy drop off or adopt a family for Christmas. My cousin works with foster kids and she said they could use help buying gifts. My suggestion would be to post wish lists and get the customers to buy for that kid."

The more Nashonna talked, the more confident I was in not being there. She was definitely handling

Blaze. "You do have the power to say something to Taz. Tell her that if she is late again without a legitimate reason, she will be terminated. Tell her she can call me but I'm going to tell her the same thing. I like the foster kid idea. Go ahead and work on that. I'll contact Pastor Billings and see if his congregation would be willing to help with that. I'll get with you later this week to iron out the details."

"Okay, Mo. How are you feeling?"

"Still sore but I'm good," I said.

"That's good to hear! I'll let you know what happens with Taz."

"Bet. Oh and Nashonna…thanks so much for what you're doing. I know Blaze is in good hands with you. You stepped up to the plate and knocked it out of the park. I can recover because I can depend on you."

"Awww thanks, Mo. But Dre has been a big help as well. He told me not to tell you, but he's been here almost every day."

I talked to Dre almost every day and he never mentioned he was going to Blaze every day. "Well, you're doing an excellent job. Let me know when you have the details."

Nashonna and I hung up and I called Pastor Billings. He didn't answer so I left him a message with our plans. When I hung up, my daddy was staring at me.

"What?" I figured I must have used profanity. I had to work really hard to not curse in front of my parents.

"I never really got your job, but you are really running things like the boss, huh?"

I laughed at my daddy. "Yes, sir, I am the boss."

"I'm proud of you."

As soon as those four words registered with me, a tear slid down my face. I tried to wipe it away quickly. Hearing that my daddy was proud of me made me feel accomplished, like I won the highest honor in owning a business. My daddy got up and kissed me on my forehead, and I saw my mama smile.

I knew this was his way of apologizing and it was then I remembered the dream I had about my brother. He said I was stuck in hurt and unforgiveness. I thought he was talking about Dre or even Nick. Never occurred to me that he was talking about my daddy. Now that forgiveness was in my heart, I was ready to go live my life.

Chapter Fourteen

Our Christmas toy drive was a huge success and Nashonna really knocked it out the park. She handled all the details, planned, and got with Pastor Billings in my absence. I was so grateful that she was there, and I told her so many times. I planned on talking to Dre to see if we could gift her with a pretty hefty bonus. I planned on giving everyone a bonus, but she deserved a little extra.

After Christmas, I was back in Atlanta. I was thankful it was my arm that was broken and not my leg because I'd be miserable if I had to be immobile. Christmas was simple, nothing like my childhood Christmas'. Keyalani came down to spend the day with me and we, along with Midori, had a blast talking in our pajamas and eating ice cream. I even took her on a tour of good ol' Americus and saw some people I hadn't seen in a very long time. My niece came over and it warmed my heart to see how well she was doing. It was so simple, but it was the break that I needed from my life. It also made me realize I needed to come home more often.

I loved Atlanta. I loved being in the city and having the amenities of city life. But Americus was slower. Not necessarily in a bad way. There was no traffic to battle. I could go in Wal-Mart and see everyone and their grandma. I could go eat at Madea's or get a chicken box from Chevron. I could ride by Boone Park and see kids playing basketball and playing on the playground. I could see the Lee Street walkers getting their miles in. I could ride by Dorthea's and see all the cars of women getting their hair done. I could go downtown to Center Stage Market and get natural, organic food. I could go to the Legion on Highway 49 and then go to Juniors for a pork chop sandwich. For the first time in my life, I missed home when I went back to Atlanta. I thought I had outgrown my hometown but every now and again I needed to go home to be revived by small town living.

It was three days before New Year's and I was trying to throw together a New Year's Eve party. I knew it wasn't going for my usual Mo Mack experience, but I had to do something for my customers. I was scrambling to get cases of wine and all the ingredients Swan needed for our special menu. Midori was going to decorate, and I sent her out with my business credit card to get what she needed. Gabby made my flier and I was sharing it like crazy on social media. I was praying we could pull this off without people feeling like it was half-assed.

I had just got off the phone with the liquor guy and I was relieved he could fill my order on such short notice. Everything was coming together, and I could breathe a little easier knowing I could cross that off my list. I was sitting back in my chair with my eyes closed trying to fight through the pain of my cracked ribs. My doctor cleared me to work as long as I took it easy. Today, Midori and I walked around trying to figure out decorations and I think I over did it. I was trying not to take pain meds because they made me drowsy. The knock at my door distracted me from the pain.

I opened my eyes and saw Nick standing in my doorway. I immediately tensed up and fear washed over me. He'd been calling and texting me non-stop, but I refused to talk or respond to his texts. He hadn't reached out to me in a few days, so I thought he finally got the message. Apparently not.

"Mo, can we talk?" he asked quietly. It didn't matter to me that his eyes didn't give me any reason to be afraid. My relationship with Nick wasn't abusive, but right now I remembered what my mama told me in the hospital.

"Nick, that isn't a good idea. I want you to leave. Please," I pleaded. I wasn't sure if he heard me because my voice was quiet and shaky.

"Please? We need to talk." He came closer to me and I began to sweat profusely. I wanted to scream but I was afraid of what he would do. I couldn't run because he was standing in the door way.

"No. Leave."

Before Nick could come any closer, Swan appeared in my door. "Hey, Mo, we need…"

He paused when he saw Nick in my office. I had never been more relieved to see anyone in my life. My staff knew what happened to me and Swan looked like he was ready to throw Nick out of Blaze. And I wouldn't object if he did.

"Are you alright, Mo?" Swan asked.

I didn't want to speak so I just shook my head no which provoked Swan to action.

"Hey, man, let's go. She doesn't want you here."

Nick scoffed at Swan. "This ain't got nothing to do with you. I'm just here to talk."

"I wouldn't give a damn if you were here to sell Girl Scout cookies. Mo said she doesn't want you here, so you need to take your ass on."

Nick didn't address Swan, he turned to talk to me. "Monica, listen. Things went south, and I know I was wrong but if it wasn't for you fucking that dude, we wouldn't be here. So, you owe me this!"

Swan left my office, leaving me perplexed and more afraid than when Nick came in. I started breathing heavy as Nick came closer to me.

"Monica, look. We can work this out. I can forgive you if you just talk to me!"

Breathing became more difficult and I couldn't catch my breath. I couldn't form words. I needed Nick to move away from me, so I could breathe. He was standing too close to me and I'd never been afraid of Nick, or any man before.

Swan reappeared in my office with Tank and Quan. "I told you to get the fuck out!"

Nick was about to yell until he saw Tank and Quan there. They all had the same "I wish this nigga would" look on their face.

Nick laughed, probably to mask his fear. Or anger. "This is probably why your ex left. You are so full of shit-"

Nick didn't get to finish his statement because Swan grabbed him and forcibly pulled him out of my office. Tank and Quan helped get him out and I was still unable to move. They were all yelling and cursing so loudly that Nashonna came to my office to see what the commotion was.

"Mo, are you okay?" she rushed around to my desk and rubbed my back. I was still having a hard time breathing and my struggle to catch my breath was making my chest hurt. "Calm down, calm down. Just breathe. It's alright. You're fine. Deep breaths, Mo. Deep breaths. There you go. Good. Just calm down."

Nashonna's calmness was doing the trick and I was slowly able to catch my breath. My kitchen crew came back in to check on me.

"You okay? I doubt you'll have to worry about him again."

"She's fine guys. Give her a second," Nashonna said. "Can someone bring her some water?"

Tank left my office and returned with a bottle of water. I took a few sips and felt myself coming back to normal. I had no idea what that feeling was, but I prayed I never had to go through that again.

"Thank you, guys. I'm okay. I'm just gonna sit here for a little while and then go home."

"Can you call Keyalani to come get you? I don't know how I feel about you driving," Nashonna informed me.

"No, I promise I'm fine. I'm going to sit for a second. I'll be cool."

"Mo, what happened?"

We all turned at the sound of Dre's voice. I was glad to see him, but I really didn't want him to know what happened.

"Nothing. I'm fine," I lied.

Swan wasn't participating in my lies. "Okay nothing. Nick showed up and we had to throw him out."

Dre cocked his head to the side as if he couldn't believe that Nick was brave enough to show his face. "And did what? Did he put his hands on you, Mo?"

"Nah, dude. If he would have even came close I would have bust that nigga in his shit!" Quan spat. I believed him whole heartedly. Quan had a criminal history and I knew he used to be about that life. He hadn't been in trouble in a while, but I was sure he'd go back if need be. I didn't want to be the reason he added to his rap sheet.

"So, what happened then?" Dre asked perturbed.

Swan gave him the rundown. Dre stared at me and I averted my eyes. I hated this fear that Nick put in me. I wasn't like this. I wasn't a daredevil by any means but there were few things I feared. A few minutes ago, I almost stopped breathing because Nick was close to me.

"Nashonna, do you have Blaze tonight?" Dre asked.

"Of course. She said she wanted to go home but I wasn't comfortable with her driving."

"I'll take her home," Dre told her.

Absently, I started to gather my things to get ready to leave. It was funny…Nick had to damn near beg me to leave Blaze. Now I'm leaving with no argument because of him.

Thirty minutes later I was at Dre's house sitting on his sofa. He tried to get me to lie down but I was much more comfortable sitting up. I hadn't mastered the art of sleeping with a broken arm and cracked ribs yet. I was still trying to work on plans for New Year's Eve, but my pain meds were kicking in and making me sleepy.

"Hey, Mo you sure you don't want to try get in the bed?" Dre asked. He had changed out of his suit and was now lounging in a wife beater and pajama pants.

He could rock a suit like nobody's business, but this man could wear a shower curtain and be sexy.

"No, I'm going to sleep here. It's hard to sleep in a bed."

" Do you mind if I sit here with you then?"

"It's your house," I laughed. "I can't tell you no."

"I guess you're right," Dre said as he sat down next to me.

Dre moved my feet and placed them on his lap. He started rubbing my feet and I closed my eyes. His hands felt amazing.

"So, how are you? Really?" he asked, interrupting my peace.

"I'm okay. Now. Earlier...I don't know what happened. I think I had a panic attack. I've never experienced that before."

"Have you given any more thought to what your pops asked you to do? I think a restraining order may be necessary."

I sighed heavily. He might be right. I really didn't feel like Nick would intentionally hurt me but the way he made me feel today...

"I'll think about it. I just don't want to make a decision that could ruin his career if he's just hurt right now. Once he gets out of his feelings, I think he'll be fine."

"I'm not trying to tell you what to do. I'm just saying...I want you to be safe."

"A restraining order is just a piece of paper. How is that going to keep me safe?"

"Monica, it will send him the message that you are done. Unless…"

"Unless what?"

He spoke without looking at me. "You don't want to be done with him."

"After today, I have no doubt we are done. I can't be in a relationship with someone that I'm afraid of."

"Are you afraid of me?" Dre asked.

His question sat on my tongue and refused to budge. My silence irritated him, and he got up from the sofa. He went into the kitchen and I heard him rumbling around in the fridge. I sighed heavily and got up.

"Dre, listen," I said.

"Nah, it's cool. I'll bring you a blanket. I'm going to bed." Dre grabbed a bottle of water out of the fridge and kissed me on the forehead. He left me standing in the kitchen. I made my way back to his sofa to sift through my thoughts. A few seconds later, he brought me a comforter and a pillow.

"Dre," I called before he could leave the room.

"You don't have to say anything. I tried to shoot my shot and you shut it down. Nothing to say."

"But it's not because of you. I just…I have too much going on and I don't want to involve you in it."

Dre chuckled and came to kiss me on the forehead again. "Mo, I've been with you during most of your mess. Most of your mess has been because of me. You're not involving me; I'm asking to be here."

He left the room, turning off the light in the process. I was so tired and drained that I should have fallen asleep quickly, but my mind was running a mile a minute.

Dre was right. He'd been there for a minute. Through all of my stuff. But the fact that he lied to me about his past and his relationship with Peaches was a glaring red flag. I didn't know what else I didn't know about him.

But I'd let him inside of my body. Being with Dre sexually wasn't just sex. It was mind blowing. He didn't make love to me, he commanded me, he controlled me. I've never experienced that with a man before and as much as it was scary, it was also exciting. I loved the passion. I loved the way he learned my body and made it obey him. I loved…him?

No. No. Noooooo. That was impossible right? I was just with Nick. And I loved him. At least I think I did. What I thought was opposites attracting was really incompatibility. It wasn't that we had different tastes in food or music. At our core, our values were different. He wanted a wife to be home when he got there with dinner waiting. He wanted a woman that would give up her life to make him happy. He thought my happiness should be found in being a wife and a mother.

Dre understood my business. He got that Blaze wasn't a 9-5 business. With the time I took off recently, I knew I could delegate to Nashonna but I really enjoyed my job. I loved being able to provide the Mo Mack Experience to people. Most of my customers have been coming to Blaze for years. I'd been invited to weddings, graduations, birthday parties, even funerals. I loved the connections I made with people. I was created to do what I do. Dre understood that but that didn't mean I needed to date him. Or even admit that I have feelings for him.

After an hour of wrestling with my thoughts, sleep finally won and I drifted off.

It seemed that as soon as I fell asleep, I felt someone waking me. "Mo, Mo, get up."

I tried to push whoever was calling my name off of me, but I was having no such luck. "No!"

"Monica, get up. It's Blaze. We have to go."

I sat up and when I saw Dre's face, I knew something was wrong. "What happened?"

"Fire. Let's go," he spoke gravely and helped me up.

The entire drive from Stone Mountain to Midtown was nerve racking. I kept nervously shaking my leg and Dre kept placing his hand on my leg to try to calm me down. I kept telling myself that it was just a small kitchen fire. Or nothing major. But nothing could have prepared me for what I saw when we pulled up.

There were a dozen fire trucks and fire fighters battling the fire that had engulfed my bar. Dre had to hold me up to keep me from falling. I watched in horror as my business, my baby, a Midtown gem was disappearing right in front of my eyes. My only comfort was that it was 5 o'clock in the morning and there were no customers or staff in the building.

After the fire was out, the fire fighters did a walk through to make sure no one was in there. The fire chief came to talk to me and if Dre wasn't there, I wouldn't have been able to form two sentences.

"You the owner?" The fire chief asked.

I nodded my head to affirm.

"Hey, I'm Chief Carlson. I'm sorry this happened to you. We're going to continue to do our walk through.

Do you have a card with your contact information? We'll keep you updated on what we find."

"What do you mean what you find? This wasn't a kitchen fire?"

"I'm not really sure right now, ma'am. Because it's a business, we want to rule out any foul play."

"You think someone did this to me? You think someone intentionally set my bar on fire?" I was about to become hysterical because Nick was the first person that popped into my head.

"I'm not saying anything yet, ma'am. I'm just saying that we need time to look around. Do you have a card?"

I shook my head that I did until I realized I didn't get my purse out of the car.

"Here, take my card," Dre said once he saw I had no cards to give. He reached in his back pocket and pulled out his wallet. He handed Chief Carlson a card. "I'm her business partner. If you have any questions or anything you can call me. I'll put you in touch with her."

Chief Carlson took the card and hurried towards the space that used to be my building.

"Come on, Mo. There's nothing else we can do here. Let's go to your place since it's closer."

Absently, I let Dre lead me back to his car. We made the short drive to my condo and once inside, I went straight to my sofa. I curled up and stared into nothing.

Dre came to sit beside me and placed his arm around me. His presence made me feel protected. Even in the midst of the tragedy I experienced tonight, I was comforted in just being with him. I snuggled up close to him and rested my head on his shoulder.

"Mo, don't worry. We'll be okay."

"How? Blaze is gone! What am I gonna do now?" I asked. I never planned for this. I never thought about life without Blaze. I had no backup. I had no other options. I had nothing.

"I don't know baby but we'll make it. I promise."

"We?"

"Yes, we," Dre informed me. "We are business partners. And even if you need to tell yourself otherwise, we are friends. I'm not going to let you go through this alone. I care too much about you to let that happen."

Hearing him admit what I'd suspected was simultaneously refreshing and scary. I was barely single and here I was letting my heart get involved with another man. I was also battling the fact that he was less than truthful with me about his past and Peaches. I had no idea how to trust him. Besides…since I met him, my life had been turned upside down.

"You know," I said sitting up. "It seems like since I met you, my life has been on a downward spiral. Nothing is going right.

Dre stared at me and his faced morphed into anger. "You're saying I did this? I set Blaze on fire?"

"No, that's not what I'm saying. But ever since we started doing business together, so much negative has happened to me. My sister tried to kill herself. I got negative publicity at Blaze. Peaches, the person that had been with me the longest quit, my boyfriend broke up with me. I got hit by a car. My business is destroyed."

"So you're saying all of this is my fault? All of this is because of me? You're a real piece of work, Mo," Dre said getting up.

"I'm not necessarily saying this is your fault, but I can't ignore this."

Dre looked at me and shook his head. "I can't take you seriously. All I did was help you expand your business and somehow, I get blamed for your fucked up life. No matter how I tried to help you. No matter how I was there for you. No matter how I loved you. All you can focus on is the negative."

Did I hear him right? "You love me?"

Dre looked at me like I spoke a foreign language. I'm assuming he didn't mean to let that slip out. "Mo, don't worry about it. If the fire chief calls, I'll let you know."

Dre left me sitting on my sofa trying to make sense of what just happened. I wasn't necessarily surprised that he felt that way about me but hearing it made it real. Right now just wasn't the time for that. I appreciated Dre for being there for me, even more so for how he bolstered my business, but what I said was true. After going into business with Dre, my whole life was turned upside down. There were some good moments but the bad overwhelmingly outweighed the good. Being in a relationship with Dre wouldn't be good for me. So why did I want to call him and beg him to come back?

* * *

Midori and I were sitting on my sofa watching *Love and Basketball*. The side eye I gave my sister when she told me she had never seen the movie was epic. Then, I felt like a failure for not being there and making her watch this classic. Granted, she was only four when the movie came out, but at some point she should have watched it. In between answering her questions about the film, I quizzed her on other movies that she should have seen, and I became more and more disappointed.

"OOOOOOOO, NO HE DIDN'T!! He went out with that other chick? Man, I swear...I would have fought everyone there!"

I laughed at her dramatics and could hardly wait until the end. She and KJ were still going strong so I knew she was going to love the happy ending. Spending time with my sister like this was refreshing. I hated it took tragedies to make us closer but nevertheless, I am grateful I wised up.

My doorbell rang and I got up to get the Uber eats order from Tin Lizzy's. Whoever came up with Uber eats deserves a Nobel peace prize. It's one of the greatest things that ever happened to me in my life, especially since I was still recovering. I didn't have to send Midori out to battle Atlanta traffic just to get something to eat and we had more choices than just pizza and Chinese delivery. This was the best thing since sliced bread.

I opened the door and was disappointed it wasn't my Uber eats order, but I was pleasantly surprised to see Dre. After I blamed him for my life the other day, he hadn't spoken two words to me. I was hurt but I didn't expect him to talk to me after everything I said.

"Dre, hey, what's up?" I said while opening the door and inviting him in. Dre stepped inside and I could tell that something was wrong. I tried to brace myself but I knew whatever he was going to say wasn't going to be good.

"The fire chief called me today," he stated with somberness in his voice. "We're going to have to go downtown tomorrow and talk to the fire chief."

"For insurance purposes?"

"Yes and no. Yes we need to discuss the insurance but we need to go talk to him for another reason."

He was dragging out what he had to tell me and it was frustrating me. "What aren't you saying Dre? Just spit it out."

He sighed heavily and looked me with hurt in his eyes. "Mo, there's no easy way to tell you this."

"Just tell me!" I raised my voice and Midori came out of the living room to see what was going on.

"Monica, the fire was arson."

Chapter Fifteen

Talking to the arson investigators was one of the most draining experiences I've had to go through. After they ruled me and Dre out as suspects, they went through my entire staff asking questions.

"Ms. Mack," Mr. Anderson, the fire investigator began. I wasn't happy with him insinuating one of my employees did this. I was over this man. "Is there anyone you can think of that did this? Anyone that you made mad? Someone that was fired recently? Anyone at all?"

My first response was to give him a resounding no but then I remembered Lisa Smith. "There was a woman making posts on social media about Blaze. I am sure it was a fake page."

"Did you report the page?"

"I didn't. It was sporadic and mostly bullsh-I mean nothing but someone with too much time on their hands."

"Are the posts still up?"

"I'm not sure but I have screen shots," I replied. I showed him the posts and he quickly handed my phone back to me.

"I'm not sure this person escalated to arson, but we will definitely check it out. Anyone else you can think of that would do this? Or had reason?"

"The only person that left Blaze recently was Peaches. But I didn't fire her, she quit."

"Tell me the circumstances around her quitting," Mr. Anderson queried with his pen prepared to scribble down what I said.

I told him the situation and didn't really care if Dre was uncomfortable. When I looked at him, he didn't seem fazed.

"Okay, we will need her contact information. Anyone else you can think of?"

"No. And I don't see Peaches doing this either. I mean, she quit but that was been before Christmas. I seriously doubt she would do this." *Would she?*

"We're not putting anything past anyone. We'll be in touch."

I stood to leave but Dre remained seated. "Aren't you forgetting someone?"

I turned around to look at him and tried to figure out what he was talking about. "Who?"

"Nick," Dre responded calmly.

"Oh my God, Dre! Seriously?" I rolled my eyes at him, flabbergasted that he would even consider Nick was capable of this.

"Who is Nick?" Mr. Anderson asked me.

"He's my ex-boyfriend."

"Mr. Restin, is there a reason you mentioned Nick?"

"Yeah, Dre. Is there a reason?" I couldn't believe he was using this arson investigation to show his jealous side.

"Oh nothing except he never wanted you to work at Blaze. He came to Blaze to tell you that in order for you two to get back together, you needed to quit. Not to mention he's the reason you have cracked ribs and a broken arm." Dre looked at me quizzically as if he couldn't believe I didn't consider Nick.

"Dre, that's bullshit and you know…" I grew quiet as what he said begin to register with me. He did tell me Blaze was one of the reasons we weren't together. He blamed my business on us not being married and having children. He despised my job. But not enough to burn it down, right?

"Monica, I'm not saying he did it. I'm just saying, he had reason."

Mr. Anderson looked back and forth between Dre and I. I'm sure he figured this was more than a business relationship. "I'm going to need his information as well."

* * *

My head was swirling with the possibility that either Nick or Peaches could have done this to me. Or even this Lisa Smith person. Whoever she was. As much as I wanted to be alone, Dre didn't think that was a good idea because if the arson team went to talk to Nick, Nick could come after me. I just didn't want to believe Nick was capable of this. But then again…he did push me into oncoming traffic. I had convinced myself it was an accident, but now I wasn't so sure.

Dre and I were at his house going over the insurance policy and talking to the insurance reps about our claim. Because it was now ruled an arson, we were having to deal with the insurance company in a different light. Blaze was a total loss. Nothing was salvageable. My insurance representative was nice enough to inform me that they would also be conducting their own investigation. This was a nightmare and I was just ready for this whole thing to be over.

We hung up after an almost hour-long conversation with my insurance rep. I was drained. "I think this is an insurance tactic. Make you so frustrated with the hoops you have to go through that you give up and say fuck the claim. This is ridiculous."

"Insurance is a scam anyway," Dre explained. "You pay your premium and then when you need them, they give you the runaround."

I sighed heavily, left the table, and went to go sit on his sofa. I really wanted a glass of wine but Dre didn't have any at his house and I wasn't about to go out. Dre followed me to the sofa but sat a safe distance from me.

"I'm just over it all. We are being treated like criminals when we pay out of ass for insurance. Now, I'm being punished for trying to use it."

"So many people have tried to get over on insurance companies. But we were making money so if they are coming with an insurance fraud angle, we don't have to worry about that."

"Yeah, I guess. I just hate we have to go through hell and high water for this." Dre looked at me and even though I blamed him for where I was in my life, his eyes still did something to me.

"Have you given any thought to what you want to do?" Dre asked.

"What do you mean?"

"Rebuild? Move? Take the money and run?"

"Rebuild, definitely," I responded quickly. There wasn't a doubt in my mind. What I told Nick was the truth: I had no desire to do anything else. Blaze was my baby.

"I knew you'd say that. So I've started looking at available spaces in Midtown, downtown and even a little further out. I know you love being a part of the Midtown scene, but I think you'll like some of the other spaces."

I looked at Dre, surprised that he was three steps ahead of me. While I was lamenting my loss, he was out making moves. I was impressed. But I wasn't up for moving out of Midtown.

"I really want to stay in Midtown. My condo is there. I'm familiar with the area. Blaze was around for ten years. If we move, we could lose some of the loyal customers."

"I get that and those are valid reasons to stay in the area. Nothing is set in stone. We can go look on Wednesday to see if anything piques your interest."

I smiled at him. In the midst of one of the most devastating events of my life, Dre was giving this situation a silver lining. "Okay, Wednesday will work. I have nothing but time now."

"Alright, I'll call you around ten."

We sat in silence. I engrossed myself in my phone but I knew he was watching me. I wanted to apologize for what I said to him but I still felt as if my life went down when he came into it. At the same time, I had never felt this connected to a man before. I wasn't sure what side was going to win.

I was debating on whether or not to apologize to Dre when my phone rang with Midori's ring tone. "Hey sis, what's up?"

"Mo, where are you?"

"I'm at Dre's. What's wrong?"

"Nick came by."

The tone of Midori's voice let me know his visit wasn't a good one. "What happened? What did he say?"

"Nothing. He just asked where you were and that he really needed to talk to you."

It was apparent that Mr. Anderson questioned him about the arson. "Are you okay? Did he say anything else?"

"No that was it. He looked...I don't know. Sad I guess?"

I felt a pang of hurt because I knew in my heart of hearts that he wouldn't burn down Blaze. I started to question why he didn't call me but I forgot I blocked him on everything. "I'm going to call him. Thanks sis."

I hung up with Midori and blocked my number then dialed Nick. As if he was expecting me to call, he answered immediately. "Nick, I heard you came by?"

Dre gave me a cold look, as if he couldn't believe I was talking to Nick. He got up leaving me in the living room alone.

"Yeah, why am I being questioned about Blaze burning down? And why was that the first I heard about it? You think I would do something like that?"

"Nick, I didn't accuse you of anything. They are investigating and going where the information leads them."

"What made you give them my name? Because of when I accidently pushed you? Come on, Mo. That's a stretch."

"Again, I am not accusing you. But it's not because of the *accidental* push. If anything, it would be because you told me I needed to quit Blaze in order for us to be together."

Nick grew quiet on the phone as if he forgot he said that. "Mo, I know what I said, but I didn't mean it. Not literally anyway."

"Yeah but-"

"Let me finish," Nick interrupted me. "Since I left the hospital, I've been doing some soul searching. I realized I was acting out of hurt and I made some terrible decisions. You hurt me and in turn, I did the same. I can't apologize enough. But I have realized that we aren't meant to be. We want two different things. That doesn't mean I'm right and you're wrong. It just means we want different things for our lives. And I was dead wrong for trying to force you into being who I needed. I loved you Mo but not really for who you were. More for who I thought I could make you. I'm sorry for everything I said and did to hurt you."

I was quiet as I took in all that he said. I was fully prepared to have to fight with him tonight. I wasn't expecting this. "Wow, Nick. I don't know what to say."

"You don't have to say anything. I just need you to know I am sorry. And I am truly sorry about Blaze."

"I'm sorry too, Nick. I know I hurt you and I wasn't right."

"I don't blame you, Mo. I pushed you away because I wanted you to be who I wanted you to be. It's not your fault. Just wanted you to know that."

Again, I was quiet. I couldn't doubt his sincerity because with everything that happened between us, Nick had every right to be pissed at me. Yet, here he was apologizing.

"I'll see you around. Take care of yourself."

Nick didn't even wait for me to hang up. I sat for a second taking in his spill before I went to the kitchen to talk to Dre.

"So let me guess, you have to go and work it out with your man." Dre replied snidely.

"Naw. Nothing like that."

I ran through the conversation I had with Nick and Dre raised his eyebrows at me. "You don't think he was just telling you that so you wouldn't suspect that it was him that burnt down your business?"

"I don't think so. Besides, even if I did believe him, that wouldn't stop the arson investigation."

Dre gave me a laugh that was laced sarcasm. He opened his mouth to speak but seemed to change his mind. Instead he left the room again. I was tired of following him around so I made myself comfortable at his island and pulled out my phone. I needed a distraction so I pulled up social media. The first post was enough to make me want to throw my phone.

> *Lisa Smith*
>
> *Someone finally took us all out of our misery! Blaze is literally blazed LMAO! Whoever did this is the real MVP and I want to celebrate with you. Mo Mack…take this as a lesson…you can't be involved in no foul shit and expect folks to take that lying down. Go on back to Americus and be the failure you are. And take Slay with you #GoodRiddance #BlazeHasBeenBlazed*

Who the hell was Slay? I was so sick of this Lisa Smith person. I took a screen shot, reported her page and blocked her because now that Blaze was gone, what else could she say. Whoever this person was was super salty but I had no idea why. I couldn't think of a single person that I pissed off to the point that my business burning down brought her joy. I was so over it. I started to go find Dre to tell him about it but I decided against it. I went to the living room and curled up on his sofa, which was uncomfortable because my ribs were still a little sore. Instead I sat up and leaned my head back and closed my eyes.

So many things were floating around in my head that I was developing a massive headache. From Nick's apology, Dre assuming his apology was flawed, to fighting with the insurance company, the arson investigation, Blaze burning down and whatever vendetta Lisa Smith had against me. All I wanted to do was be a successful business owner. Scratch that. I wanted to be a successful black woman that owned a business. I wanted to give back to my community. I wanted to give the grown and sexy the Mo Mack Experience that included good food, good music, good drinks, and a good time. I wanted to be known in the Atlanta bar and lounge scene. Right now, I was a failure. That was one thing Lisa Smith got right.

"Mo, did you see this post?" Dre came into the living room and interrupted the thoughts that were running rampant.

"Yeah," I replied, not even bothering to open my eyes. "I'm over it. I don't want to deal with this right now. Or anymore."

I was definitely drained. My emotions were all over the place and all I wanted to do was run away and recharge. Matter of fact, that's exactly what I was going to do. I got my phone and went online to see what flight and hotel deals were available. Since I had no concrete destination in mind, I was open to going pretty much anywhere.

"We need to go to see Mr. Anderson. I know who Lisa Smith is."

* * *

"Are you sure? Are you absolutely sure?" Mr. Anderson queried.

"Yes. I'm Slay. In my former life, that's what people called me. Peaches loved that lifestyle. No one has called me that in years."

"So you're telling me she committed arson because of the history between you two?" Mr. Anderson looked skeptical as did I. I just didn't want to believe that Peaches was behind all of this.

"It makes sense, though," Dre explained. "When I walked into Blaze the first day, before I even approached Monica with our business deal, Peaches was there. She barely spoke to me. When I came back to talk business, again, she was nonchalant. It was when she suspected there was something more between Monica and I that all this stuff started going down."

I cut my eyes at Dre. "You suspected this? And you didn't tell me?"

"At the time, I didn't suspect anything. Once the deal was signed, she texted me and asked what my angle was. She didn't believe that I was legitimately just trying to make money. She thought that I was using Blaze to push drugs and she wanted in."

I was on the verge of cursing Dre all the way out but he held up his hand to stop me. "Mo, I know I should have told you. At the time you didn't know about my past and I worried you would have yanked the deal. I apologize. But after I told her I was done with that life, she told me I'd gone soft and she was glad she was over me. I didn't think anything else would come from it."

I thought back to how Peaches started acting once Dre came around. Surely her behavior was because she wasn't over him and her suspicions that we were sleeping together probably rubbed her the wrong way. So she tried to attack Blaze. And she was the one that sent Nick the pictures of Dre and I.

I walked over to Mr. Anderson's window and stared out of it. I couldn't believe that Peaches did this to me. Kevin told me to draw the line between friends and employees and I didn't listen. I trusted Peaches with Blaze. She had access to deposits and money but she didn't want that. She wanted me to suffer. She wanted me to hurt like she did. And if that was what she was going for, she certainly succeeded.

Chapter Sixteen

Keyalani and I were sitting at the courtyard pool at the Riviera Hotel on South Beach. While Georgia was battling cold temperatures, we were in Miami enjoying weather that was almost ninety degrees. It was a little after seven and we were taking advantage of the complimentary drinks. About thirty minutes ago, we indulged at Mas Cuba Café on the premises of the hotel.

Our two-queen suite was divine and we hadn't ventured from the hotel since we got there yesterday. The room looked like something straight out of an HGTV home makeover show. The art décor was stunning and a great back drop for helping me to unwind. We'd done nothing but eat and sleep. Even though Blaze had been gone for weeks, getting out of town was refreshing.

Keyalani coming with me proved to be one of the best things for me. We stayed up talking and laughing and she really helped to get my mind off everything. I was also grateful that she didn't bombard me with Blaze/Peaches/Dre business. When I asked her to come with me, I told her I needed a break from life. So she understood that talking about what happened would have to come on my terms.

We were people watching while enjoying the complimentary drinks from the bar. I had a drink at dinner so I was sipping my drink slowly because even though I wanted to be intoxicated, it was too early in the day to do so. We planned to go to Miami Beach after sunset. I was sipping my drink, loving the balance between the vodka and the cranberry. Sometimes bartenders either used too much vodka or too much cranberry; a good bartender could make the drink go down easy. Like Peaches.

I told myself I wasn't going to think about Blaze, Dre, Nick, or Peaches yet here I was. I was still in disbelief that she was the person that wanted to ruin me. After she was arrested, Peaches didn't deny anything. She was angry and she was hurt. She told the investigator that she just lost her mind for a second.

Peaches knew Dre when he was a big-time drug dealer. She loved that life, even when she almost took a charge for him. Even when she lost her child. For her, this was love. Drugs, fast money, cheating, hurt…this was what she was accustomed to. Once she saw Dre changed, how he was legit and how he was into me, she became frustrated that he wasn't like that with her. I became her enemy, not him. She figured that if we didn't have Blaze, there would be no more "us".

After she was arrested and sitting in jail, she became remorseful. Against, my better judgement, I went to go see her. She cried and apologized over and over. I believed she was sorry but I couldn't really forgive her. She planned and plotted to bring me down when I did nothing but treat her like family. What she did was unforgiveable. I left the jail and headed to the airport to catch my flight. Before we took off, I told Dre I was going out of town for a few days and I would call him when I got back. He asked me a lot of questions, but I put my phone on airplane mode and prepared for take-off.

I was almost done with my drink so we stopped by the bar to get another on our way to the beach. According to Google, it was about a ten-minute walk. We decided because the weather was decent we wouldn't use Uber and headed off to the beach. As soon as we stepped out of the hotel, we ran smack dab into Dre and Swan.

"In a rush?" he asked smiling at me.

Lani ran to Swan and practically jumped into his arms. I knew things were going great between them but this just solidified that she was really into him. I was glad to see my friend happy after having to deal with so many losers in her life. Swan wasn't her "type" but he treated her like a queen and she loved every second of it.

"What are you two doing here?" Even though I saw him damn near every day, the way he looked at me, the light of his eyes, the charm of his smile still got to me. Looking at him made me weak. It took a lot for me to pull myself together and act normal.

"Swan missed his woman and I didn't know how Keyalani was going to act with him popping up so I came. You know, for moral support," Dre explained.

Hearing his name, Swan whipped his head in our direction. "Really, Dre? You're gonna put this on me? You're the one that asked me to come with you!"

Dre smiled sheepishly. "Come on, Swan! Help a brother out!"

Lani and I laughed. I'm sure she was ecstatic to see her man while I was on the fence about Dre.

"Yeah, I wanted to know if you were alright. Since you weren't returning my texts or calls."

I was ignoring him because I was just drained with talking about Blaze and Peaches. "I just needed to recharge."

"I get that. I was just worried about you." His voice was earnest; I knew he was being truthful. I felt bad for disappearing; it pissed Nick off to no end but this was what I did. "Where are you guys headed?"

"To the beach. It's a ten minute walk." Keyalani announced with her arm entwined with Swan. I already knew that her support of me was done since Swan was here. I wasn't mad at all; she deserved to be happy and not have to pull me up out of my pit.

"Hey baby," Swan said to Lani. "Let us check in and then we will walk with you."

They left to go check in while Lani and I sat down in the lobby. Like our room, the lobby was tastefully decorated.

"Are you okay? With him being here? I swear I didn't know they were coming," Lani said.

"Yes, I'm fine," I informed her. "I love seeing you happy. You deserve this."

"Thank you, Mo. Swan is so different than anyone I've ever met. He's made me realize why no other relationship ever worked out. I think I love him."

Out of nowhere a tear fell from my eyes. I tried to wipe it away before Keyalani saw me but I had no such luck.

"Oh my God, Mo are you crying? Why?"

I laughed at her dramatics. "With all the shit that went down, this is the one good thing that's come out of it. You found love."

"Awww, Mo! That is so sweet. But maybe something else good can come out of this, too." She gave me a side eye while I rolled my eyes at her. "Listen, Dre cares about you. Maybe he was wrong for not telling you about Peaches but when everything fell down, he was the one there. He could have walked away, Mo, but he's still here."

I heard what she said and I shooed her away with my hand. The guys came down and we started our walk to the beach in silence. Once we got there, we found a semi empty spot. Swan pulled towels, a bottle of wine and cups from his book bag. Swan poured two cups for Dre and I and he and Lani moved a little further away from us. Dre spread out the towel and gestured for me to sit down.

Once we got settled, I was immediately taken in by the sound of the ocean. It was so peaceful, so relaxing. I was already starting to decompress.

"So how are you feeling?" Dre interrupted my serenity.

"If you don't mind, I don't want to talk about anything business related. I just want to relax," I informed him.

"Not a problem."

We continued to sit in silence. I think the ocean lulled us both into a space of peace. I'm not sure what Dre was thinking about but I knew I put this apology off long enough. I put my cup down and turned to him.

"Dre, I'm sorry." I announced breaking our quiet moment.

He turned to me and seemed almost perturbed that I interrupted his thoughts. "Sorry for what?"

"For saying my life went downhill after I started doing business with you. That was unfair of me."

"It's cool," he replied nonchalantly. "It's kind of true though. I wasn't honest with you and things got out of hand...it really was because of me."

"It kinda was," I laughed. "But I made the choice to get involved with you. Outside of a business relationship. So I have to take some responsibility myself."

"What do you want to do? About us?" he inquired.

I thought I heard him inhale sharply. As if my answer was going to make or break him. I really didn't know what I wanted to do. I couldn't deny that I had feelings for him but that didn't mean I needed to make a relationship out of it. "Dre, I don't know. I have feelings for you. I can admit that but...so much has happened. I really don't know."

"I understand, Mo. I'm not going to pressure you. The ball is in your court."

I was relieved to hear he wasn't going to pressure me. On one hand, I felt like I needed to take some time to get myself together. I needed to be alone and be single for a second. On the other hand, Dre had the potential to make me happy. I didn't want to risk losing him. Maybe Lani was right. I scooted closer to him and rested my head on his shoulder. His very presence was calming, almost like the ocean.

Once again, Dre and I were sitting comfortably in our peace when Swan and Lani announced they were going back to the hotel. It then dawned on me that I was going to have to spend the night with Dre. Lani looked at me with pleading eyes. There was no way I could deny her this. I rolled my eyes indicating that I was going to take one for the team. Swan and Lani couldn't leave fast enough.

"Looks like it's just me and you. Anything in particular you want to do?" he asked.

"I'm fine right here for now," I answered. I rested my head on his shoulder again. Dre and I sat on the beach for another thirty minutes before he announced he was hungry. He pulled up restaurants in the area and decided on Sylvano's because it wasn't too far from our hotel. I wasn't too hungry but I decided I could just get an appetizer. After looking over the menu, we decided on the prosciutto and mozzarella pizza.

We made small talk and drank wine until our food arrived. I wasn't hungry but the pizza was so good that I couldn't stop myself from eating two slices. I heard Mas Cuba Café had good breakfast but I would be eating this pizza in the morning.

We wrapped up our meal and made our way back to the hotel. Since Swan and Lani hijacked my room, Dre and I made our way to the room he was supposed to share with Swan. When we walked in, I was stunned. The room was a suite and it was magnificent. I thought our room was nice, but this one was absolutely gorgeous. There was a living room and a separate bedroom where I found my stuff tucked away in the corner. It was then that I knew this was all planned.

"I'm gonna kill Lani," I announced playfully.

"Don't kill her. I begged her. Profusely," Dre said closing the space between us. "I know I said I wasn't going to pressure you but Mo...I'm in love with you."

I was quiet as I tried to take in his words. They rested in my head and slowly begin to travel to my heart. "Dre, I'm...I'm scared."

"I messed up with you one time before. I promise I'm not going to do it again. I know this isn't the best situation but I promise that the way I feel about you is real."

Instead of answering, I threw caution to the wind and kissed Dre. I think I caught him off guard but he quickly recovered and kissed me with the intensity I remembered. He led me to the bed where he made love to me, not in the gentle way this moment began. Instead, Dre controlled me and commanded me in the fashion that let me know that not only did he admire my body but he also wanted inside my heart.

Chapter Seventeen

One year later...

This was my second grand opening but this didn't stop me from being nervous. We were opening our new bar and lounge, Diamond Ultra Bar and Lounge. It was basically Blaze 2. We made changes to the décor but most of the other things were the same. This space was bigger with space for Karaoke, open mic, and small concerts with local artists. We also added a pool hall and darts. We were fortunate enough to be able to stay just outside of Midtown but the buzz on social media was that our location wasn't an issue; folks were just ready to get back to the Mo Mack Experience.

After the arson investigation, the insurance had no leg to stand on and had to pay out. We looked into remaining in the same space but it would cost so much more to gut it and start over because the smoke damage was so bad. Diamond Ultra was a standalone building and that alone sold me.

Dre and I decided on Diamond Ultra because diamonds form under pressure. After everything that happened in the last year, we were definitely tested and fortunate to come out as diamonds. After the getaway in Miami, Dre and I decided to give our relationship a chance. So far, I had no regrets. Because he lived in Stone Mountain, Dre practically moved in with me while we were getting Diamond Ultra up and running.

It's funny that I fought Nick tooth and nail on this, but with Dre it just came so easily. At the time, I didn't know what was stopping me from moving in with Nick but part of it was his pressure. Dre and I worked well together. We could work most of the day together at Diamond Ultra then come home and decompress or talk business. There wasn't a demand for me to be anything but the business woman I was born to be.

My sister and KJ found their own place and I thought I was going to be relieved that she was gone but I missed her. I made it a point to take a day or two out of my week to do something with her, even if it was nothing but ordering a pizza and having a Netflix day on a Sunday. She had a small break down about three months ago when she became overwhelmed with school. Because she still went to therapy, she was able to recognize she was slipping and went to an in-patient facility for a few days. It was difficult to see her there but I was relieved she had the willpower to get herself help.

We had our soft opening two weeks ago and tonight was our grand opening. Dre came across a few deals on houses so he was doing a few flips in the middle of getting Diamond Ultra ready. I called him a few times today, ensuring he was going to be here tonight. He assured me, for the millionth time, that he would.

My sister was old enough to come to my place now and I was so happy to see her walk through the door. I fully expected her to come in with KJ but she brought some girls from class with her. I imagined part of it was to do things without him but the other part was to show them what she did. As with Blaze's remodel, Midori handled the decorations at Diamond Ultra. I was beyond proud of what she did and my customers raved about the décor.

Finally around 8:30, Dre came in followed by Keyalani. I told her to be here around 6 and I wasn't surprised she was late. She was six months pregnant and either there was another baby hidden in there or she was going to have a big son. Swan was ecstatic to be having his first kid, a son at that.

Keyalani came to give me a hug before going to the kitchen to speak to her man. Dre and I were walking around and greeting customers when I heard the music change from the hip hop medley Tyrin was spinning to "Never Letting Go" by Anthony Hamilton. While I loved the song, I had no idea why Tyrin was playing it.

I was about to head to the booth but Dre stopped me. Out of nowhere, I heard Swan's voice over the speaker.

"Keyalani, you are the most amazing woman I've ever met. You carrying my son is one of the best gifts a man could ever ask for. But there is only one thing missing."

I finally saw Swan walking towards Keyalani who was sitting in one of the oversized chairs near the bar. Once he made it to her, I saw tears running down her face. Swan walked to her, dropped to one knee, and donned a ring. Immediately my water works started and Dre came behind me and wrapped his arms around my waist. Swan put the microphone down so we couldn't hear the rest of his speech but whatever he said made her drop her head and cry harder. Finally, he slipped the ring on her finger. He helped pull her up, feigning like it was so hard which caused everyone to laugh. He hugged her as tight as he could to the cheers from everyone in Diamond Ultra.

I ran over to Keyalani and hugged her tightly. "Oh my God Lani!! I'm so happy for you!"

"Mo, did you know about this?" she asked while wiping tears. Swan stood proudly by her side, almost refusing to leave Lani's side.

"I didn't. I had no clue. Swan, you could have let me know!"

"Nah, Mo. I know you women can't hold water sometimes. I couldn't risk you letting it slip."

I hit him playfully and hugged him too. "This is because of you two," Swan said motioning to Dre and I. "If it wasn't for you two, I never would have met my fiancé or have a son on the way."

Even with everything that happened in the last year, this moment let me know it was all worth it. Everything around me came falling down but out of the debris came something worthwhile and beautiful. With Dre by my side, I knew that I was doing what I was meant to do and that I was with who was meant for me.

Acknowledgments

I cannot believe I am here already...book number 2! This is surreal, but it wouldn't be possible with my amazing support system...

To my parents Joseph West and Bishop James and Ossie Lundy: There aren't enough words to describe how grateful I am for you guys. Mama, thank you so much for your encouraging words and for your support for my first book. I love you!

To Trabian, Tyler, and Jade: I couldn't ask for better children. You guys have been my motivation and my reason for working as hard as I do. I want you guys to know that your dreams are obtainable and I will be right here to support you when you smash those goals! I love you guys to the moon and back.

To Jamaal...babe you have been my rock for years and I don't know what I would do without you in my corner. You are my peace, my strength, my sounding board, my encourager. If I've ever wondered what love is, this is it. I love you, King.

To my sister Amy: Thank you for everything! I love you and thank you for your support, your encouragemen,t and just being an awesome woman. Hey ya'll, check out Pink Sky Dreams for travel ideas, inspiration, and travel tips!

To my niece Amia: Thank you for my love muffin! And for being an awesome supporter!

To my nephews Jordan and Jalen: Auntie loves you guys so much!

To Randae: Where would I be without you? I don't even want to think about it. From story ideas to editing to laughing to getting me together...I couldn't ask for a better friend. You define friendship for me and I love you for that!

To Manda: 26 years later, this friendship is still everything. You have supported me since 6th grade and I couldn't ask for a better person in my corner. I love you!

To STEPHANIE: I love you so much! You have been there and have been my boo for years and I cannot thank you enough for being in my corner. I have to get you all my books. With bows!

To Britney: You are the most motivational, inspirational, water drinking, devotional reading, dramatic, powerful person I know! You have inspired me and I am so glad you are a part of my circle. Thank you for all your support and dealing with all my story questions!

To #GreenGrands: You guys are the best cousins a girl could ever ask for! I don't have to beg or plead...my family just shows up right on time! To my Hamilton family: I thank everyone for supporting me! You have proven that family is truly everything! Thank you to my cousin Monika for your awesome design work on my cover! You are the best!

To my grandma Mamie Jackson: Years ago when I was a little girl, you always made me feel like I was one of your favorite people. Even now, you still have that power. I love you grandma! To my Jackson family: Thank you for all your support and love!

To Bishop Melvin McCluster: Thank you, thank you, thank you for your continuous pouring of love and support! You have spoken life into my gift and supported me for years! I sincerely thank you for all the time you have spent preparing a word that I needed to hear.

To my family at Friendship Missionary Baptist Church: If no one else thinks of me as a celebrity, you guys do! Thank you!

To Ms. Shirley "Star" Barksdale: 4 years ago you became my "mother in law" and you've been supporting me ever since. From reading and sharing my stories, I am blessed to have you in my corner!

To Amanda and the Divine Legacy Publishing Family: Listen. There are not enough words in the English language to talk about how much I love and appreciate you. From the advice to the talks to the laughs, you have been the most AMAZING editor ever in life! And you hooked me up with some pretty awesome people: Nicki Charest, Michelle Warren, Kaylin Greer, and Samika Johnson. You are without a doubt my favoritest SG-Rho!

To my beta reader: Virgilia Edge...girl. You inspire me with your words and I am so so so proud of you for publishing your book! You are an awesome writer and I am glad you are in my circle.

To Lakinia Ramsey: TWIN! You are my girl and practically my cousin! Thank you for your support and for just being an awesome writer. Hey ya'll check out Good Intentions 1 and 2 by Lakinia. You won't be disappointed.

To Aisha Douglas: Someone will show you this I'm sure but thank you for helping with names and story situations. I know I get on your nerves but it pays off!

To Jimiyah aka Dr. Carter: I love you girlie! I'm putting this in writing so it can be real...You will do great things! Go conquer the world!

To everyone who supported me, shared my stories, bought or gifted my book and told a friend about my book, I thank you. I cannot name every single one of you guys because I know I will leave someone out. My Facebook, Twitter, and IG friends...I thank you guys so much for being awesome supporters!

Connect with the Author

Website: www.authorjenniferrobinson.com

Facebook: Author Jennifer Robinson

Instagram: authorjenniferrobinson

Creative Control With Self-Publishing

Divine Legacy Publishing provides authors with the guid-ance necessary to take creative control of their work through self-publishing. We provide:

Writing Coaching

Professional Editing

Author Branding

Self-Publishing Coaching

Graphic Design

Website Design

Let Divine Legacy Publishing help you master the business of self-publishing.